Hair of the Dog

The Erin O'Reilly Mysteries
Book Fourteen

Steven Henry

Clickworks Press • Baltimore, MD

First publication: Clickworks Press, 2021
Release: CWP-EOR14-INT-P.IS-1.1

Sign up for updates, deals, and exclusive sneak peeks at clickworkspress.com/join.

Ebook ISBN: 978-1-943383-85-6
Paperback ISBN: 978-1-943383-86-3
Hardcover ISBN: 978-1-943383-87-0

Also by the Author

The Erin O'Reilly Mysteries
Black Velvet
Irish Car Bomb
White Russian
Double Scotch
Manhattan
Black Magic
Death By Chocolate
Massacre
Flashback
First Love
High Stakes
Aquarium
The Devil You Know
Hair of the Dog
Punch Drunk (coming soon)

Fathers
A Modern Christmas Story

The Clarion Chronicles
Ember of Dreams

For Andy, who always had my back.

We've got a bonus story for you!

We're so grateful for the love and support you've shown for Erin and Rolf. As a special thank you, we want to give you a free bonus story starring Lt. Harry Webb, *before* he was a lieutenant.

Keep reading after Hair of the Dog to enjoy

Pinot Noir
A Harry Webb Story

Drugs, seduction, money, murder, and film; it's a classic Hollywood story, shining a spotlight on Lieutenant Webb's past.

Hair of the Dog That Bit You

Any alcoholic drink taken the following morning to treat a hangover.

Chapter 1

Sean O'Reilly would never really stop being a cop. He might be retired. He might have less hair and more gut than when he'd walked a Patrol beat in Queens. His mustache might have turned white. He might have to wear reading glasses to make sense of the morning paper. But his instincts were still razor sharp. He could take the measure of a man in an instant, recognizing potential threats or weaknesses. He always knew who was in the room with him and where they were. He liked to put his back against the wall, so no one could get behind him. And he always, always watched the other guy's hands.

He'd drilled the mantra into his daughter years before Erin O'Reilly had put on her own shield and gun: *What will hurt you? Hands will hurt you. Watch the hands.*

Now Sean stood in the living room of his oldest son's house facing Erin and the man at her elbow. He hardly glanced at his only daughter, though she knew he loved her more than he'd ever been able to say. With his veteran policeman's eye, he'd zeroed in on her dinner date.

The two men watched one another with the wary respect reserved for a dangerous opponent. It was like a pair of chess masters squaring off before making the first move, Erin thought. Or maybe a couple of gunslingers in some dusty street in the Old West.

"Evening, Mr. O'Reilly," Morton Carlyle said in his distinctive Belfast brogue. "I'm pleased to meet you under such pleasant circumstances." He extended his hand.

Sean didn't move. He watched that hand and its mate. Both were empty, clean, with well-trimmed nails. They were the hands of a businessman, the wrists resting in sleeves of Italian silk. Carlyle was wearing one of his best suits, a charcoal-gray Armani accented by a burgundy necktie and matching pocket handkerchief.

Erin had been dreading this meeting for months. Her father and her boyfriend had successfully avoided one another as long as they could. The last time they'd met face-to-face had been almost twenty years ago, when Carlyle had been a young gangster and Sean an ordinary Patrol cop. Carlyle, with his usual conversational deftness, had reminded Sean that their previous encounter had been less pleasant, but ultimately useful. It had probably saved Sean's career by giving him the information he needed to escape a corruption scandal. Sean had distrusted and resented Carlyle ever since. Finding out his daughter had fallen in love with the mobster had not improved his view of the man.

Carlyle's hand hung in the air, an unanswered offer.

Erin fought the urge to roll her eyes. Instead, she slipped her own hand into Carlyle's left, interlacing their fingers. Her message was clear. They were a unit now, and Sean would have to accept Carlyle because Erin already had.

Sean's mustache twitched irritably. "Glad you could join us," he said, sounding anything but. However, he did take the offered hand at last, giving the other man a brisk, firm handshake.

Erin let out the breath she'd been holding. The other adults in the room also relaxed, feeling the release of tension. Erin's brother Sean Junior and his wife Michelle came forward. Michelle put her arms around Carlyle's shoulders and gave him a kiss on the cheek. Sean Junior offered his own hand.

"How's the stomach?" he asked.

"Grand," Carlyle said. "You did a fine job stitching me up. I'm well mended, I'm thinking. I'd be happy to give you a glowing reference."

"I get too much business as it is." Sean Junior was a trauma surgeon at Bellevue Hospital. "Just do me a favor and try not to stop any more bullets. I hate having to redo my work."

Michelle had moved on to the last guest in her home. "Ian!" she exclaimed. "I was hoping you'd be joining us, too. Welcome back!"

Ian Thompson, Carlyle's driver and chief bodyguard, shifted uncomfortably. He wasn't used to being greeted with such enthusiasm. But he managed the closest thing to a smile Erin had ever seen on his face and submitted to Michelle's hug and kiss. Once he'd disengaged, he made his way to the front window and kept an eye on the street, probably looking for potential hitmen.

Anna and Patrick, Erin's niece and nephew, were already engrossed in a game with Erin's partner Rolf. Anna had a tennis ball which she was trying to hide. Rolf, an expert at search-and-rescue, nosed it out wherever she put it, retrieving the ball from under the couch, behind the seat cushions, and the base of the curtains. The German Shepherd K-9 was having a great time, his tail wagging eagerly, his gigantic ears fully upright. Erin approved. It was training, of a sort, and good for both of them.

The dinner party had been Michelle's idea, of course. Shelley was a romantic at heart, and ever since meeting Carlyle, she'd been planning to bring him together with Erin's folks. In her view, it would help cement them as one big happy family. She didn't seem to realize just how complicated the situation was, or how awkward Erin's position in it might be.

"Where's Mom?" Erin asked.

"In the kitchen, naturally," Michelle said. "She's just putting the finishing touches on one of her famous triple-berry pies. It should be out of the oven by the time we're done with dinner."

"What's cooking?" Erin asked.

"It smells lovely," Carlyle said.

"Roast chicken with asparagus," Michelle said. "It's in a mustard cream sauce, with tarragon, garlic, and shallots. Boiled potatoes on the side."

"I don't like asparagus," Anna announced, pausing in her game. The tennis ball was poised in her hand. Rolf, transfixed by the ball, stood with one paw raised, waiting.

"When's the last time you tried it?" her mother replied.

"At Debbie Lynn's house," Anna said. "It was yucky."

"Then Debbie's mother didn't cook it properly," Michelle said.

Rolf barked, reminding Anna that she'd forgotten something important. Anna tossed the ball. Rolf snagged it neatly out of midair.

Erin only listened to the others with half an ear. Her attention was still on her dad and Carlyle. The two men were definitely on their best behavior. Carlyle was more outwardly relaxed than Sean, but they continued to watch one another. She hoped her dad had left all his guns at home.

Carlyle was right. Dinner did smell delicious. The O'Reillys and their guests sat down around a table full of good things. Ian made a halfhearted effort to stand clear of the meal, explaining he was on duty, but Michelle was having none of it, so he ended up seated between Anna and Erin.

"Would you like to say grace, Mr. Carlyle?" Michelle asked.

He was startled, but covered it with a pleasant smile. "I'd be honored," he said. They all bowed their heads while the Irishman began the traditional Catholic table blessing. "Bless us, O Lord, and these, Thy gifts, which we are about to receive from Thy bounty. Through—"

Erin's phone buzzed.

"—Christ, our Lord. Amen," Carlyle finished.

"I hate those things," Mary O'Reilly said. "Our generation got on fine without them."

Erin looked at her phone's screen and sighed. "I have to take this," she said, pushing her chair back from the table and thumbing the smartphone. "O'Reilly."

"I know you're off duty," Lieutenant Webb said. "So I'm sorry to call you. But there's a situation."

"What is it?" she asked, sudden anxiety sharpening her voice. Something was wrong. Webb didn't sound normal. Maybe an officer had been wounded, or even killed. Maybe there'd been some sort of terrorist incident. Maybe—

"How fast can you get to Long Island?" he asked.

"I'm at my brother's in Midtown," she said. "Maybe twenty or thirty minutes?"

"Make it twenty," he said. "It's a Brooklyn address. I'll text it to you."

"Sir, what's going on?"

"I caught a body," Webb said, and that was weird, too. He usually would have said "we," not "I."

"Is there a problem, sir?"

"No problem, O'Reilly. Just get here as fast as you can." And Webb hung up.

Erin looked around at the expectant, worried faces at the dinner table. "I have to go," she said lamely. "Work."

Sean nodded his understanding, as did Erin's brother. Both of them knew the Job sometimes came first, even before a meal cooked by Michelle O'Reilly, who was the family gourmet.

Erin didn't want to go. She ought to be here, chaperoning the encounter between Carlyle and her father, making sure things didn't get off on the wrong foot. But that strange note in Webb's voice nagged at her. Webb was a tough, cynical old gumshoe, and he'd sounded different. He'd sounded almost scared.

"Rolf," she said, standing up. The Shepherd sprang up instantly, awaiting instructions. *"Komm,"* she said, using the German command he'd been taught as a puppy in Bavaria.

Criminals didn't keep respectable business hours. The Job was calling, so it was time for Detective O'Reilly to go to work.

* * *

The address Webb sent to Erin's phone was on Marlborough Road in Prospect Park South, a small, upscale Brooklyn neighborhood. The houses tended to be fancy, with spacious porches, bay windows, and round towers. It wasn't the sort of neighborhood a Major Crimes cop expected to be summoned to.

"I guess people get killed everywhere," she said to her K-9.

Rolf didn't argue. He was glad to be out with her. As far as he was concerned, chasing down bad guys was even better than lurking under Anna's chair waiting for food to get dropped.

Erin pulled up in front of what was either a large house or a small mansion, depending on context. She parked behind the familiar shape of Vic Neshenko's unmarked Taurus. The other car on the street was a slightly rusty Oldsmobile, a car about as out of place in this swanky area as a street bum at a black-tie dinner. She didn't see any officially-marked NYPD vehicles, which was strange. She also saw no sign of an ambulance or of the coroner's van. In fact, if not for Vic's car, she would have assumed she'd come to the wrong address.

"Something smells about this," she muttered, taking a moment to strap on her Kevlar vest and do a quick chamber check on her Glock, ensuring the gun was loaded and ready.

Rolf wagged his tail. He liked smells. Maybe they'd get out of the car soon and find something to sniff.

Erin opened her Charger's door and stepped onto the street. It was about seven o'clock. The sun was low in the sky, shadows stretching across the pavement. She saw a light over the door of the house, another shining through the living room blinds. The ordinariness of the scene made her skin crawl. Something was wrong, she just didn't know what.

"*Your old man's a cop,*" her dad had once told her. "*You bleed blue, just like me. It's in your veins. If your gut tells you something, listen to it. Your insides know more than you think they do.*"

Erin unloaded Rolf from his compartment and strapped on the dog's body armor. Then she walked quickly up the sidewalk to the front door, going up the porch steps on the side instead of in the middle so they didn't creak. She paused at the door, leaning in and listening, one hand holding Rolf's leash, the other resting on the grip of her pistol.

She heard voices coming faintly through the woodwork and relaxed. She recognized Webb and Vic, along with a third voice she didn't know, a woman. No one sounded violent, or even particularly angry.

She knocked on the door. "It's me," she announced loudly. "O'Reilly."

Vic Neshenko opened the door. The big Russian detective was an intimidating sight, his bulky six-foot-three body topped by a face with a crooked, twice-broken nose. But Erin found him comforting. He was rock solid in a fight and much smarter than he looked.

"What's the deal?" Erin asked, trying to see past him into the house. Vic tended to fill up a doorway.

"Got one victim, male, multiple GSW," he said, pointing a thumb in the direction of the living room. "One witness, says she was upstairs. I don't know more, I just got here myself. I was visiting my folks down in Little Odessa, so at least I was already on Long Island."

"I skipped out on a family dinner," she said.

"You're welcome," he said.

She made a face. "Not everyone's family is totally screwed up."

He looked surprised. "You sure about that? That hasn't been my experience."

"Where's the first responders?" she asked, changing the subject.

"We didn't need a bus," he said. "Hell, I could see that the moment I got here. The guy's as dead as I've seen."

"I mean the Patrol unit," she said. "Didn't they stick around to secure the scene? Come to that, why isn't the scene secured? Where's the uniforms?"

Vic got a funny look on his face. "Only guy when I got here was the Lieutenant."

"And that didn't strike you as strange?"

"I live in New York, Erin. I want strange, all I have to do is look out my window. So many things seem weird to me, it's become normal." He stepped out of the doorway. "C'mon in and have a look."

The living room was well furnished but looked somehow artificial to Erin, like the interior decorator had copied it out of a picture in *Good Housekeeping*. She had a hard time imagining anyone actually living there. The sterile magazine-inspired beauty was spoiled, in any case, by the dead body sprawled on the throw rug next to the glass-topped coffee table. The dead guy looked to have been a middle-aged gentleman, clad in a white terrycloth bathrobe. The front of the robe was now deep, dark crimson and had fallen open to reveal a stout, hairy torso with at least two extra holes punched in it. The man's eyes were wide open with the shock of his last moment on Earth.

Lieutenant Webb was standing by the divider that separated the living room from the dining room. He was talking to a woman who looked to be about the same age as him, but in somewhat better repair. She had a pleasant face with a splash of freckles framed by brown hair with a hint of red. Erin suspected the red tint might not be entirely natural. The woman was clearly distraught. One hand was toying nervously with her hair. She was dressed like a well-to-do white-collar woman: silk blouse, professional skirt, expensive shoes. She wore no wedding ring.

"Got here as fast as I could, sir," Erin said.

"Thanks, O'Reilly," Webb said. "This is Catherine Simmons. Cath, this is Detective O'Reilly. She's our K-9 officer and my second-in-command."

Vic's face twitched slightly at that last bit, but he didn't react. After all, it was true. Erin was a Detective Second Grade, while Vic was stuck at the bottom of the Major Crimes promotion ladder until he learned how to play nice. In other words, forever.

Cath, Erin thought. *Not Ms. Simmons.* All of a sudden, it hit her. She knew why no uniformed officers were here. And she knew why Webb had called her and Vic, even though they weren't on duty.

She exchanged a look with Vic and saw the same knowledge in his eyes. Webb knew the witness. There was a shared history, it was obvious from the way they stood, the way they looked at one another.

The first rule of police work was very similar to the first rule of being a gangster, a lesson straight out of *The Godfather*. *It's just business, don't make it personal.*

This case was personal for Lieutenant Webb. That meant it was going to be an absolute mess. And Erin had stepped right in the middle of it

Chapter 2

"How long before Levine gets here?" Erin asked. She expected the Medical Examiner was already on the way. Doctor Levine more or less lived in the basement morgue at Precinct 8 and was usually available on very short notice.

"I'll call her in a minute," Webb said.

"You haven't called her?" Erin said in disbelief. "Sir, you know the fresher the scene, the better—"

"I'm aware of that, O'Reilly," Webb snapped.

Erin stared at her commanding officer. "Sir," she said, trying to choose her words carefully. "Is there something we need to know about this situation?"

"Did you shoot him, sir?" Vic wasn't so circumspect.

"No, dammit," Webb said. "I didn't even see it happen. I wasn't here."

"Is this your house, Ms. Simmons?" Erin asked the woman.

"I... no," she replied. "I don't live in New York."

"Where do you live, ma'am?"

"Los Angeles."

That sparked another connection for Erin. Webb was from LA, had transferred out of the LAPD when he'd come to the Big Apple.

"Now, Cath," Webb said. "You already told me a little bit about our victim here. I'm going to need you to repeat it for my colleagues."

"Did you have to call them?" she asked, twining a loose strand of hair around her finger and chewing on her lower lip. "I was hoping we could keep this more unofficial."

"I'm a professional police officer, Cath. And there's a dead man lying in this house. I can't just make it disappear."

Catherine Simmons appeared to wish very much that Webb would do that exact thing, but she didn't say so.

"I'm going to do what I can for you," he went on. "But I need you to tell us what happened."

"Why don't you start with who he is," Erin said, indicating the body.

Catherine averted her eyes from the bloody mess at her feet. "His name's Vernon Henderson. He's a realtor."

"Self-employed, or part of a company?" Vic asked.

"Shady Acres Development," she said.

"What's your relationship to the victim?" Erin asked.

Catherine flinched and said nothing.

Erin and Vic exchanged yet another look. The woman couldn't have been more obvious about hiding something.

"Ma'am," Erin said. "This man is wearing a bathrobe. Obviously, he wasn't dressed for going outside. Is this his house?"

Catherine nodded.

"Are you a guest in this house?" Erin pressed.

The woman nodded again.

"Did you see the shooting?"

Catherine shook her head. "I heard it," she said quietly.

"Where were you?" Webb asked.

"Upstairs. In the... the bedroom."

"This place looks like it's got more than one," Vic observed. "Which one were you in?"

"Why does that matter?" Catherine asked.

"We need to establish where everybody was," Webb explained. "It helps us figure out what happened."

"I was in the room on the left when you get to the top of the stairs," Catherine said.

"Is anyone else in the house?" Erin asked, receiving another head shake in reply.

"Do you own a gun?" Vic asked abruptly.

"What?" Catherine said. "No! Of course not!"

"What about Henderson, here?" he asked.

"No. That is... I don't think so. He never said anything about having one."

"I'm gonna clear the house," Vic said. "Unless you already did, sir."

"Good idea, Neshenko," Webb said. "You do that."

"I think maybe I'd better do it," Erin said, twitching Rolf's leash. "We're trained for this."

"I was in ESU," Vic reminded her. "I know how to clear a building."

"Rolf's better at it than you."

He shrugged. "Okay. You want backup?"

"I'll be fine. Why don't you stay here?" Erin's unspoken coda was *and keep an eye on these two.* She tried to say it with her eyes.

Vic gave the slightest of nods. "Sure. Want me to call the coroner?"

"Before we do, I have something to ask you, Cath," Webb said. "I'm sorry, but I need to. You didn't shoot Mr. Henderson, did you?"

"Harry!" Catherine exclaimed in a horrified tone. "How could you even think that?"

Harry, Erin thought. That just confirmed her suspicions. She needed to know what the hell was going on between those two. But for now, she had a house to search. At least this would give her the perfect excuse to poke around a little and see what turned up.

"Rolf, *such!*" she said, giving him his "search" command.

She and the K-9 did their usual search pattern, checking every room. The Shepherd was trained to detect explosives and human beings, dead or alive. If anyone was in the house, he'd find them.

They didn't find anything interesting on the ground floor. Erin continued to have the feeling she was in a show house, not a place where people actually lived. The kitchen was too clean. The furniture was too carefully coordinated. Nothing was out of place.

"Not a robbery," she muttered to Rolf. "Or if it was, they knew what they were looking for." Break-ins tended to be very messy. Drawers would be pulled out, papers strewn around, doors left open. By contrast, this was definitely one of the tidier murder scenes she'd encountered.

The upstairs was the same, until she came to the master bedroom. If everything else hadn't been so orderly, she might have missed it. But the comforter looked lumpy. She pulled it back, not sure what she was expecting, and found the sheets rumpled and disarrayed.

Rolf sniffed at the bedclothes with professional interest and moved on. His job was to look for people or bombs, and since neither was present in this room, it was obviously a waste of his time and talents. He started tugging toward the next room to continue their search.

Erin hesitated. She was putting pieces together. The man downstairs in his bathrobe, the bed quickly covered up, the woman upstairs... it all suggested one thing.

"They were sleeping together," she told Rolf.

The K-9 wagged his tail and pulled toward the hallway again. He didn't care.

On an impulse, she checked the dresser. It was completely empty.

"It's like no one lives here," she told Rolf, who cocked his head but stayed in the doorway, waiting for her to remember what was important.

Erin also saw a suitcase and an overnight bag. She pulled on a pair of disposable gloves from the roll she always kept in her car and checked the luggage. The suitcase struck her as feminine, which turned out to be accurate. It had women's clothes and cosmetics, along with a laptop computer and the other electronic accessories of a twenty-first century professional woman. The overnight bag had some men's clothing crammed into it with no attempt at folding. Everything was just wadded up and stuffed in.

Rolf trotted over, snuffling. Then, suddenly, he sat in front of it and stared.

That was his signal for explosives. Erin looked at the bag and considered. She was living with a retired IRA bomb-maker, and that had given her a slightly different view of things like drawers, doors, automobiles, and discarded luggage. She got down close and peered more closely at the clothing. Half-buried beneath a T-shirt was a cardboard box of .38 caliber bullets.

Erin opened the box. Six bullets were missing.

* * *

"Levine's on her way," Vic said when Erin and Rolf returned to the living room. "We should have some uniforms coming from the Seven-Zero any minute."

Erin nodded. They were in the 70th Precinct's Area of Service, so the Seven-Zero would be the ones sending Patrol units. "There was a gun in the house," she announced.

Webb looked up sharply. "Where?"

"I think our victim brought it with him. I found some ammo. Thirty-eights, so probably a revolver."

"But no gun?" Webb asked.

"No."

"Cath, did you ever see a pistol in Henderson's possession?" he asked.

"I told you, Harry," Catherine said, sounding petulant. "Don't you ever listen to me, even when you're working?"

Webb rubbed the bridge of his nose. "Cath, not now," he said wearily. "Look, we're going to need you to come down to the station with us. We'll need an official statement and—"

"I can't do that, Harry! I've got a flight leaving in three hours. I should be getting ready to go to the airport right now!"

"That's not going to happen, Cath. I'm sorry. Don't you realize what's going on here? You're a person of interest in a homicide. When you called me and said you needed help... God, I didn't think you meant *this*."

Catherine drew in a deep breath, preparing a scathing comeback. Webb was saved by a knock at the door and a voice announcing that more of New York's Finest had arrived. Vic let in a pair of uniformed officers.

"This is a new one," said the older of the two, a tough-looking woman with a strong Brooklyn accent. "We don't usually get here after the detectives."

"We just need you to establish a perimeter," Webb said.

"Copy that," she replied. "It beats having drunks throwing up in the back of your squad car."

"So, Cath," Webb said. "You were upstairs, so you didn't see anything. What, exactly, did you hear?"

"The doorbell rang," she said. "I heard the door open. Then Vernon started talking to someone. The other man sounded angry. They were shouting at each other. I started toward the stairs to see what was going on. Then I heard some sort of struggle and a couple of really loud bangs. I guess they must have been gunshots. They didn't sound like they do on TV. They were a lot louder. I... I froze. I knew I should do something, but my legs wouldn't move. I had to tell myself to take a step. How silly is that? When I came downstairs, I saw Vern like... like that."

"You said a couple of bangs," Vic said. "Do you mean two?"

"No, it was three, I suppose."

"Are you sure?"

"Yes. Three."

"Looks like all three hit him," the other Patrol officer observed, looking down at the body. "Either our shooter's a good shot, or it was real close range."

"I don't see any brass," Vic said. "Our guy wouldn't have had time to collect his casings, so I'm thinking revolver."

"Sir," Erin said in an undertone. "Can I talk to you for a moment?"

"What is it, O'Reilly?" Webb asked.

"Just you," she said, flicking her eyes Catherine's direction.

He nodded and they stepped out onto the front porch and closed the door. "Okay, now what is it?" he asked.

"Sir, what is your relationship with Catherine Simmons?"

He put his hands on his hips. "What's that supposed to mean?" he answered in a dangerously quiet voice.

Erin pushed on. "You know as well as I do that this could be a domestic shooting. No sign of forced entry, no sign of robbery. I've got a box of bullets upstairs, conveniently placed in our victim's overnight bag, and a woman with a convenient story who was obviously in a physical relationship with the deceased. Remember that apartment shooting? The one we thought was a home invader?"

"Cath's not a murderer, O'Reilly."

"Cath's a suspect!" she shot back. "Who is she? How do you know her? For God's sake, sir, I've been working for you over a year now and you don't use my first name, but she's not Catherine, she's not Cathy, she's Cath!"

"She's my ex-wife, okay?"

The words hung in the air. Erin blinked. She'd known this was awkward for Webb. She hadn't been expecting it to be *that* bad. "Really?"

He sighed. "Yes, really. "We divorced just before I left LA. She's ex-wife number two, to be precise. That's why she called me. She knew I was with the NYPD and she thought she was in some trouble here."

"She's right! You know she did exactly what a guilty person would, right? Don't call 911. Call in a favor from a guy you know."

"We'll check her for GSR," he said, referring to gunshot residue, the particles left on someone when a firearm was discharged nearby. "I don't think we'll find any. Will that convince you?"

"No. She had plenty of chance to clean up. Did you notice our victim isn't wearing any clothes, but she is? She got dressed before she called you. And she did a quick clean in the bedroom. The bedsheets are rumpled, but the comforter was pulled over the top. And it's just the one bed. The others are made. It's not bedtime yet, so it's unlikely one of them was just taking a nap."

"Okay, I get the picture. You don't have to go into details."

"Sir, this is my point," she said. "In a case like this, knowing these people were in a physical relationship is important information. The details matter. If you're not prepared to hear them, maybe you shouldn't be calling the shots on this one."

"You're lecturing me on appropriate boundaries between the Job and our personal lives?" Webb said coldly. "*You?*"

Erin licked her lips. "That's not what I meant, sir."

"That's exactly what you meant. I've been giving you every bit of slack I have, O'Reilly. Have I asked you one question about your relationship? One? Or have I been trusting you to maintain your professionalism and do your goddamned job? Is it too much to expect you to return that courtesy, or are you the only one who ignores the rules whenever you feel like it? At least I stopped sleeping with Cath when she kicked me out of the house."

She flinched, as much from the pent-up anger in Webb's voice as from his words. She tried to think of something to say that would convince him she was right, because she *was* right. He was compromised in this investigation. Just being here now, he was already putting the case in jeopardy. But he was also right that she'd stepped over the line herself, not long ago.

"Just think about it, please, sir," she said, trying to moderate her own tone. "For the good of the case. And the Department."

"I'll take it under advisement, O'Reilly," he said. Then he softened just a little. "You're trying to help. I know that. Otherwise I wouldn't have called you in."

That didn't comfort her. He damned well should call her in on a homicide. That he'd even consider not doing so in this situation only proved her point.

"Let's get back inside," she said, setting it aside for the moment. "See what we can find before CSU turns up."

Chapter 3

Sarah Levine walked into a tense, awkward crime scene. Fortunately, she either didn't care or, more likely, didn't notice. The moment she saw the dead body, the Medical Examiner went straight for it. Without saying a single word, she got down next to the corpse and began her external examination. Levine and social awkwardness were old friends.

The Crime Scene Unit techs arrived only a minute or two behind her and also got to work, setting out little yellow plastic numbers next to pieces of evidence, looking for footprints outside the windows, dusting for fingerprints, and photographing everything in sight.

The detectives retreated into the dining room, taking Catherine with them. None of them said much as they watched their colleagues' familiar routines.

"I didn't know you were in town," Webb said after a very long silence.

"It was just for a few days," Catherine said.

"So, who's Vern?"

"A guy I know."

Webb waited. He was good at using time as a weapon in interrogations. Catherine became uncomfortable, then irritated.

"What do you want me to say, Harry? That I was sleeping with him? Okay, what if I was? We've been divorced for *years*, Harry. I can see whoever I want. It's none of your business."

"Cath, it became my business the moment he got murdered," Webb said. "As long as your boyfriends stay alive, I don't care what they do or who they are. In fact, I'd prefer not to know about them. I might question your taste, but like you say, that's not my problem."

"I've known I had bad taste ever since I met you."

Vic winced and mouthed the word "ouch" to Erin behind Webb's back.

"You called me, Cath," Webb reminded her. "You could've just dialed 911. You probably would've gotten a Brooklyn Homicide detective assigned to the case, a complete stranger."

"Who would have just as soon arrested me as talked to me!" she shot back.

"Why do you think they might do that?" Erin asked quietly.

"I'm the only one in the house. He had a gun, so you tell me, and it's missing. I watch *CSI*. I can do the math."

"Because prime-time TV will make you an authority on police work," Vic said, flat deadpan.

"How long had you and Vern been seeing each other?" Erin asked, thinking the question would go over better from her than from Webb.

"About three months, I guess," Catherine replied.

"How did the two of you meet?"

"At a seminar."

"What was the topic?"

"How to get rich in real estate."

"Cath, you're a divorce lawyer," Webb said. "Were you thinking of switching careers?"

"I was selling the house," she said. "And I got to talking with the realtor, and he asked if I wanted to go with him to the seminar, and he made it sound interesting."

"I bet he did," Webb said. "Don't you see he was just trying to hit on you?"

"Of course I saw that, Harry. I'm not stupid. And I'm not a nun. Do you want to know how many dates I've been on since we split up? How many men I've gone to bed with?"

"No, I do not," Webb said.

"So you went to the seminar and met Vern?" Erin prompted.

"That's right," Catherine said. "He was much more pleasant than Hector."

"Hector was your realtor?"

"Yes. I ended up talking with Vern over hors d'oeuvres. We had a lot in common. He was only in LA for the weekend, but we spent almost the whole time together. He really was very charming, funny, likable. We exchanged information and started up a long-distance relationship when he went back to New York."

"What do you know about him?" Erin asked.

"He's divorced, like me. No kids. He's a realtor, like I said. He likes hiking in the woods, long walks on the beach, jazz music, and Long Island iced tea."

"What do you know about his financial situation?"

Catherine frowned. "What do you mean? He makes a good living. He has alimony, of course."

"Did he owe money to anyone else? Do you know if his assets were heavily leveraged? Any gambling problems?"

Catherine shook her head. "We weren't at that point in our relationship yet. If he was having money troubles, he certainly didn't tell me about it."

"And this is where he lived?" Vic asked.

"Yes, of course."

Vic snorted softly but audibly.

Catherine put her hands on her hips. "What do you mean by that, Detective?"

"Nobody lives here," Vic said. "Just look at the place. It's a showroom."

"I beg to differ, Detective. Vern had the key, he knew where everything was. It's his house."

"He's a realtor, lady," Vic said. "Look, why don't you come outside for a second and we'll check something. If I'm wrong, I'll apologize. But I'm not."

They trooped out of the house after Vic, who went across the lawn to the curb. It had gotten fully dark by now, so he pulled out a pocket flashlight and panned it across the ground. It took a moment, but he pointed triumphantly.

"There! See?"

Erin saw what the others did: a square hole about four inches on a side, sunk into the dirt a couple of feet back from the street.

"That was a 'For Sale' sign," she said.

"I'm betting we find the sign in the garage," Vic said. "Sorry, lady. He was playing you."

"The bedroom dresser was empty," Erin added. "Didn't you think it was a little strange that he had an overnight bag with him?"

"I..." Catherine began. She cleared her throat and started over. "That doesn't mean a thing. I don't blame a man for wanting to impress me. If *someone* had tried a little harder to impress me, maybe we wouldn't be in this situation at all."

Webb didn't bother replying to that. He was holding an unlit cigarette, staring hungrily at it as if his eyes could transfer the nicotine directly to his bloodstream.

"Let's see how Levine is coming along," Erin suggested, as much to get past the moment as anything.

The CSU guys had finished photographing the body, so Levine had moved on from her initial visual examination to taking the temperature of the body and probing the wounds.

"I think you should wait in the dining room, Cath," Webb suggested. She bit her lip, nodded, and moved away.

"How's it look, Doc?" Webb asked, coming to stand behind Levine where she knelt on the floor.

"Caucasian male, between forty and sixty, weight about ninety kilograms," Levine said without looking up. "Preliminary cause of death is a bullet, probably either nine-millimeter or .38 caliber, overpenetrating the left ventricle and exiting between the ribs. The victim also sustained two additional bullets, likely of the same caliber, one of which collapsed the right lung. The other struck the lower abdomen and perforated the large intestine. Due to the absence of exit wounds from these two shots, I anticipate discovering one bullet in the thoracic cavity and the other in the abdominal cavity."

"Got your third bullet here, Lieutenant," a CSU tech called, pointing to a hole in the plaster on the far side of the room.

"What else can you tell us about the shooting?" Erin asked Levine.

"Presence of powder marks on the victim, together with this scorched patch of cloth, suggests the shooter was nearly in contact with the victim, particularly for the shot to the abdomen, which I theorize was the first."

"Makes sense," Vic said, nodding. "Our shooter shoves the gun into his gut and triggers it off. Our victim stumbles back, but he doesn't go down yet, so our guy hits him twice more. He had to still be standing for that round to hit the wall. Those two shots do the trick and he hits the floor."

"His hand looks a little funny," Erin said. She was looking at Henderson's right hand. The index finger was bent at an unusual angle.

"I was getting to that," Levine said with a touch of annoyance. "The right index finger is broken. I see indications of a thin strip of something hard, probably metal, digging into the flesh on the underside."

"That's from a trigger guard," Erin said. "The victim had the gun at first. He probably drew on the shooter."

"But our killer was too close," Webb said.

"Or our victim hesitated," Vic added.

"Either way, the shooter twisted the gun out of his hand," Erin said.

"Cath wouldn't have the strength to do that," Webb said quietly.

"It's not hard to do, sir," Erin said, and that was true. If you could get to one side of a pistol's muzzle and get your hands on the gun, a little leverage would let you twist the hand, trapping the finger inside the trigger guard. You could disarm your opponent and break his finger simultaneously, which would almost guarantee an easy, close-range shot with the victim's own weapon while he was temporarily incapacitated with pain. It was risky to pull a gun on someone at close quarters, particularly if you weren't ready and willing to use it.

"I guess we know where the gun from upstairs went," Vic commented. "Our shooter took it with him."

"Or hid it on site," Erin said. She glanced Catherine's direction.

"I'm telling you, O'Reilly, it wasn't her," Webb said through gritted teeth.

"Is that the evidence talking, sir?" she asked gently.

"I was married to her for five years. I would've known if she was the type."

"What if he attacked her?" she asked. "What if he pulled a gun? Did she have any self-defense training?"

Webb was looking at his cigarette again with helpless longing. CSU would throw a fit if he lit up at their crime scene. "Yeah, I encouraged her to go to a couple of sessions. You never know what's going to happen to an attractive woman in LA after dark. She tended to work late. I was worried about her."

"So she had means and opportunity," Erin said. "What about motive?"

"If a guy and a girl are screwing each other, there's always motive for murder," Vic said, giving Erin a meaningful look. "Especially if the guy's a scumbag who's lying to the girl."

"Sir, you don't have to like it," Erin said. "But you need to do the right thing."

"She asked me for help," Webb said, and for just a moment his world-weary façade cracked to show a hint of the idealism he must have had as a younger man.

"What do we say when we want a guy to turn himself in?" she asked. "We tell them it's for their own good. I don't know about you two, but I mean it when I say it."

"So do I," Vic said. "If they don't give up, they're liable to get shot. Usually by me."

"Not what I meant, Vic."

"Okay," Webb sighed. "We'll take her to the Eightball. We need to get her statement anyway. We'll check her for GSR and particulates. Hell, a DNA swab while we're at it, but that won't tell us anything we don't already know. Cath's not going to like this."

"Hey, she already kicked you out of the house, right?" Vic asked. "What's she gonna do, make you sleep on your own couch?"

* * *

Before leaving Long Island, they canvassed the neighbors, hoping someone had seen something. Erin was particularly hoping for a physical description or a car sighting. Unfortunately, this was the sort of neighborhood where gunfire was unheard-of, so if anybody had heard the shots inside the house, they hadn't attached enough importance to it to notice anything. No one had seen anybody who didn't belong in the area. The car that got most of the attention was the beat-up Oldsmobile parked out front, but that was Webb's.

"You drive this thing?" Vic asked as they walked past it at the end of their expedition. He reached down and flicked a chunk of rust the size of a quarter off the wheel well. "Sheesh. No wonder we take my car when we're working."

"I keep it in a long-term garage," Webb said. "Just in case I need it. I was a little surprised it started. The battery's pretty flat. Now let's get Cath out of here before the meat wagon arrives."

"You don't want her meeting Hank and Ernie?" Erin asked, suppressing a smile.

"Are you crazy? I don't even want her to know they exist." Webb shook his head. "Look here. You're not on the clock. The Captain's been getting heat about paying out too much overtime. Why don't the two of you go on home? CSU will be a while yet processing the scene, and Levine will need time to do the post-mortem. You've got lives to get back to."

"Not me, sir," Vic said. "If the Department wanted me to have a life, they would've issued me one along with the gun and shield."

He gave Erin a very quick sidelong flick of his eyes as he said it. She took his hidden meaning. He'd be keeping an eye on Catherine Simmons, just in case.

"Thanks, sir," Erin said. "I'll see you tomorrow." She checked the time. It was after nine. Dinner would be long over. She could only hope her dad hadn't picked a fight with Carlyle. But there was nothing to do but find out what had happened, and maybe pick up the pieces. At least Carlyle was retired from the bomb-making business, so the pieces would be metaphorical. Probably. She'd check the police-band radio in her car on the way, just in case.

*   *   *

"The house is still standing," she told Rolf as she parked. "That's a good sign."

Rolf's tail was already wagging. He knew this house very well, and always looked forward to visiting.

Erin didn't see any squad cars. No ambulances, no flashing emergency lights. Carlyle's Mercedes sat against the curb, next to her dad's Crown Vic. Sean O'Reilly didn't like change, so his retirement car was a decommissioned squad car. It might not have the flashers or the radar scanner anymore, but it still packed eight cylinders of power under the hood and handled like a champ.

She climbed the stairs to the brownstone's front door. She didn't hear shouting or gunfire. The windows appeared to be intact. Smoke wasn't billowing out the roof. So far, so good. She took a deep breath and rang the bell.

Michelle opened the door, wearing a smile that widened when she saw Erin. "Hey! Glad you were able to get back! I hope everything's okay."

"Yeah. Well, I mean, I work murder cases, so it's not like everybody's okay but..." Erin trailed off. "Anyway, I'm fine," she finished lamely. "Looks like everyone's still here. How's it going?"

"Of course they're here. Your dad and your boyfriend are talking in Sean's study. Junior's gone to the hospital, naturally. Overnight ER shift. Ian's playing with Anna and Patrick."

"Ian's... playing?" Erin echoed.

"Come in and have a look," Michelle said.

In the living room, sure enough, they found Anna, Patrick, and Ian on the carpet. They'd combined Patrick's wooden train set with Anna's My Little Ponies and, at first glance, looked to be engaged in some sort of Wild West game. One of the trains had derailed, but that was okay, because Anna's pastel ponies were galloping to the rescue. And Ian was...

Ian was *smiling*. It was the only time Erin had ever seen him look genuinely happy. It made a tremendous difference to his face. The former Scout Sniper usually radiated calm intensity, giving the impression of tightly-coiled potential violence. Here, playing with a couple of young kids, he just looked like a pleasant young man with a short haircut and a few interesting scars. Mary O'Reilly sat in an armchair watching them contentedly.

"They just love him," Michelle confided to Erin in a low voice. "Patrick especially. I think he's decided Ian's some sort of big hero."

"He is," Erin whispered back. "He's got the medals and everything. But don't say it to his face. He won't thank you for bringing it up. Sorry I missed dinner, Shelley."

"I understand," her sister-in-law said. "I've lost count of the times my husband's had to run out on me because some idiot walked out into traffic or cut off a finger chopping vegetables. I can heat up the leftovers, or whip up something else if you want. Have you eaten?"

"No, I haven't," Erin said, her stomach gurgling. "Leftovers are fine. Just let me check on the guys first."

She left Rolf in the living room, to Anna's delight, and walked down the short hallway to Sean Junior's study. She put her hand out to knock. Then she paused. She could hear voices through the door.

It was impolite to listen at doors, but it was the sort of thing police were used to doing. Feeling only a small twinge of guilt, she put her ear to the woodwork.

"...wasn't that I didn't want to do detective work," her dad was saying. "Walking the beat, and I mean *walking* it, was what I liked. It was better than being in a radio car. You can really feel the city's pulse when you're out there doing foot patrols. You talk to people, you get a real sense of what's going down. I swear, I could actually feel it through my shoes sometimes."

"Oh, aye," Carlyle replied. "A lad can tell when people are restless. It's in the air, like a storm that's coming. In Belfast, sad to say, we'd more stormy days than calm ones when I was a wee lad."

"What'd you think of the Irish cops?"

"The RUC?" Carlyle said, referring to the Royal Ulster Constabulary. "Well, to us in the Brigades, of course, they were turncoats and traitors, the whole sorry lot of them. We treated them about the same as the British soldiers, only we respected them less for doing the occupier's dirty work. Though I'll grant they did their best to clamp down on those UVF bastards, too. Those are the ones who got my wife."

Erin grimaced. Carlyle was talking about the Ulster Volunteer Front, a paramilitary terror group that, while ostensibly fighting on the same side as the United Kingdom during the Troubles, had been more like a bunch of psychopathic murderers than an organized military force. The UVF had gunned down Carlyle's wife and their unborn child.

"Sorry about that," Sean said, so quietly Erin almost couldn't hear him. "If something happened to Mary... well, I don't know what I'd do. Probably something Charles Bronson would like."

There was a pause, and Erin decided it was as good a moment as any. She knocked and called, "I'm looking for the men in my life."

"Come on in," Sean said.

Erin opened the door to find Carlyle standing to greet her. Her dad was in her brother's leather office chair. Both men had bottles of beer close at hand. They seemed remarkably relaxed.

"Glad to see you haven't killed each other," she said, mostly joking.

"Oh, we're just bonding over fermented beverages and vigilante justice," Carlyle said with a smile. "Discussing our families, that sort of thing. I imagine I'm being interviewed for a particularly demanding job."

"Which is?" she asked.

"I've got to know if he's good enough for you," Sean said.

Erin put a hand on her hip. "Well?"

"Hmph," Sean said ambiguously, the sound getting mostly lost in his mustache.

"I think what your da's trying to get across is that no one's good enough for his only daughter," Carlyle said. "He's right, of course, particularly with respect to me. And he's looking for something he can use as an excuse, but I've given him nothing to work with. While he found that frustrating at first, he's coming around. I credit this excellent Guinness."

"He's a smooth talker," Sean said grudgingly. "But that doesn't mean I like him. Or trust him."

"Of course not," Erin said, keeping a poker face. "I'm just wondering how old I need to be for you to stop passing judgment on my boyfriends."

"Seventy-five," Sean said. "No, better make it eighty."

"That young?" Erin asked, raising an eyebrow.

"Hey, if you're going to risk tying yourself to someone, you have to be sure they're the right one," Sean said. "You land the wrong guy, you're setting yourself up for years of misery."

Erin thought about Webb and Catherine Simmons. Maybe her dad had a point.

Chapter 4

"Okay, spill," Erin said.

"What is it you're wanting from me?" Carlyle asked. They were back in their apartment above the Barley Corner, sitting on his couch with glasses of Glen D whiskey in hand.

"Dad. What did he say?"

Carlyle rubbed his chin. "Words to the effect that he knew who I was. Furthermore, he knew *what* I was, and if he ever heard of me mistreating his daughter, or disrespecting her in any way, or of returning to my wayward so-called career, he'd forcibly feed me my own entrails."

"I knew it," she growled.

"After those initial pleasantries were out of the way, we got along rather well," Carlyle said, smiling. "He doesn't trust me, naturally. And I couldn't tell him what's truly going on, sad to say."

Erin stared at the ceiling in exasperation. They were both under very specific orders not to tell anyone, not other cops, family members, or even family members who *were* retired cops, about their undercover arrangement. Vic had figured it out, and she suspected Webb might know too, but it had to stop there. It made the family situation much more difficult and complicated.

"Nonetheless," Carlyle continued, "we'd more in common than he'd like to admit. As we've discovered, you and I, those in the Life and those on the Job share the same world. I flatter myself I was able to bring him partway round. I've convinced nastier fellows than he that I'm a good lad to keep alive."

"So I guess it was a success," she said. She took a drink.

"I'd say so, aye. And Ian was a grand success with the wee ones."

"Yeah." Erin grinned. "I didn't know he could do 'happy.'"

"It was a surprise to me," he agreed. "But I've not seen the lad around children much. I'd suggest we bring him there more often. It'll do him good. But something else is troubling you, darling."

"Am I that obvious?"

He touched her cheek. "To me, aye. But I pay closer attention than most."

"It's got nothing to do with you, with us. It's this case we caught. I'm afraid Webb might be compromised."

"Surely not." Carlyle clearly hadn't been expecting that. "I've looked into your Lieutenant. He's as square as they come, solid to the backbone. I'd not believe he could be bought."

"His ex-wife is our suspect. Our only suspect, so far."

"Oh." He sat back and bought some time by taking a slow sip of his whiskey. "What do you know of their marriage?"

"Practically nothing. He hardly ever talks about his personal life. I know she's his second wife. He told us once that his first one got the kids, his second one got the house."

Carlyle chuckled. "I've heard it said that the only thing more expensive than marriage is divorce. But I meant, do you know whether the separation was amicable?"

"I don't know. Webb isn't a very amicable guy, so I'd guess not. What difference do you think it'll make?"

"It's hard to say. Obviously, if he still considers her a friend, he'll want to assist her. But at the same time, if he feels he let her down somehow, he may want to prove himself. Or he may want revenge. It all depends on his own feelings."

"We're watching him," she said.

"Do you suspect he'll do something untoward?"

She shook her head. "Not deliberately. But it might be more subconscious than that. I think he's got a mental block. He's refusing to consider the possibility she might be capable of murder."

"Nearly everyone's capable of murder, in the proper circumstances."

"What about Rose? Your wife?"

"I'd absolutely have killed for her."

"That's not what I meant. Would she have killed someone?"

He blinked. "I see your point. I honestly don't know. She was a sweet lass, but she'd a fierceness to her as well. I imagine if she'd been spared, and we'd had our child, she'd have killed to protect him... or her." A shadow of old sadness passed over his face at the thought of what might have been. "Bad lads will kill for hate. Good ones are more likely to do it for love. Anyone may do it from fear."

"In my line of work, the usual motives are money and love."

"Who was killed in this case of yours?"

"The ex-wife's lover."

"I see why you suspect her. I suppose your next step is clear."

"Yeah. We look into whether our victim had other girlfriends. Jealousy is one of the main reasons a girl will off her boyfriend."

"Should I be worried?"

She smiled mischievously. "Depends. Do you have another girlfriend?"

"You're my one and only. You know that."

"And assuming we strike out on the girlfriend angle, we look into his finances," she said, returning to the original subject. "Catherine says he wasn't having money troubles."

"But what lad would tell the truth about that to a lass he wanted to impress?"

"My thoughts exactly. When we find motive, nine times out of ten, we find the killer. I'd also like to find a gun."

"If it's firearms you're needing, I know a lad. But haven't you a few of your own?"

"I need a particular one," she said. "The murder weapon isn't on scene."

"If it's a professional hit, the lad will already be rid of it."

"I know. But this feels like a spur-of-the-moment killing. It was the victim's own gun, from what we can tell. We think he pulled it, then got disarmed and shot with his own piece."

"And you think the lass may have done it?"

"Yeah. But she was still on site, so unless she was clever enough to run off and dump it, the gun will still be somewhere at the house. Rolf didn't sniff it out, but CSU might find it. If they do, it's probably open-and-shut. We'll have DNA on the handle."

"Is there anything else to be done about it tonight?"

She shook her head again. "No. Not for me."

"Then set it aside, darling. I've a few meetings yet this evening, so I fear I'll be up late. You know my lads. They live by night. So you needn't wait up for me."

"Are you going to be wearing a wire?"

"Aye. No fear, it's well hidden." He'd had a couple of his suit coats fitted with concealed recording wires by Phil Stachowski's people.

"Okay. Just be careful."

"Erin, darling, these are lads who'd as soon kill me as walk past me in a crowd. I'm always careful. That's why I'm still breathing."

* * *

Erin was awakened by Rolf. The K-9, always a lighter sleeper than she, was on his feet and alert before she could rub the bleariness out of her eyes. She heard quiet footsteps approaching the bedroom. Rolf didn't bark or growl, so she knew he'd recognized the scent. Still, she breathed a little easier when she caught her own faint whiff of Carlyle's cologne.

He came in without turning on the lights. She flicked on the bedside lamp. The clock on her nightstand read 4:14. There he stood in his stocking feet, shoes held in one hand, the other at his throat loosening his necktie.

"Sorry to wake you, darling," he said.

"Not your fault," she replied. "Rolf's hard to sneak up on. Everything okay?"

"With these lads, any meeting you walk away from went well," he said, hanging up his coat and tie and starting to unbutton his shirt. "Just typical business. Mickey had some concerns. I've locked the recordings in my personal safe."

"Mickey?" She sat up, alarm bells chiming in the back of her brain. "You do know he wants to kill you, right?"

"Of course he wants to kill me, darling." Carlyle took off his shirt and unbuckled his belt. "But the more he talks, the more we have on him. Aren't you familiar with the advice from *The Godfather*?"

"'Keep your friends close, and your enemies closer?'" she quoted.

"Precisely. Speaking of which, Mickey and Veronica are working rather closely these days."

Erin nodded. Veronica Blackburn ran the O'Malley drug and prostitution business. The streetwalker-turned-madam liked to attach herself to strength.

"Mickey had a number of questions about cleaning," Carlyle continued.

"Cleaning what?" Erin asked, still fuzzy from sleep.

"Money."

"Mickey's an enforcer," she said. "He just does muscle work. Why does he need to know anything about money laundering?"

"He doesn't. Unless he's about to be promoted."

"Promoted? Evan wouldn't put that guy in charge of anything more than he's already got."

"You're right," Carlyle said grimly.

"Oh," Erin said as pieces clicked into place. "You think he's planning to take over from Evan?"

"It's possible."

"You need to tell Evan."

Carlyle smiled coldly. "I very much doubt Evan wants my views on the subject. Mickey's a violent psychopath, agreed, but he's always been loyal. If I suddenly tell Evan his chief leg-breaker's plotting against him, without any proof, what good will it do? He knows there's bad blood between Mickey and me. Besides, darling, I thought you didn't care what happened to Evan. We're working to bring him down, after all."

"That's different. Mickey isn't planning to just throw a few guys in jail. We're talking about murder. Multiple murders, probably. Besides, if he takes Evan out, who's he going to go after next?"

"Now you're thinking like a gangster," Carlyle said approvingly. "No fear, darling. I wasn't forthcoming on the subject of underworld banking. Though Mickey did let something interesting slip."

"What's that?"

"He's looking for Evan's ledger."

"He told you that?" Erin and Carlyle had been trying to figure out where Evan kept his books ever since they'd started building their case against him. Thus far, they'd had no luck.

"Not in so many words. But the manner of questions he was asking told me what he was looking for."

"What'd you tell him?"

"I told him the truth, which was that I couldn't help him with that line of inquiry. Now, darling, I'm rather worn, so if you've no further questions, I'd like an hour of sleep before the sun comes up."

* * *

And just like that, Erin's night was over. She found herself getting out of bed a few minutes later, leashing up Rolf, and going for a quick jog and grabbing a shower before heading in to the station.

To her surprise, Vic was already at his desk in Major Crimes, accompanied by a two-liter bottle of Mountain Dew. He was drinking straight from the bottle and glaring at his computer.

"Morning," Erin said, making for the break room and the sweet smell of the coffee machine.

"If you say so," Vic grunted.

She emerged with a steaming cup, stirring a packet of creamer into it. "I wasn't expecting to see you so early," she said. "It's not even eight yet. What time did you leave last night?"

"I didn't."

"Did you get any sleep?"

"I'm missing a couple hours, so either I went to sleep or I blacked out. Didn't find a bump on my head, so I guess I slept a little. Why do you care?"

"I don't. Just making conversation. Where's the Lieutenant?"

"He went home around midnight."

"What about Cathy Simmons?"

"She went with him."

"Vic? Are you telling me we've got a person of interest sleeping with one of our detectives?"

He gave her a look. "Wouldn't be the first time."

"I wasn't the first either," she said. "Remember Tatiana?"

"That's a low blow."

"You started it. Don't dish it if you can't take it." She looked at the whiteboard. Vic had put up pictures of the crime scene and notes detailing what he knew about the victim. She started reading.

"Henderson's a realtor, just like the Simmons chick told us," Vic said. "He used to work for a Manhattan real-estate firm. He just went into business for himself a couple years back."

"Any Mob connections? Sometimes they're into construction."

"Nothing obvious. He seems pretty vanilla. He's got no record."

"What about his financials?" Erin knew that following the money was always a good place to start.

Vic spread his hands helplessly. "I'm an ESU doorkicker, Erin. Do I look like a goddamn CPA. I got my degree in criminal justice, not accounting."

"You have a degree?" she asked, feigning shock.

"You got something against community college?"

"I didn't, until I learned they let you in."

"I can't make head or tails out of his financials," he admitted. "We're gonna need someone from Forensic Accounting to look at it. He's got a lot of money coming in and out of his personal accounts, and then there's his business accounts. The guy's got something like a dozen credit cards on top of checking and savings accounts with every major bank in the five boroughs. Seriously, I swear I've seen whole corporations with less complicated bank records."

"Nobody needs that kind of setup," she said.

"Not unless they're hiding something," he agreed. "But if we can't figure out what, it doesn't help us."

"Did Cathy Simmons have GSR on her?" Erin asked, deciding to get off the subject of money. She wasn't an accountant either.

"Swabs came back negative," Vic said. "But she'd showered, remember? Even sweat can be enough to wash it off."

"Oh well, worth a try," Erin said. Both detectives knew gunpowder particulates were less than reliable as a means of figuring out who'd fired a weapon, but if they'd found residue on Catherine, it would have at least suggested she'd been in the room when the gun had been fired. "How about the blood-work?"

"Levine was here all night, same as me. She sent up the report about four in the morning. Nothing unusual. She said he had a slight BAC, under the legal limit. Oh, and she did find one drug in his system."

"What was it?"

Vic smirked. "Viagra."

Erin spotted where Vic had written that bit of information on the board. He'd used blue marker; his idea of subtle humor. "Webb's going to love seeing that when he gets in. You sure Simmons is staying with him?"

"I don't know where she went after she left," he said. "She wasn't under arrest. We've got no evidence tying her to the shooting. Webb said he'd look after her. For all I know he put her up in a motel. Hell, maybe he airmailed her back to LA."

"Maybe it was a home invasion," she said. "Maybe Henderson was just in the wrong place at the wrong time."

"Could be," Vic said. "The house was on the market. Maybe some meth-head decides to break in and rip out the copper pipes so he can sell them for smack. He thinks the place is deserted, then he runs into Casanova here in the living room. Lover-boy is all jazzed on blue pills and hormones, he decides to be a hero. He whips out his piece, meth-head takes it away from him and pops him. What do you think?"

"Could be," she echoed. "But here's what I can't figure. He's shacking up at his love nest with this woman. He just got laid. He's in his bathrobe. Who the hell sticks a .38 in his bathrobe pocket if he's not expecting trouble?"

Vic nodded. "You got a point. You think he knew the guy was coming? If so, why didn't he put on some clothes?"

"It had to be short notice," she said. "Maybe he got a phone call..."

Her voice trailed off. She turned back to the whiteboard and looked at the pictures of the living room. She scanned the list of evidence CSU had taken from the scene.

"What're you looking for?" Vic asked.

"His phone," she said. "The guy's a real-estate agent. He'd have his phone with him pretty much constantly. So where is it?"

"Bedroom, maybe?" Vic guessed.

"I didn't see a phone," she said. "And Simmons didn't say anything about him getting a call. We'd better go over the place again. But I don't think we'll find it."

"I guess the shooter took it, along with the gun," Vic said.

"Why? Even a junkie would know we can trace a phone. They're not valuable enough to be worth the risk."

"Then what do you think happened to it, Sherlock?"

Erin smiled tightly. "I think our victim talked to someone right before getting shot. I think the shooter took it so we wouldn't know who."

"I'll look at his phone records," Vic said. After a few minutes, he sat back with a quiet but heartfelt curse.

"What?" Erin asked.

"I pinged the cell that's registered to Henderson," Vic said. "Guess what?"

"Turned off?" she guessed.

"Nope. Up and running... in an apartment in Queens, according to its GPS."

"That's great!" Erin was already on her feet. Rolf bounced up, tail in motion, ready to go get the bad guys. Then she saw the look on Vic's face. "Not so great?"

"Specifically, it's the apartment currently being rented by Vernon Henderson, realtor," he said.

"Oh. So he didn't have his phone with him after all." Erin sank back into her chair. "It was worth a try."

"Think outside the box, Detective Second Grade," Vic said. "Think like a sleazy real-estate agent. He was entertaining his out-of-town girlfriend at a house that wasn't his. I bet he leases a car, or uses a company vehicle. Nothing about this guy is genuine."

"You think he had a separate phone," she said. "Maybe a prepaid one?"

"I wouldn't be surprised."

"Which doesn't help us if we don't have the phone," she sighed. "Since it wouldn't be in his name. Which is probably why it got stolen."

"Right," Vic said morosely. He sucked down about a hundred calories' worth of Mountain Dew and stared into space.

"Anything else on the postmortem?" Erin asked, trying to find something they could latch onto.

"Just cause of death," he said. "Bullets, naturally. Levine fished two .38 slugs out of him, probably a match to the one CSU found in the living-room wall."

Erin nodded. If they could find the gun, that would be something. At the moment, the ballistics report wasn't going to be particularly useful. She started sorting through Henderson's financial records, got confused, and decided to look into his personal details instead. A search of public records turned up his marriage and subsequent divorce, so at least he hadn't been lying about that. He had his license from New York to sell real estate. And she found his company, Shady Acres.

A very quick look at the company's records told her two things: first, they'd need a court order to get to the good stuff; and second, even if they did, Vic was right. They needed a forensic accountant.

What they got was a cynical, tired-looking Major Crimes Lieutenant. Webb arrived a little after nine, looking like the tail end of a bad weekend.

"Good morning, sir," Erin said.

"Where's our person of interest, sir?" Vic asked.

"At my place," Webb said. "Asleep."

"Um, sir?" Erin said.

"What is it, O'Reilly?" Webb was already on his way to the coffee machine.

"Should we be doing that?"

Webb's answer had to wait until he emerged with a cup of black coffee. "Doing what, exactly?" he asked.

"Sharing living space with a person of interest?"

"That's all we shared, O'Reilly," Webb said, taking a premature sip of coffee and wincing as it scorched his tongue. "She got the bedroom, I got the couch, if you must know. And my back's not thanking me for it."

"I didn't mean..." Erin began.

"What she meant was, it looks bad," Vic said. "It could screw up the case, whether we bring charges on her or not."

"For the last time, Neshenko," Webb growled. "Cath's not a killer."

"Whatever she is," Erin said, "we need information from her."

"Like what?" Webb replied. "We've got her statement."

"Like Henderson's phone number," she said. "We've got reason to believe he was keeping multiple phones, in addition to his complicated financial arrangements."

"This guy was dirty," Vic said. "I guarantee he's hiding something."

"If we can figure out what, we may be able to find a motive," Erin said. "That'll help Ms. Simmons. Do we have anyone who can do an audit of his accounts?"

"Not on short notice," Webb said. "It'll have to get in line."

"They'll take a month to even start looking," Vic predicted. "Those guys are too busy going after white-collar assholes for tax fraud and crap like that. They wouldn't want to get mixed up in real crimes."

"Do either of you have any accounting experience?" Webb asked.

"I do my own taxes," Erin said uncertainly.

"I just wait for the IRS to tell me how bad I screwed up and write 'em a check," Vic said.

"Do we know anyone who can help with this?" Webb asked.

"I've got an idea," Erin said. "But you aren't going to like it."

"Why not?"

"Because it'll involve Internal Affairs."

Chapter 5

The flight of stairs that led up to the Internal Affairs office wasn't really longer than any other stairway in Precinct 8, it just felt that way. It reminded Erin of trips to the principal's office back in Middle School. She could feel herself hesitating, dragging her feet.

It was a stupid mindset. She wasn't in any trouble. At least, no more than usual. Every cop existed in a gray area of mild infraction. The Patrol Guide was just too big and complicated to follow everything all the time. Ordinary cops felt about IAB the same way the average motorist felt about the Highway Patrol. Sure, he probably wouldn't pull you over, but had you *really* been obeying the speed limit?

"We're fine," she told Rolf, who wagged his tail agreeably. His conscience was clean.

The Internal Affairs Department consisted of Lieutenant Keane and four underlings. Erin didn't know three of these, and avoided Keane himself as much as possible. Keane was in on her secret, but she still didn't like or trust him. But the final member of the unit was a friend.

"Hey, Kira," she said.

Kira Jones looked up from the file she'd been reading. She was wearing a conservative suit coat that stood in contrast to her hair, which was spiky and dyed electric blue. When she saw Erin, a mix of surprise, pleasure, and nervousness played across her face.

"Hey, Erin," Kira said.

"You got a minute?" Erin asked.

"Sure." Kira stood up and came around her desk, revealing a modest skirt and a pair of knee-high black leather boots. She put down a hand for Rolf, who sniffed it and wagged. The K-9 liked Kira.

"You miss Major Crimes yet?" Erin asked. Kira had been a member of their squad prior to her transfer to IA.

"Sometimes. Until I remember what being shot at feels like."

"You dyed your hair again. Looks nice."

"Yeah, having to wear business clothes is depressing enough. I had to do something or I was gonna go crazy. What's on your mind?"

"I need some help."

The nervousness sprang up again in Kira's face and she lowered her voice, shooting a quick glance around the room at the other IAB cops. "Can you talk about it?"

"This is nothing to do with me. I was just hoping you could spare a little time to look at something in a case we caught. It's an accounting thing."

"Oh." Kira was relieved. "Just give me a sec. Meet you downstairs in five?"

"Copy that."

Kira came down to Major Crimes as promised. Webb greeted her with a weary smile. Vic scowled.

"Hey, don't I know you?" he growled. "Didn't you used to be a cop or something?"

Kira flinched.

"Knock it off, Vic," Erin said. "She's here to help."

"Because Internal Affairs is always there to help," he said, oozing mock sincerity.

"Just ignore him," she told Kira. "He's just grouchy because he misses you and won't come out and say it."

Vic snorted.

"Come have a look," Erin said.

The two women sat down at Erin's computer. Kira listened as Erin explained Vernon Henderson's situation, nodding thoughtfully.

"Okay," she said at the end. "I'll take a look. I've been taking some Accounting classes at night."

"The better to screw hardworking cops out of their pensions," Vic said darkly.

"Don't do anything wrong and you've got nothing to worry about," Kira said.

"I've heard that line before," Vic said. "Hell, I've *used* it before. That don't make it true."

Kira took Erin's advice and ignored that and further sniping from Vic. After a few minutes of examination, she sat back.

"Okay," she said again.

"Okay what?" Erin asked.

"I agree, it looks like this guy was hiding something."

"Like what?" Webb asked.

"I can't possibly tell that without a closer look, sir," Kira said. "Give me a day or two to go over this."

"Two days?" Erin said, unable to mask her disappointment.

"These records are complicated," Kira said. "It'll take some time to unravel. And I do have a day job. Two days is fast for this kind of thing. And I can't guarantee a particular result."

"Just get us what you can," Erin said. "I appreciate it."

Kira jotted down Henderson's information and got up to go. As she walked toward the stairs, she motioned Erin with a slight tilt of her head to follow. Erin obeyed, Rolf trotting beside her.

"Erin," Kira said in a very quiet undertone, once they were out of earshot of the others. "I heard about what happened with you and Carlyle and that shooter. Are you okay?"

"I'm fine," Erin said. "I didn't take any bullets."

"That's not what I meant. I... Jesus, I didn't realize this whole thing with him was so serious."

"I can't talk about it."

Kira nodded. "Okay, I get it. Believe me, I understand trauma. I just wanted to say, if you do need to..."

"Kira?"

"Yeah?"

"I can't talk about it."

She saw confusion, followed by recognition, in Kira's eyes. "I don't know about any investigation," Kira said. "You're cleared for duty."

"I know."

"Then what...?"

Erin stared at Kira and shook her head ever so slightly. The other woman shrugged.

"Okay," Kira said. "Need-to-know bullshit. Copy that. Just one question. Are you really living with him?"

"You're IAB," Erin said. "You've got my current address on file."

"Yeah, but I mean, are you *with* him?"

"Yeah."

"For real?"

"For real."

"And the Captain and Keane know about it?"

"Yeah. And that's way more than one question. That's all you get."

"Okay, okay." Kira ran a hand through her spiked hair, which sprang right back up. "What a mess."

"You're telling me. And we've got another one happening right now."

"What's that?"

Erin opened her mouth to explain about Webb and Catherine Simmons. Then she remembered she wasn't just talking to her friend, she was talking to an Internal Affairs detective. She closed her mouth again.

"Erin? What's going on?"

"Forget about it. You don't want to know. Thanks for your help with this."

* * *

The next logical steps in the investigation were to check Henderson's apartment and talk to his ex-wife. Webb told Vic to find the woman and instructed Erin to take Rolf down to Queens and look over Henderson's place.

"Why do I have to do the notification?" Vic asked. "Erin's better at this than I am."

"Just because you pad it out with a compliment doesn't mean you're not whining," Webb said. "I can't stand it when a grown man whines."

"Besides," Erin added. "She's his ex. She might give you a hug for bringing her good news."

"I want O'Reilly at the apartment in case her K-9 sniffs out anything strange," Webb said. "It looks like he had a gun at the crime scene, and it sure as hell wasn't legally registered. O'Reilly, I've asked a CSU team to meet you there. Make sure they go over everything, and I mean *everything*."

"Yes, sir."

So Erin went down to the garage, loaded Rolf into her Charger, and drove back to the borough where she'd grown up and learned the ropes of police work. Queens might not be the most glamorous part of New York, but she liked it. She knew the people, the community, the rhythm of the streets. It didn't have the bravado and reputation for toughness that Brooklyn or the Bronx did. Queens was working-class New York City, mostly just ordinary folks trying to live their lives. Crossing the East River really did feel like coming back home.

Erin spent the drive thinking about divorce. She'd been raised Catholic, in a household where her parents' marriage had been taken as much for granted as the fact that the sun came up in the morning. In her book, if you weren't going to stay married, you shouldn't get married in the first place. But clearly not everyone felt that way. Webb had gone through the whole dance, start to finish, twice over.

"No wonder he's a pessimist," she told Rolf.

Rolf thrust his snout through the opening between the front seats and snuffled at Erin's ear. He was one hundred percent on the side of commitment. Also, he tended to agree with Erin on general principle.

Erin had fallen in and out of love a few times. It was hard to hit your mid-thirties without getting your heart broken at least once. But marriage was something different, something special.

Wasn't it?

"Look what happens when you get divorced," she told Rolf. "You wind up lying on the floor of your love nest with three bullet holes in you."

Rolf nosed her again, a little more uncertainly.

"You're right," she told him. "That doesn't always happen. Hell, his ex probably had nothing to do with it. If he pulled the gun, why did he throw down on her? I guess we'll just wait and see what Vic finds out from her. And what's Webb doing? He's screwing up the whole case."

She glanced at her onboard computer to double-check the address. They were getting close. "Yeah, I know," she went on, using Rolf as her sounding board. "I screwed up even worse. But that's different. I still love Carlyle. Webb and Cath went their separate ways. Didn't they want to be done with each other? But when she gets in trouble, he's the first guy she calls."

Maybe that was the point. Once you'd been married to someone, a part of you never really forgot it, whether things ended in divorce, death, or the elusive happily ever after. Erin laughed at her sister-in-law's fairy tale view of the world, but she had to admit, a big part of her expected to find her own Prince Charming.

"Maybe I already did," she said. "But if he's a prince, he's a prince of thieves."

Rolf wagged his tail. He had no idea what she was talking about, but that was okay. She was talking to him, and they were on a car ride together, and that was what was important.

"Besides," Erin added. "Shelley's marriage is no bed of roses. She's getting restless. My brother better step up his game or they're going to have problems one of these days."

She pulled up to the curb outside Henderson's apartment. The CSU van was already there, a pair of techs sharing a cigarette on the boulevard. Erin had the search warrant ready to go. Henderson had lived alone, and as the victim of a homicide, his apartment was fair game for the NYPD once they got a judge to sign off, and that was really just a legal formality.

The apartment was an ugly box of red brick piled up on 99th Street, looking like the architect had wanted to build a warehouse but had decided to turn it into housing at the last moment. She got the landlord to let them in. He was a guy who looked to be about thirty, skinnier than the stereotypical New

York landlord and with more hair. He was more interested than annoyed, and insisted on reading the whole warrant while Erin and the CSU guys twiddled their thumbs.

"This is neat," he said. "Am I gonna be on TV? Like, on *Cops*?" Then, inevitably, he had to sing a few bars of the theme song, inquiring what the bad boys were gonna do.

Erin pasted a polite smile on her face and waited for him to take a breath. When he did, she asked, "Do you see any TV cameras?"

His face fell. "Aw, man! My girlfriend loves that stuff! Can I keep this?" He held up the warrant.

"Yeah, you can keep a copy," she said.

"Would you autograph it for me?"

Erin blinked at him. That was a new one for her. "Judge Ferris already did," she said, pointing to the signature at the bottom.

"Cool," the landlord said. Then, once he opened the door to Henderson's second-floor apartment, he tried to follow them in. The CSU guys insisted he stay in the hallway, where he craned his neck around the doorframe and snapped pictures with his cell phone while they worked.

Erin was used to rubberneckers from her Patrol days, so she ignored him and tried to concentrate on the apartment. This wasn't a crime scene, but she was still looking for clues. Mainly, she was trying to figure out what sort of man Vernon Henderson had been. That might lead to a motive, which could get them their killer.

She started by doing a quick once-over, just looking for a sense of the man's life. She saw a bachelor apartment, one-bedroom, not particularly clean. The kitchen sink had dirty dishes in it. The counter had empty takeout containers piled next to the microwave. She could see why Henderson would have taken his girlfriend to another place.

Erin moved on into the living room, Rolf keeping pace at her side. The coffee table was covered with books and brochures about New York real estate and the main treasure—a laptop computer.

The first question the evidence guys always asked, when they went through a victim or suspect's home, was "Where's the computer? Did you get the computer?" Erin pointed to it. One of the CSU guys pounced almost before she had her hand up, bagging the machine.

"Rolf," she said quietly. "*Such.*"

The K-9 began sniffing eagerly. He was looking for people and explosives. It would've been helpful if he was trained to find narcotics, too, but it wasn't a good idea to do too much cross-training for a police dog. A dog getting confused when a bomb's timer might be ticking down was potentially disastrous.

Erin didn't expect much, but Rolf almost immediately alerted. He sat in front of Henderson's couch and stared at the left-hand cushion.

"Guys," Erin said to the CSU team. "Back off a second."

She didn't explain, but her tone told them plenty. They immediately exited the living room. Erin, not knowing what was there, moved cautiously. She very gently probed the cushion, finding the zipper at the back of the cover by feel. Before trying to open it, she went over the exterior with her fingertips. When she felt the familiar outlines of a handgun, she relaxed. She'd been hanging out with Carlyle too long. This wasn't a bomb.

"Got a pistol in here," she announced.

"And a shotgun over here," one of the CSU guys replied from the bedroom.

"Really?"

"Yeah. Sawed-off Mossberg twelve-gauge. Guy had it under the bed. Loaded. Geez, was he expecting World War Three or what?"

Erin shook her head. She had no answer. But she knew if they'd found two weapons, there were probably more, so she turned Rolf loose to keep looking. Their search turned up a snub-nosed revolver in a kitchen drawer and several boxes of ammunition in the bedroom. She also found some back issues of a scary-looking far-right magazine with an emphasis on self-defense. And at the end of the sweep, Rolf led her to a duffel bag in the front closet. She knew what that was right away. She'd seen a similar one in Ian Thompson's apartment once.

"Go-bag," she said. It was a bag pre-packed in case Henderson needed to run for his life on a moment's notice. In the bag was a change of clothes, a passport, a roll of bills, a survival knife, and one other thing.

"Holy shit," she said.

"What?" a CSU tech asked.

Wordlessly, Erin reached into the bag with her gloved hands and removed a gun. Vic, with his encyclopedic knowledge of firearms, would have been able to identify it immediately. Erin wasn't sure of the exact make and model, but she knew an assault rifle when she saw one. She popped the magazine and saw neat rows of shining bullets, stacked on top of the spring, ready to be fed into the chamber.

The CSU guy whistled. "Damn," he said. "That's an AK. I'm no detective, but I can only think of two reasons for a guy to carry something like that around."

Erin raised her eyebrows.

"One," the tech said, "he's compensating for something."

"Or two?" she prompted.

"He was scared shitless."

"Yeah," Erin said. "But scared of what? Or who?"

Chapter 6

Erin and Rolf walked back into Major Crimes to find Vic engaged in a pleasant conversation with a beautiful woman. That was so unexpected that Erin did a genuine double-take. The woman was about Erin's age and of mixed ethnic background, with a lovely caramel complexion, dark, almond-shaped eyes, long, wavy black hair and a knockout figure. Webb was nowhere to be seen.

"Hey, Vic," Erin said. "Introduce me?"

"Sure thing," Vic said. "Faith, this is Erin O'Reilly and her sidekick Rolf. They're working with us to find out about Henderson. Erin, meet Faith Copeland. She used to be married to Henderson."

"Pleasure," Erin said, extending a hand.

"How ya doin?" Faith said, giving Erin a firm handshake. Her voice was pure street Bronx, very much at odds with her appearance.

"I'm good," Erin said. "Did Vic bring you up to speed?"

"He told me somebody busted a cap in Vern," Faith said. If she was upset by the news, or even surprised, she hid it well.

"Where were you last night, between five and seven PM?"

"Wow, you get right to it." Faith's smile was breathtaking, but it had a cynical, nasty edge. "I left work about five, got some Chinese takeout, went home and ate it. Watched some TV."

"Can anybody vouch for you?"

"Maybe the lady at the restaurant counter, but I don't think she speaks English too good. You gotta point to what you want on the menu."

"Do you live alone?"

"I got a cat. Stray tabby, just turned up at my door one day. You know how it goes, you're livin' alone, and then suddenly you got a cat that never leaves. Had him a couple months now."

"What kind of work do you do, Ms. Copeland?"

"Staffing. I find people who need jobs, get 'em hooked up with apartments, schools, that kinda thing. Janitors, grounds-keepers."

"I was just talking to Faith here about Vern," Vic said. "If you're done getting her alibi, that is."

Erin thought it was a pretty lousy alibi, but one which sounded plausible. "Just one more question," she said. "Where's your office located?"

"Brooklyn. Storefront on Prospect Avenue."

Erin looked at her mental map of Long Island. Prospect Avenue was fairly close to the murder site. Faith would've had plenty of time to drive down and blow Henderson away, even if she'd had a tighter alibi.

"Okay," she said, filing the information away for future consideration. "So, you were saying?"

"You were telling me about being married to Vern," Vic prompted.

"Yeah, he was okay," Faith said. "It was good, for a while. A guy like that tries to impress you, y'know? But then after a while, it wears off. He was a nice guy, I'll give him that. Never hit me, never tried anything sketchy. But he started getting weird."

"Weird how?" Vic asked.

"Suspicious."

"He was suspicious of you?" Erin asked. "Do you mean jealous?"

"Nah, I mean he was acting like he was hiding something. I thought maybe an affair, he was screwing some other girl. He had this chick working for him, she was younger than me, I figured maybe there was something goin' on there. He always said no, of course, but guys always deny it, unless they're bragging to each other."

"So what did you do about it?" Vic asked.

"I followed him," Faith said nonchalantly. "He went to this real iffy neighborhood. It's late at night, I'm thinkin' he's getting' drugs, maybe, or pickin' up a hooker. I don't get it, how some guys gotta pay for it. I mean, seriously, what's some skanky ho got that I don't, that she's gonna charge a hundred, two hundred a pop? I'm thinkin' maybe I shoulda started chargin' him, y'know?"

Vic tried unsuccessfully to disguise his snort of laughter.

"So what was he doing?" Erin asked.

"He was meetin' a guy, not a girl," Faith said. "Creepy dude. All pimped out, fancy suit, even a cane with a gold head, you believe that shit?"

"Sounds like maybe a pimp," Vic allowed.

"White boy, though," Faith said. "Not a brother. Y'know how some of those boys do, right? Try to look gangsta?" She smiled that hard-edged smile again. "They're not foolin' nobody."

"So what did they talk about?" Erin asked.

"Dunno. I couldn't hear 'em. But Vern was askin' questions. This other boy started pointing at shit with his cane, like they was sightseein' or something."

"What was he pointing at?" Erin asked.

Faith shrugged. "Wasn't nothin' there but some old apartments and shit, broken-down neighborhood."

"Where was this?" Erin asked.

"Borough Park, around 48th."

"When did this happen?" Vic asked.

"Six months ago. When he got home, I asked him where he'd been. He fed me some bullshit about hangin' with friends. So I knew he was lyin' to me, but I didn't know why. Thing is, how am I supposed to trust a boy who's gonna give me shit like that? And then, when he brought a piece home, I knew that was it. I was done."

"A piece?" Erin said. "Do you mean a gun?"

"Hell yes," Faith said. "I don't want none of that shit around me. I grew up in a bad part of the Bronx, okay? Dumbass brothers poppin' off rounds at each other all night sometimes. You people comin' into our homes lookin' for guns and dope. My family never had nothin' to do with that, and I swore I was never gonna be around it. I wanna have kids someday, y'know? You think I want my kid pokin' around, findin' his dad's gun? I knew a kid died that way. In my class. Third grade, nine years old. First funeral I ever went to. Fuck that. I told Vern, either the gun goes, or I go."

"What'd he say to that?" Vic asked.

"He said he needed it," she said, rolling her eyes. "For protection. Guess he thought I was bluffing. I went down to the courthouse next morning and filed the papers. Finalized six weeks later."

"Was he scared of this other guy?" Erin asked.

"Maybe. Or maybe he was into drugs. How the hell do I know?" Faith shrugged. "I thought, I found a guy in real estate, he's normal, he's safe, y'know? Turns out he's just another asshole."

"Lot of those around," Vic observed.

"You know it," she said. "Hell, I bet you keep guns and shit at home."

"Who, me?" Vic was surprised. "Well, yeah, but I keep them safe. I wouldn't let a kid get his hands on one."

Faith wasn't impressed. "Yeah, they all say that. Guns don't kill people? Please."

Erin was at her computer while Faith and Vic talked, bringing up a map of Brooklyn. "Can you point to where you saw this encounter?" she asked.

"Sure, I guess." Faith bent over Erin's shoulder and pointed. "That block, right there. That side of the street."

"Would you know the man Henderson was talking to if you saw him again?"

"Nah, it was dark, and it was a while ago. He was a white boy, like I said, but he was wearin' this big fancy hat. Couldn't hardly see his face. Had a bunch of rings on his fingers. Gold cane, like I said, and flashy suit."

"Have you ever used a gun, Ms. Copeland?" Erin asked.

Faith twisted back as if Erin had slapped her. "Hell no! You hear a word I said? I don't touch those things. Dope and guns killed more kids in my neighborhood. My mama taught me better than that."

"Thanks for coming up," Vic said. "You've been a big help."

"I knew it," Faith said. "The moment you showed up, I knew you were gonna tell me Vern got popped. I told him, guns don't mean shit for protection. All they do is get you shot."

* * *

"She's a character," Erin said after Faith Copeland had left the building.

"Yeah," Vic agreed. "Wonder how she ran into a guy like Henderson."

"Girl from a bad neighborhood meets a cheap con man?" Erin said. "Good question."

"Irrelevant to the case, of course," Vic said.

"I'm not sure about that," she said. "The guy was in real estate. According to Copeland, she followed him to a broken-down part of Brooklyn. Where'd she sound like she was from?"

"To me, sounded Bronx."

"Me, too." All NYPD street cops developed an ear for the different accents of the boroughs. "I'd be very interested to know what parts of New York were being sold off by Shady Acres."

"Could be it's a cover for something else," Vic suggested. "Drugs, maybe. Or guns. Or laundering money for a gang. I'm thinking gang hit."

"Vic, gang hitmen don't kill a guy with his own weapon. They bring their own guns."

He looked disappointed, but nodded. "Good point, I guess. I'll look into Shady Acres." He yawned. "Even thinking about real estate makes me sleepy. That's why I rent."

"I thought it was because they don't pay us enough to buy Manhattan properties."

"That too."

"Say, where's Webb?" she asked.

"Dunno. He got a phone call and took off a little before you got back."

"Really? Did he say anything to you about where he was going?"

"Erin, he's my boss. I call him when I'm not gonna be here, not the other way round. Plus, he's, like, fifty years older than I am. I'm not his damn babysitter."

"How old are you, Vic?"

"I'm thirty-two. What's it to you?"

"That'd make Webb over eighty. You really think he's that old?"

Vic considered. "Well, some of his organs, when you consider the extra mileage he puts on them..."

"Any idea how long he and Simmons were married?"

"Just how the hell am I supposed to know that?"

She shrugged. "State of California public records?"

Vic gave an exasperated sigh. "You really think I've got nothing better to do than look up my commanding officer's marital history?"

"It's pertinent to the case."

"Yeah? How?"

"Because it might tell us what kind of emotional attachment he's got to her."

"Because how long a guy's been married tells us that? That's been your experience?"

"I don't know, Vic. I've never been married."

"Me neither. Thank God."

Erin tried to put her mind and the conversation back on track. "Okay, Vic. Here's the thing. Webb has a history with one of our suspects. We don't know how strong that attachment is. Now he's gone off the reservation. That could be a coincidence, but here in Major Crimes, we don't believe in coincidence."

"You got that right," Vic said.

"So in the absence of our Lieutenant, as ranking detective, I'm calling the shots right now. The way I see it, we have a few avenues of investigation. One: Shady Acres. I want to know what properties they currently have, and any others they may have recently sold or been looking to sell. Two: Faith Copeland. She claims not to like guns, but from the way she talked about her background, it sounds like there may be violence in her history. The way she was denying things seemed a little too strong. We need to check her criminal record. Three: Catherine Simmons. She meets a guy for a weekend and then comes clear across the country for him? Either Henderson made one hell of an impression, or there's something else going on between the two of them. Four: Vernon Henderson. From everything we've seen, he was a con man, and that means he's probably got a record. If a guy lies as much as he did to Simmons, he does it for a living."

"I'm not sure about that last one, Erin. Guys always lie to girls when they want to get them in bed."

"Not everybody's like you, Vic."

"Nope. Plenty of guys with weaker muscles and smaller dicks."

"Oh, good. I was wondering how long it'd take for this to turn into dick-measuring. You lie to Piekarski?"

"Not about anything important. But I wasn't trying to get her in bed. It was the other way round."

Erin shook her head. "And there I thought she had better taste than that."

"I think I know how she tastes better than—"

"Stop, Vic. Just stop right there. I do not want to know."

"Okay. But if you don't think your guy lies to you, you're lying to yourself."

"He doesn't."

"How would you know?"

"I'm a detective, Vic. I sniff out lies for a living."

"And everybody lies to us. Why should he be any different?"

Erin let it go. "You've got Shady Acres, right?"

"Yeah. And I'll run Faith's background."

"Sounds good. I'll look into Simmons and Henderson. How about we get lunch from that Thai place down the block?"

"Copy that. Some pad Thai will help keep me awake. The spicier the better."

* * *

Fortified by hot and spicy takeout, Erin and Vic attacked their respective targets. Erin logged onto LEEP, the Law Enforcement Enterprise Portal. This was a centralized online database for information sharing between police agencies nationwide, which gave her an opening to look into Catherine Simmons and her California history. Erin plunged into cyberspace. Rolf snoozed next to her desk.

The results were reassuring from a human viewpoint, but disappointing to a cop. The only marks on the woman's record were speeding tickets and a single DUI. Curious, Erin called up the DUI. Catherine had pled out on the charge and received probation—a slap on the wrist. Had Webb used his influence with the Department to get her out of trouble? Still, that was pretty small potatoes and didn't suggest Catherine was a murderer. It just meant she ran to Webb when she got on the wrong side of the law, and Erin had already known that.

And could Erin really blame her for that? If you had a hook, you used it. That was the way the world worked. How many times had Carlyle told her? She could hear his voice, that smooth Belfast brogue, saying it in her head.

"The world runs on favors, darling."

Gangsters weren't the only ones who operated that way. But she'd have to talk to Webb about that. It wasn't a conversation she was looking forward to.

Vernon Henderson was more promising than his girlfriend. Erin's hunch about him had been right on the money. He was a lifelong con artist with half a dozen busts. He'd managed to avoid doing serious jail time, but he'd been in for a ninety-day stint once, and thirty days on another occasion, for petty larceny. He'd paid fines on the other four occasions. He'd also been arrested for Criminal Impersonation, but those charges hadn't stuck.

The afternoon wore away with no sign of Webb. Erin considered calling him, but reasoned that if he wanted to talk to them, he'd call or show up. If Vic wasn't a babysitter, neither was she.

"What've you got?" she asked Vic a little before five.

He sat back from his computer, flexed his shoulders, and rubbed his eyes. "Faith Copeland is squeaky clean," he said. "But I did find one thing. Her dad got murdered twenty years back."

"What happened?"

"A couple drug dealers had a difference of opinion and started swapping bullets. A stray nine-millimeter went through a window and caught Mel Copeland right in the head in his own easy chair. Just bad luck. Wrong place, wrong time."

"He was sitting at home, minding his own business, and got shot by accident? No wonder this woman hates guns."

"Yeah. Wonder why she didn't tell us about her dad."

"You were saying everybody lies to cops," Erin reminded him. "It's probably the worst memory she's got. You think a woman wants to bring up something like that in front of a couple of strangers? She was trying to be tough. It's hard to put up a tough façade while you're crying."

"I guess so. Anyway, Faith was never into anything shady."

"Speaking of shady, what about the real estate company?"

"Now that's a little more interesting. Henderson bought Faith's building."

"Really?" That got Erin's attention. "I guess that's how they met."

"Yeah. He bought the whole apartment block. Then he sold it again, less than two months later."

"So he flipped the property. It happens. New York real estate is crazy. He probably just got wind of a bargain and snapped it up, then turned around and cashed it in to some chump."

"Yeah. Something's funny about this, though."

"What?"

He shook his head. "I don't know. Add 'realtor' to the increasing list of things I'm not, right under 'babysitter' and 'accountant.' I just think the deal looks a little off. Look, this apartment block was a big, steaming pile of urban shit, okay?"

"Colorful, but accurate, I suppose. What's your point?"

"That kind of property only really changes hands when a developer's got big plans to turn it into a shopping mall or a big-ass coffee shop or whatever. Otherwise, no one wants it. What matters is what it can be turned into, not what it is."

"Still waiting for you to get to your point, Vic."

"So how come the apartment's still there?"

"Come again?"

"No development. No urban renewal. No gentrification or whatever the hell you call it. It's the same slums. No one's even working on tearing them down. I've been trying to track down the permits and I can't, 'cause they're not there. So why's a white boy go to the Bronx and buy a falling-down inner-city apartment, just to sell it again?"

"I have no idea, Vic."

"Do you at least agree that it's weird?"

"Yeah, I guess so." Erin stood up. "It's time for me to get out of here."

"Going home? Good idea." Vic got to his feet and stretched. His back and neck made popping sounds Erin could hear from ten feet away. "Gonna hit the gym, I think."

"I'm not going home," she said.

"What's on your plate, then?"

"Brooklyn. I'm going to see what's on that block Henderson was so interested in. If I'm lucky, I can figure out who he was talking to."

"Copy that. I'm in."

"What about the gym?"

"The weights can wait. That was what I wanted to do before I heard there was a chance to get in a street fight with a pimp."

"Vic, I am not going to Brooklyn to pick a fistfight. If everything goes well, nobody's going to get hurt."

"Yeah, but as long as there's a chance it goes sideways, I want to be there. Tell you what, you lead, I'll get the Taurus and trail you."

"On one condition."

"You're starting to sound like the Lieutenant," he warned her.

"You don't start a fight."

"I finish more fights than I start."

"Is that a yes? Remember that date-rapist we ran into? You picked a fight with him and he broke your nose. Again."

"Okay, fine. I won't start anything."

Chapter 7

"It doesn't look so bad," Vic said. He, Erin, and Rolf stood on 48th Street, looking up at a six-story apartment building.

"I've seen worse," Erin agreed.

"I mean, sure, the bushes could use a trim," he went on. "And that fire escape isn't up to code. It's so rusty it'd probably fall right off the wall if anyone tried to climb it."

"And the brickwork is falling apart," Erin added. "Cheap cement. See, at the corners? And those windows over there are boarded over. But they've got AC units in some of the windows, the lights are on, and nobody's dealing meth on the front step, so on the whole..."

"Not bad," they said in unison.

A handful of pre-teen kids were playing just outside the main door. As the detectives approached, they looked up with curiosity that sharpened to interest.

"Five-oh," one of them said, nudging his buddy with his elbow. Then, without any further word, the kids scattered, leaving the cops alone outside.

"What the hell was that for?" Vic wondered. "They weren't doing anything illegal. At least, I don't think so."

"I think they were just practicing," Erin said. "For when they get older. Or they could be lookouts for dealers."

"And you say I have a depressing outlook on life," he said sourly.

"Or it could be part of their game," she said. "Cops and robbers, only with real cops. Hell, maybe they didn't even make us as NYPD."

"You think anybody sees me, they don't see a cop?"

"If you got a neck tattoo, they might mistake you for a violent felon."

"Really?" Vic looked surprised and a little pleased. "So, how do you want to play this?"

"Let's find the landlord."

They found the office easily enough, but it was locked. Knocking produced no results, as did identifying themselves as law-enforcement officers and demanding the occupant open up.

"Guess he's not here," Vic said.

"There's supposed to be someone on duty," Erin said.

"And everybody's always exactly where they're supposed to be," he said.

Erin caught sight of a young woman carrying a laundry basket down the hall. She walked quickly after her, Rolf keeping pace. They caught up with the woman at the door to the laundry room. Erin put out a hand and opened the door.

"Thanks," the woman said. Then she caught sight of the K-9, or maybe just processed the color of Erin's skin, and that of the big Russian coming down the hall toward them. Her face became unreadable, as if steel shutters had snapped down behind her eyes.

Erin sighed inwardly. She'd seen this more times than she could count. This was clearly a neighborhood where the cops and the citizens weren't on the best terms. "Sorry to bother you, ma'am," she said. "I was just hoping you could tell me who owns this building."

"I wouldn't know about that," the woman said. "I just pay my rent, first of the month, like everyone."

"Who do you pay the rent to?"

"There's a slot in the door," the woman said, cocking her head toward the office. "I just slide the check inside. Why you care?"

"Who runs things around here?" Erin asked.

"What you mean?" The woman was more skittish now. Her eyes darted from side to side, as if she was looking for escape routes.

"White guy," Erin said. "Fancy suit. Gold cane. What's his name?"

"I don't want trouble," the woman said. "I got a kid."

She was already telling Erin things, chiefly that she was right. This guy was bad news. He had a street rep as a man not to be trifled with. "This will be the last you hear from us," Erin promised. "Just give me a name and I'm gone."

"I don't know his right name," the woman said. "He goes by 'Dog.'" Her gaze slid down to Rolf for a moment. "He keeps a couple mean dogs, them black ones with the pointy ears."

"Dobermans?" Erin guessed.

"Yeah, those. He comes around sometimes, and sometimes he got them dogs with him. When he does, I keep my kid inside."

"And he has a gold-headed cane and dresses sharp?" Erin pressed.

"Yeah, that sounds like him. Now I got laundry to do."

"Right. Thanks for your help, ma'am."

"Don't need no thanks. Thanks don't put soap in the machine."

*   *   *

"Dog," Vic repeated once he and Erin were back outside.

"That's what she said. Let's run it as an alias and see what pops." Erin walked back to her Charger.

"Sounds like your kind of crook," Vic said.

"If he's trained his dogs to attack people, he's probably an asshole who abuses animals," she said. "In which case I'll take great pleasure in cuffing him and hauling his sorry ass in."

"You trained your mutt to attack," he pointed out.

"No," Erin said. "Rolf's trained to apprehend and restrain. He's no killer."

"You might be surprised," Vic said. "The beast's always there, right under the surface."

The two of them glanced at Rolf, who stared back with his intense brown eyes. Maybe he had a beast inside, he seemed to say, and maybe not, and did you really want to find out?

Erin got on her computer and punched in the street name. She got a bunch of results. Apparently, "Dog" was a nickname liberally applied to men in the underworld. But by localizing her search to Brooklyn and narrowing down the ethnicity, she got the search to just a few. Then she cross-referenced it with animal attacks.

"I think I got him," she announced.

Vic had found a tennis ball in the gutter and was bouncing it off the apartment wall, catching it on the rebound. Rolf was watching him with interest. Tennis balls were always worth watching. Vic snagged the ball and tossed it to the dog, who caught it before it could hit the ground.

"So who's our boy?" he asked, coming over and poking his head into the passenger window.

"Clay Dodgson," Erin said, showing Vic a mugshot of a square-jawed, cold-eyed man with a nasty scar on his jaw.

"Independent operator. Started out doing protection rackets. Did a nickel upstate for breaking a man's jaw with a tire iron when he was nineteen. Once he got out, he started moving up in the world. He started shaking down landlords and superintendents. That's when he got interested in dogs. Looks like he's got a semi-legitimate business breeding Doberman Pinschers. He sells them as guard dogs to junkyards and people who like to live in fenced-in yards."

"Sounds like a typical nice guy," Vic said. "How is this loser not back in prison?"

"People don't like to testify against him," she said. "Looks like the last time someone tried, the guy's mom got mauled in an animal attack. Not much detail in the file, but there's pictures." She glanced at them and grimaced. A big dog could do a lot of damage.

"I guess word got around after that," Vic said. "But if this is our guy, how come Henderson didn't get his face bitten off?"

"I didn't say Dodgson shot Henderson," Erin said. "But if he was meeting with him, I want to know why. What do you say we go visit a dog breeder? Looks like it closes at six. We've got a few minutes yet, and it's just down the street."

"Okay. But I'm not getting a puppy."

"What if he's really, really cute? Piekarski might like a puppy."

"No puppies."

*　　*　　*

It wasn't a good sign, in Erin's book, when a dog breeder operated out of a basement. Dogs needed clean air and sunshine. This was a seedy concrete cellar with a sign advertising the one misspelled word JAWZ. She shifted her grip on Rolf's leash and set her own jaw.

Vic opened the door and paused in the doorway as a storm of barking exploded in front of them. A bare concrete hallway stretched ahead, lined with chain-link fencing on both sides. That fence was flexing and bending under the impact of frantic, short-haired bodies.

Erin wondered whether she ought to have left Rolf in the car. The Shepherd was generally calm around other dogs, but this was a high-stress canine environment. Rolf's hackles rose. He didn't growl or bark, but she could feel the tension radiating off him. He was stiff-legged and alert at her side, ears laid back against his skull, eyes searching for threats.

She couldn't leave him behind now. He'd be frantic, thinking she was going into some sort of trouble without him. And that might be true. So she tried to project a quiet, soothing energy and walked in behind Vic.

They walked a long gauntlet of snarling muzzles, snapping teeth, and wild eyes. These Dobermans weren't under any sort of control, either internal or external. If one of the chain-link barriers gave way, Erin and Vic would probably have to shoot that dog, and both of them knew it. Vic's fingers were curled around the grip of his Sig-Sauer automatic, ready to draw as a reflex.

The JAWZ office was at the far end of the hall. Erin understood why. The walk past the kennels served a dual purpose, intimidation and a twisted kind of advertising. But Erin didn't intimidate easily. Bullies just pissed her off. All the same, these dogs unsettled her. She liked dogs, on the whole, and dogs liked her. These animals weren't acting normal. They'd been broken by their training, turned into something unnatural and dangerous.

The office door was made of steel. Vic knocked, his knuckles making an echoing metallic sound. Without waiting for an answer, he twisted the knob and went in. Erin and Rolf followed.

Erin saw pretty much the office she'd expected. The floor was bare concrete, just like the kennels outside. A battered desk and chair, a couple of olive-green metal file cabinets, and a poster from a Spike Lee movie were the only furnishings. The windows were just a few inches wide and near the ceiling, crisscrossed by iron bars. A pair of crates on the far side of the room held a matched set of very large Dobermans who stared balefully at the newcomers. They didn't bark or growl, which was somehow even more unnerving than their noisier brethren. They just stared. Sitting in the chair, fingers interlaced across one knee, leaning back, was the most overdressed man Erin had ever seen.

Everything about the room was cheap, bare-bones, and unpleasant. The man at the desk was dressed like he'd walked right off a Hollywood red carpet. His suit was white in the harsh light of the bare bulbs, and Erin would bet twenty bucks it was silk. He wore a blue silk shirt under it and a white necktie. His wrists sparkled with diamond cufflinks and his fingers were studded with gold rings. A white fedora with a black band sat on the desktop next to him and a cane with a gold dog's head handle leaned beside it.

The man was handsome, in a rough street way. He had a strong jaw and a deep, intense stare. Even at the end of the day, his chin was smooth-shaven, showing an old scar. He gave Vic a quick once-over, measuring him. Then he smiled at Erin. The smile was charming, but not exactly nice. The polite thing to do would have been to stand up. He didn't.

"Evening," he said. "Nice dog you got there. Purebred German Shepherd?"

"That's right," Erin said, sweeping the door shut behind her and muffling the sound of the maniacal barking. "Police K-9.

This is Detective Neshenko, Major Crimes. I'm Detective O'Reilly. Are you Clay Dodgson?"

His smile widened, showing very white teeth. Erin suppressed a start. He'd filed his canine teeth to sharp points. "I am, Detective O'Reilly, and you're a very fine-looking woman, if you don't mind me saying so." Now he did stand up. "As a professional, I recognize good breeding stock."

Vic's eyes narrowed. Erin let the comment go by.

"Are you in the market for a dog?" Dodgson went on. "I have a couple available if you're interested. Unneutered males, of course. I understand that's what cops like." He gave her a very appreciative look, head to toe.

"We're here to talk to you about Vernon Henderson," Erin said. "And Shady Acres Real Estate."

"Henderson? I don't think I know any Henderson." Dodgson came out from behind the desk. He moved with an easy, confident grace. Erin realized what his wardrobe reminded her of. It was the spitting image of Michael Jackson's "Smooth Criminal" suit.

"You were talking to him about an apartment building," Erin said. "A few weeks ago."

"Strange," Dodgson said. "You'd think I would've remembered something like that."

"Are you in the real estate business, Mr. Dodgson?" Erin asked.

"I'm in the dog business, Ms. O'Reilly," he said. He offered his hand to Rolf.

Rolf took a step back, bristling. Now he did growl, low in his chest. Dodgson laughed, showing those sharp teeth again.

"Careful," he said. "You got a lawsuit on a leash there."

"Rolf's never bitten anyone I didn't want him to," Erin said evenly. "Can you say the same about yours?"

"Love and Hate, here?" Dodgson said, indicating the caged Dobermans. "Yeah, actually, I can. They just need to know who's boss. You show 'em a firm hand and they belong to you. That's the thing about a bitch, O'Reilly. Someone's always in control. It can be you, or it can be them."

"Love and Hate?" Vic repeated. He was keeping a wary eye on the dogs.

"Hate's not so bad, but Love's one mean son of a bitch," Dodgson said. "Better keep your hands to yourself if you like being able to count to ten. It'd be interesting to put Love and your K-9 in the ring, let 'em go a couple rounds."

"Section 351 of the Agriculture and Markets Law has something to say about that," Erin said.

"Oh? And what's that?" Dodgson inquired.

Erin didn't have Kira Jones's head for the New York Penal Code, but she knew the sections that pertained to dogs by heart. "If you're talking about setting up or participating in a dogfight, it says you owe the state four years and twenty-five grand," she said. "Anyone shows up to watch, they're looking at a year and a thousand bucks."

"I think you may have misunderstood me," Dodgson said. "I was just wondering how they'd stack up in a theoretical kind of way. Like fantasy football at the office water cooler."

"That gets me thinking," Vic said. "I wonder how, say, you and I would stack up. Maybe we should put on some gloves and go a couple rounds. Or just forget the gloves. Theoretically."

"Where were you last night, between five and seven o'clock?" Erin asked suddenly.

"Hold on, lady. Are you accusing me of something?"

"Please answer the question, Mr. Dodgson."

He snapped his fingers. "O'Reilly! I knew the name was familiar. I've heard about you. *Detective* O'Reilly. Your partner here in on it with you?"

"What the hell are you talking about?" Erin retorted.

Dodgson winked. "Okay, that's how you want to play it, I get it. All in the game, right? Okay, last night I was here until six. Then I went to a club, got some dinner, found myself one fine-looking bitch, and we went back to my place."

"What's this woman's name?" Erin asked.

"Now that's the funny thing. I can't quite recall. But she was a good piece of ass. Not quite as good as what I'm looking at here, but close." He let his eyes rove up and down her with absolutely no shame.

"What club were you at?" she asked, ignoring the petty sexual harassment. He was just looking for a reaction.

"Little place called B66," Dodgson said, naming one of the more popular Brooklyn clubs. "Maybe you've heard of it. I got an idea. I was about to close up shop here. Maybe you and I could go get a drink, if you're off duty, and get to know each other a little better."

"If you've really heard about me," Erin said quietly, "you should listen to what you hear before you start hitting on me."

She and Dodgson exchanged a long look, and she saw in his eyes that he did know who she was. That made sense. The O'Malleys had a presence in Brooklyn. For the first time in the conversation, Dodgson's eyes slid off to the side and he broke contact. He might be willing to bluff and bluster in front of a cop, but he wanted no trouble with Morton Carlyle or Evan O'Malley.

"How come you're here, talking to me?" Dodgson asked.

"Word has it, you're the guy who runs things around here," Erin said. "Someone put three bullets in Vernon Henderson and I think you know who."

"Like I told you, O'Reilly, I don't know any Henderson. Sorry. Now, I really do have to close up. I've got places to go. Obligations."

"Of course you do," Erin said. "Have a good night, Mr. Dodgson."

Chapter 8

"You were kind of quiet in there," Erin observed. They were back on the sidewalk in front of Dodgson's psychopathic pet store.

"You told me not to pick a fight," Vic said. "This is me being nice."

"You challenged him to a fistfight."

"A theoretical fistfight. Erin, the guy's a sleazeball. I would love to toss his dentist some work. If somebody talked about my sister that way, they'd need a metal detector and a proctologist to retrieve his fillings."

"But I'm not your sister, Vic."

"No, you're my partner. That's even worse."

"Stop it. I can take care of myself. These guys are all assholes. They stink and they make ugly sounds. If I don't let it bother me, why should it bother you? Anyway," she added. "You say worse stuff to me all the time."

"Yeah, well, that's different. Of course we slag each other. Difference is, he means it."

"Forget about it, Vic. Let's work the case."

"Okay. What do we know now that we didn't going in?"

"He's definitely the guy Henderson was talking to."

"Yeah," Vic agreed. "I saw the way he brushed us off when you brought our victim up again. So what?"

"So Henderson was definitely into something with him, something shady. First thing in the morning, I'm going to pull the title deed for that building and see whose name is on it. I'm also going to check the property's history."

Vic yawned. "Sorry. Whenever I hear that word, it takes me back to Mr. Brecker, my tenth-grade history teacher. Most boring man on the face of the earth. You know those ceiling tiles, the white ones with the little holes in them?"

"Yeah. What do those have to do with anything?"

"You ever wonder how many holes are in each of those?"

"Not really."

"About five thousand one hundred. The exact number varies, depending on the tile. I know that because of Mr. Brecker. I must've counted every hole in every tile."

"You must've been a great kid to have in class."

He shrugged. "When I wasn't in detention, I did all right. You going back to the Eightball?"

"Yeah, just long enough to update the murder board. You?"

"I guess I'll take off. I still need to do my weights. It's arm day today."

"Isn't it always? See you tomorrow."

Vic climbed into his Taurus, Erin and Rolf got in her Charger, and they went their separate ways.

*   *   *

The lights were off in Major Crimes when Erin got there at quarter to seven. The sun was getting low enough that the Manhattan skyline blocked the direct sunlight from reaching the windows, so the office was dim, illuminated by reflected golden magic-hour light.

Erin walked over to the whiteboard, intending to just scribble down what they had on Dodgson and get out of there. A tall glass of Guinness and a bowl of Irish stew at the Barley Corner sounded really good right about then. She was tired, hungry, and ready to go home. She picked up a dry-erase marker and raised her hand to start writing.

Rolf stiffened and looked at something to Erin's left. She turned.

Lieutenant Webb was standing in the shadows a few feet back from the window, hands in his trench coat's well-worn pockets, staring out at the New York streets.

"Sir," Erin said. "I didn't see you there. I thought everybody had gone home."

Webb took a hand out of his pocket and plucked an unlit cigarette from the corner of his mouth. He stared at it, as if he was talking to the Camel instead of to Erin.

"Cath always said I should quit," he said quietly. "She can't stand the smell. She said it was a barrier to intimacy. Like a beard. I never wanted a beard, but I guess when I had to choose between keeping these damn coffin nails and Cath, I loved smoking more."

"Are you okay, sir?"

He laid the small white cylinder down on his desk and turned to face her. Erin thought she'd never seen her commanding officer look so tired, so old.

"I think maybe it's time to hand in my shield," he said.

"Sir?" Erin took a step toward him, trying to read his face.

"Some jobs, you can have a bad day, you don't have to bring your 'A' game," Webb said. "But some you can't. A brain surgeon can't just go through the motions, and neither can we."

"Some cops do," Erin said, trying to inject a little levity.

"You have an off day here, on the Job, and people die," he said, ignoring her words. "A murderer walks, maybe, and kills someone else. A rapist goes on and ruins the lives of ten, twenty, a hundred women. A robber keeps right on stealing. Or maybe you're a little too slow and another officer, one of your brothers, goes down. And you end up standing next to his widow while they hand her a folded flag.

"If I can't bring it, O'Reilly, I've got no business being here. And this time I can't do it."

"Why not, sir?" She wanted to reach out, to touch him, but that wouldn't be appropriate. Not here.

"The light was like this," he said. "Sun just going down. November. Even in LA, it can get chilly. Not like here, but enough to get in your bones. It'd been raining, but the sun came out right at the end of the day. I went to the house to tell Cath I was done with La La Land. I was moving out here. That was the last time I saw her, until last night. I thought we'd both moved on, and figured I'd at least done it with a little dignity."

Erin waited and said nothing. In an interrogation, when the subject was talking, you let him talk, even if he wasn't answering your question directly. He was giving you information. True or false, it told you something about him, and that was useful.

"Cath's a good woman," he said. "By and large. Our marriage didn't break up because of anything she did. I guess it was mostly on me. Of course, she knew who I was when we got together. Maybe she thought I'd change. Or she would. Or we'd figure something out. I didn't know until yesterday that..."

He stopped. He took off his battered fedora and ran a hand along a scalp that was nearly bald. "You've never been married, O'Reilly."

"No, sir."

"But you've been in love." It wasn't a question.

Erin nodded. She wanted to say, "Still am," but decided not to.

"When you fall out of love, it goes a couple of ways," he said. "Either you stop caring, go numb, or you turn it into hate. Divorce is like an amputation. Like getting an arm or a leg chopped right off. And most days you don't feel it, but you know what phantom pain is, right?"

Erin nodded again.

"Phantom love," Webb sighed. "It's still in there, and it can pop right up again when you least expect it. Maybe it never goes away. I'm compromised, O'Reilly. I don't believe Cath killed Henderson. I *can't* believe it. I could've found her with the gun in her hand, still smoking, and maybe I still wouldn't."

"Because you still love her," Erin said softly.

"Yeah," Webb said. "Isn't that a kick in the balls? You find out years too late that you should've stuck it out, should've worked the problem, should've kicked the damn bad habits. You know I hate cigarettes?"

Erin blinked. She didn't know what to say to that.

"I hate them and love them. Just like Cath. Maybe I can't kick either habit."

"Maybe you should take some time, sir," Erin said. "Just a few days of vacation. Let Vic and me handle this."

"What kind of commander does that?"

"The right kind," she said. "The kind who trusts his people to bring it home. The kind who understands why they don't let doctors operate on family members."

"But what if she did it?" Webb asked, and for the first time Erin saw open, naked fear in Harry Webb's eyes. It shook her more deeply than she'd imagined it could, but she forced her voice to be calm, steady, and reassuring.

"Then we'll find out the truth," she said. "I don't know if she killed him. But I do think she knows more than she's told us. Can you get her to cooperate?"

"I can try."

"All we want is the truth," Erin said. "You're not helping her by covering it up."

He nodded. "She's at my place," he said. "I told her not to leave town. But I almost put her on a plane myself, today. I wanted to."

"Because you love her," she said.

"Because I love her," he echoed. "And she asked for my help."

"You're helping her," she said, and she laid a hand on his arm, protocol be damned. "Whether she knows it or not."

"Okay, O'Reilly," Webb said. "You win."

"I don't understand, sir."

"You want this case, it's yours." He straightened his back, and just like that, ten years seemed to fall from his shoulders. "I'll tell the Captain first thing tomorrow. And then I'll keep an eye on Cath for you. I'll keep her here until this whole thing is cleared up. But this is on you now, Detective Second Grade. You got this?"

Erin tightened her jaw and looked him in the eye. "I've got this, sir," she promised. "I won't let you down."

* * *

Erin went into the Barley Corner the back way. A few of the guys spotted her, but she managed to slip upstairs without attracting much notice. She found Carlyle in his office, working at his computer. When he saw her, he got up and met her in the doorway with a kiss.

Something in the kiss made him take a step back and look her over with sudden concern. He put his hands on her arms just below the shoulders.

"What's the matter, darling?"

"I'm fine," she said.

He didn't move. "I'm certain it's nothing you can't handle," he said. "Because there's nothing I've seen that's beyond you. But I'd like you to tell me."

"You're going to think I'm silly."

"I've never thought that. Fiery, impetuous, a mite reckless, aye, but never silly."

She smiled. "Don't take this the wrong way, but I'm thinking about marriage."

"And that's troubling you?"

"Something a guy told me earlier this evening. He's divorced, but he's still hung up on his ex. And it's getting him in trouble. I guess I'm just realizing what a big deal it is."

"Marriage?"

"Yeah. It's not something you can take back."

"Few things are," he said. "Have you heard the saying, you can't put words back in your mouth or bullets back in your gun?"

"Yeah," she said again. "But I've got a dead divorcee in our morgue and a live one screwing up the investigation. What do you think about it?"

"Are you talking about your case, or the institution of marriage?"

"Marriage, I guess."

He looked straight into her face. "I've always believed it's a lifelong decision. Perhaps not for everyone, but for me. That's what my faith tells me, and more to the point, it's what's in my heart. If Rose had been spared, I'd be her husband today."

"What if you fell out of love with her?"

"Why do I get the feeling we're not talking about my wife, darling?" His tone was light, but his eyes were thoughtful.

Erin looked away. "I said you'd think I was being silly."

"Erin," he said, putting two fingers under her chin and gently turning her face back toward his. "We're bound together by more than love. Are you proposing to me?"

"I... what? No!" she exclaimed. Then she stammered, "I mean, it's not that I'm against the idea. I'm just not ready. There's too much going on right now." She felt like an idiot and wondered what she could do to get out of that room with a little dignity intact. Even better, maybe she could just erase the last five minutes. But as he'd just reminded her, words couldn't be taken back.

"It's a conversation we ought to be having," he said. "But not just now, I agree."

"Can you imagine the service?" Erin said, suddenly giggling. "You wouldn't want to sit on the wrong side of the church. On my side there'd be all the boys in blue, and on yours..."

"Hard lads with tattoos on their arms and prison terms in their pasts," he chuckled. "With a few IRA hardheads thrown in for good measure."

"And your best man hitting on all the bridesmaids," she said.

"Maybe two or three at once," he agreed. "Corky always said weddings and funerals were the best places to look for stray lasses."

"Funerals? Really?"

"You'd have to ask him about that. He's in favor of a theory that grief makes women emotionally open and therefore available."

"Just as long as he's not hitting on the widow," she said.

Carlyle made a slight, apologetic shrug.

"He didn't!" Erin exclaimed, believing wholeheartedly that James Corcoran was completely capable of it. Thankfully, their joking had broken the tension of the moment. Whenever they tried to think about the future, they both shied away from it. Erin wanted—needed—to know where their relationship was going, but right now, she didn't dare. Divorce might be the best outcome in store, because it assumed they'd both live long enough to get sick of each other.

"Can we get supper sent up?" she asked, pushing the whole business aside. "I don't really want to eat downstairs this evening."

"I'll be happy to order it up, darling, and I'll join you for a quick bite. But remember, my day's just getting started while yours is ending."

"I know," she said. "I used to work nights, remember? Just don't stay up too late, and try not to get killed."

*   *   *

They'd just finished a late supper of hearty bowls of Irish stew with fresh-baked oatmeal rolls, washed down with Guinness. Carlyle had set off downstairs, leaving her resting comfortably on the couch, when Erin's phone rang.

"Not now, Webb," she groaned. Rolf, curled up beside her, lifted his head and perked his ears. He was cozy, but he wanted her to know that if they needed to chase someone, he was ready and willing.

But the caller ID wasn't the Lieutenant. It said "Michelle." That meant it was her sister-in-law's cell. Erin thumbed the phone and put it to her ear.

"Hey, Shelley," she said.

"Hey, sis," Michelle said.

"What's wrong?" Erin asked, sitting up. Michelle's voice, usually so bubbly and cheerful, was quiet and subdued. Rolf, sensing the change in Erin's energy, stretched and got to his feet, tail wagging anxiously.

"I maybe shouldn't be calling you," Michelle said. "Not about this."

The warning bells went off in Erin's head again. "Are you okay?" she asked. "What about the kids? And Junior?"

"They're all fine. Anna's excited about her graduation. She's going to be done with third grade in just a couple of weeks here. They're having a presentation and the dance team will be performing. She's been preparing all spring. And Patrick got a gold star on his spelling test and... and..."

And with that Michelle started to cry.

Erin held the phone awkwardly and wondered what to say. She had no idea what was going on. Put her in a gunfight or a bar brawl and she knew what to do. She could take on two drunks at once, six if she had Rolf. She could reduce a perp to tears in the interrogation room. But she was never much good at making the tears stop.

"Shelley..." she said. "It's okay."

"No, it's not," Michelle sniffled. "I have a beautiful family and a wonderful life. There's food in the fridge and money in the... in the bank account. I have a lovely son and daughter and I love them. My husband is brilliant, and handsome, and he's a good man, I know that. And I just put Anna and Patrick to bed, and I'm sitting here all by myself, and I'm wondering... I mean, it would be so stupid to throw it all away, but I just thought..."

"Shelley, what are you talking about?"

Erin had to wait for several sniffles and throat-clearings.

"I hardly ever see him," Michelle said at last. "The hospital upped his hours. He's always working, and when he's home, he's not really *here*. He's so tired, and whatever energy he has, the kids take up. They miss him too and they get so needy. I'm starting to just feel like the help, Erin. I cook, I clean, I take the kids places."

"Shelley, did Junior say or do something? Are you mad at him?"

"Well... no. I wish he would do something. We don't have any spark, Erin. When's the last time you think he and I made love?"

"Shelley! This is my brother we're talking about. I don't need to know this!"

"I'll bet your man took you to bed more recently," Michelle said. "You know why? Because you've got the spark. And we don't. Not anymore."

"Have you been reading romance novels again, Shelley?"

"Well... maybe a few." Michelle sounded slightly embarrassed. "There's this series I've been reading, about this nurse in Scotland who goes back in time to the Eighteenth Century, and they're making it into a TV series that looks like it'll be really good, and sexy, and..."

"Spare me the details," Erin said. She preferred thrillers and action movies. "Look, Shelley, it sounds like you're just going through a dry spell. Things will get better. You and my brother... I can't even imagine you apart. You're family."

"I know, Erin, and I do love him. I love all of you. It's just... there has to be something more than this. I gave up a career. I gave up everything for my family and maybe I'm wondering what's in it for me. Don't ever get married, Erin. And don't have kids."

"What?" Erin couldn't believe her ears. Michelle loved her children, practically worshiped them. "Shelley, you don't mean that."

"I do. Once you have them, it's too late, because you'll love them so much you'll give up your whole life for their sake. And then you'll wake up and you'll be looking at the wrong side of forty and your life will be over."

Erin had nothing to say to that. She just let her sister-in-law talk, working out the frustrations of quiet, prosperous, married life. Maybe the grass really was greener, Erin thought as she listened.

At last, Michelle swallowed noisily and cleared her throat one more time. "Sorry," she said. "I think I just needed to get it out of my system. I'm okay. Don't worry, I won't do anything. Please, don't say anything to your brother, okay? We'll sort it out between us. The last thing I want is for you to get caught in the middle. You're the sister I wish I'd had growing up. You're easy to talk to."

"It comes from all the time I spend in interrogation rooms," Erin said. "People like to tell me things. Then sometimes I lock them up."

Michelle laughed shakily. "I guess so. Thanks for lending an ear, sis. I'd better go now. I've got some things to take care of, household stuff. Have a good night."

"Good night, Shelley," Erin said. She stared at the phone for a long minute after the call disconnected. Then she shook her head and looked at Rolf. He looked back, cocking his head quizzically. She ruffled the fur behind his ears.

"Thanks," she said to him. He was so uncomplicated, so completely devoted and faithful. "Carlyle was half right when he said I needed a gangster. What I really needed was a dog."

Rolf's tail thumped against the cushions. If she needed him, he was right there.

Chapter 9

Hair still damp from her shower, muscles pleasantly sore from her morning run, Erin felt a lot better. With a day of work in front of her, she shoved Michelle's midlife crisis to the back of her mind. Webb's personal problems had more direct bearing on the case, but she could handle that. This was a standard homicide, no more and no less.

Vic was already in Major Crimes, his usual gigantic cup of Mountain Dew on his desk. He had bags under his eyes, but he looked reasonably alert and cheerful, which by Vic's standards meant he wasn't scowling.

"You're in early," Erin commented as Rolf curled up in his place beside her desk.

"SNEU took down a major score around two this morning," Vic said. "They're really stickin' it to the Lucarellis in Little Italy. Sergeant Logan's team got a tip and hit a stash house, grabbed a couple kilos of the good stuff. Piekarski was all amped up when she got off duty. I'm at home fast asleep this whole time. First I know of it, she's practically kicking my door down. She's lucky I'm only half-awake and can't get to my gun safe in time. I'm just barely figuring out what's going on. When that woman's high on the Job, it's like getting mauled by a wild dog. But in a good way."

"That was a lot more than I needed to know about your love life," Erin said. She looked at him a little more closely. "You've got blood on your face. Cut yourself shaving?"

"Like a wild dog," Vic repeated. Then he grinned. "You sure you don't want more info?"

"Pass," she said. "I swear, everybody at the Eightball is hopped up on hormones. We ought to have Levine test our water supply." She sat down, logged onto her computer, and checked her messages. To her surprise, she had one from Kira Jones.

It was a detailed breakdown of Vernon Henderson's personal and business finances. Erin did a quick scan.

"Got our victim's account details," she said.

"That was quick," Vic said. "What's the word?"

"I have no idea. Kira may understand this, but I don't."

"Is she on site?"

"I think so. This e-mail was sent twenty minutes ago."

"Then get her down here."

Erin looked at him. "I thought you were pissed at her."

"I am. So what? I'm pissed at you, remember? It's my natural state of being."

"You ever think about anger management?"

"I'm Russian. In Russia, you don't manage anger..."

"...Anger manages you," she finished for him as she picked up her desk phone and called upstairs. Two minutes later, Kira was down in Major Crimes, looking over one of Erin's shoulders. Vic was on the other side. Rolf was asleep.

"I don't see what's so confusing," Kira said. "You just need to follow these check tracers here, and as this footnote says, he made cash withdrawals on these dates. Then he redeposited, but slightly different amounts. I guess he thought that would be clever, so the banks wouldn't be able to track him. But since he opened this account under his own name, and this one under his wife's..."

"Ex-wife," Erin corrected.

"You don't see what's so confusing," Vic said flatly.

"Kira, we appreciate you doing this," Erin said. "Because Vic and I don't have the training or the eye for it. And you do. We don't need to know how you did it, we just need to know the result."

"Oh. Right. Sorry." Kira took a second to order her thoughts. "Your guy was trying to hide his money. And I'm guessing not all of it was his. At least, he didn't declare it on his taxes."

"You got a look at his tax returns?" Vic asked.

"I talked to the CSU guy who got his computer," Kira explained. "He had his returns on the hard drive. Unencrypted, even."

"How'd you know we had his computer?" Vic demanded.

"You were checking him out," she said. "You went to his place. Of course you took his computer. You're not morons."

"That's the nicest thing you've said to me in a long time," he said.

"Then I take it back," Kira said with a sweetly insincere smile. "You're as dumb as a bag of hammers."

"That's more like it," Vic said.

"So he was laundering money?" Erin asked, trying to keep them on track.

"Trying to," Kira said. "This was more like giving it a quick rinse. I don't think he really knew how to do it right. I mean, he was using personal accounts, just moving it around. The IRS would've got onto him sooner or later."

"What was the money for?" Erin wondered.

"Best guess?" Kira replied. "Real estate. At least that's what he was buying. These withdrawals correspond to the acquisition dates of these properties, if you look on this other spreadsheet..."

Erin felt her eyes glazing over and tried to stay alert. Beside her, Vic's eyelids drooped. "Why was he buying these lots?" she asked.

"I can't possibly answer that on the basis of his financial records," Kira said.

"I'm asking for opinions. Suggestions."

"My opinion is that our commanding officer needs to get his ass in here and pull his weight," Vic said.

"Webb's recusing himself from the investigation," Erin said.

"He's what now?" Vic was definitely awake.

"He's out," she said. "This is still our case, but I'm in charge of the investigation."

"Since when?"

"Since last night."

"Can he do that?" Vic asked Kira. "You're Internal Affairs. You know this shit."

"If he's personally involved with the case, he'd be putting it in jeopardy if he didn't step aside," she said. "Sounds to me like he's doing the right thing."

"I knew it," Vic growled. "If IAB is on board, you know somebody's getting screwed."

"Wait," Kira said. "You wanted me to disagree with his decision?"

"No, then you'd be showing you didn't trust the boots on the ground."

"So there was no right answer? What the hell did you ask me for?"

"I guess she isn't a moron either," Vic said with satisfaction.

"If you two could stop acting like you're married to each other and answer my question, I'd appreciate it," Erin said.

That worked. Vic and Kira both made grimaces of disgust and turned back to the matter at hand.

"Maybe he's got inside info from City Hall," Kira suggested. "If there's some project about to be approved, and the city needs the land, maybe?"

"He met his ex in one of these towers," Vic said. "Maybe he was looking for girls."

"Then what was he doing chasing a skirt out in California?" Erin asked. "He bought and sold houses, but he also went for slums. I feel like if we can figure out why, we may know why he's dead."

"I got nothing," Vic said.

"Buy low, sell high," Kira said. "It's definitely some of the cheapest real estate in the five boroughs. Not that that's saying much."

"Was he selling high?" Erin asked.

"No," Kira said. "Not really."

"Who owns Faith Copeland's building now?" Erin asked, the thought suddenly striking her. "I think we need to talk to him."

"Have fun with that," Kira said. "I need to get back upstairs to my real job."

"Thanks for your help," Erin said. "It means a lot."

"Yeah," Vic added. "Do it again sometime and I may start thinking you're a cop or something."

"So," Erin said to Vic. "Want to take a drive to the Bronx?"

*   *   *

Erin and Vic stared at the tenement where Faith Copeland had grown up. It stared back out of broken, boarded-up windows. Rolf, unimpressed, sniffed the crumbling corner of the building and cocked a leg.

"Your mutt's got the right idea," Vic said. "What a toilet."

"I'm surprised Faith got out," Erin said. The cycle of poverty was always hard to escape.

"Yeah," he agreed. "I'd expect her to have popped out a couple babies by the time she was nineteen. Then she'd be living on welfare or peddling her ass to make ends meet."

"Don't be such a..." Erin said, searching for the word.

"Realist?" he tried. "Social commentator?"

"Asshole," she decided. "I know I was lucky. I grew up in a home with two parents, middle class, white. Check your privilege, Vic."

"And my mom's a florist," he said. "I went to community college. I'm not exactly an Ivy Leaguer. What's your point?"

"If my dad had caught a bullet like hers did, I might've turned out worse," she said. "These are the people we're supposed to protect. It's hard to look after people when you're looking down on them."

"Okay," he said. "I'll be the first to admit, people in neighborhoods like these have been pretty thoroughly screwed, and that's not their fault. But I dare you to tell me half the homicides in the city don't happen in slums."

"So maybe we need to figure out how to fix things so people don't have to live in slums anymore."

He snorted. "That's not your job or mine. We just pick up the pieces when people get killed. You want to fix the system, go into politics. You think people hate you when you're a cop, try being a politician. Now, where's this guy who owns this place?"

The name on the apartment title was Kenneth Parker, but he was nowhere to be found. The detectives braved the building's filthy hallways, fighting nausea at the smells of trash and stale urine, knocking on doors. They finally found the super's office on their fourth try. The door was unlabeled.

Inside, they found a trio of young men dressed like gangsta wannabes, complete with baseball caps, sports jerseys, low-hanging jeans, and gold chains. The room was thick with cigarette smoke and body odor.

The kids eyeballed Vic and Erin, giving her lingering, appreciative looks. Vic replied with his standard badass stare and cracked his knuckles. He probably weighed more than any two of them put together.

"We're looking for Kenneth Parker," Erin said.

"He ain't here," said one of the kids. "What you need?"

"We'd like to talk to him," she said.

"You a Narc?" the second kid asked, looking at Rolf.

"No," she said. "We're with the NYPD, but we're not investigating drugs."

"Unless you've got some," Vic added. "In which case, you're all under arrest."

"He joking?" the first kid asked.

"Do I look like I'm joking?" Vic replied.

"Hey, man, just 'cause we're Black, you think we're selling drugs?"

"No, I think you're dealing drugs because you're dressed like drug dealers and acting like drug dealers."

"Which one of you is in charge of this office?" Erin asked, stepping in front of Vic. He was getting back at her for ordering him not to pick a fight with Dodgson.

The three kids looked at each other. None of them said anything.

"Look," Erin said. "You obviously know Parker. Either I'll talk to you or I'll talk to him. So who's calling the shots?"

She saw two of them glance at the third. It was just for a second, but it was enough for her practiced eye.

"You," she said, pointing to the third kid. "What's your name?"

"Andre," he said.

"Your last name?"

"I don't have to tell you shit."

"You're required by law to identify yourself when a police officer asks," she said. "I don't want to take you downtown. That'd waste your time and mine. I'd rather take care of this now, without trouble."

Andre thought it over and decided not to make it an issue. "Parker," he said.

"And Kenneth is your... what?" she prompted.

"My uncle."

"So you know where he is."

"What you want with him, anyway?"

"I want to know how he bought this property from Vernon Henderson," she said.

"I don't know nothin' about that," he said, but the flicker of recognition in his eyes gave him away.

"Tell me about Henderson," she said.

"What about him? He a white boy who don't belong here, just like you," Andre said defiantly, glaring at her and Vic.

"I agree," Erin said. "That's why I'm curious about him. Why did he want this building?"

"He didn't."

"Then why did he buy it?"

"He sold it to my uncle right away," Andre said. "He didn't want to keep it."

"So he flipped the property?"

"If you say so."

"What was the deal?"

"I dunno."

"Here's the thing, Andre. I think you do." She stepped closer to him. "I think you're smarter than you're acting. So be smart. Give me what I want, and I walk away. Otherwise, I'm going to call up some buddies in the Street Narcotics unit and they'll turn this place upside down. They'll find something, I know it. You may be clean, but I'll be there's people here who aren't. Then we'll ID all your friends and see what we've got on them. Basically, we can turn your life into a never-ending shitshow. Your uncle's life, too. And when he asks why the NYPD is giving him such a hard time, you can explain it's because you didn't answer the detectives' nice, reasonable questions. How old are you, kid?"

Andre didn't answer.

"Your uncle gave you this job," Erin said. It was a guess, but she thought it was a good one. "He wants to see if you've got what it takes to work for him. If you screw this up, he's going to think of that every time he looks at you. Do you really want that?"

"You two stay right there," Vic said, glaring at Andre's friends, who were sidling toward the door. "Your buddy's trying to decide whether you all leave here in handcuffs or not."

"What you care, anyway?" Andre asked. "What's this Henderson punk to you?"

"He got shot," Erin said. "So unless you can convince me your uncle was on good terms with him, he's a suspect."

"And so are you," Vic interjected.

"I didn't kill nobody!" Andre protested. "Neither did Uncle Kenny!"

Erin looked at him and waited. "If your uncle didn't kill Henderson, he's got nothing to worry about," she said.

"They was in business," Andre said at last. "Uncle Kenny got the property, this other boy got a cut of things."

"What things?" Erin asked.

"Everything, lady! Whatever was goin' down! A percentage, like."

"Rent?" she asked.

"That, too."

Erin understood then. "Okay," she said. "And how does Uncle Kenny feel about the arrangement?"

"He's cool with it. Everybody gets paid, no hard feelings, you feel me?"

"Yeah, I do," she said. "Thanks, Andre. You have a good day."

Vic let them get halfway to the car before he burst out, "Why are we walking away from those losers?"

"You think we should've arrested them?" Erin asked.

"Hell yes!"

"On what charge?"

"You heard the kid! He practically confessed to drug dealing, protection rackets, whatever!"

"Not in any way that would hold up in court," she said. "Vic, he only talked because I threatened to haul him downtown. The second I cuffed him, he would've shut up. Yeah, I know he's dirty, and so is his uncle. But at least we finally know what Henderson was up to."

"He was flipping run-down properties to slumlords in exchange for cash kickbacks off the books," Vic said. "And a cut of the illegal business."

"Yeah," she said. "That's basically how the Mafia got started in Little Italy back in the day. Small-time protection rackets. He was selling run-down buildings to criminals, building his own little empire."

"No wonder he got whacked," Vic said. "He didn't have the muscle for that kind of work."

"And no wonder his apartment was full of guns," she said. "But this wasn't a hit."

"Because hitmen bring their own guns," Vic said. "I know, I know. But it's gotta be connected."

"Yeah," Erin said. "But here's the thing that gets me. The killer knew where to find Henderson. How? It wasn't his house."

"Beats the hell out of me."

"Me, too. But there's one person who might know."

"Yeah, Henderson. Unfortunately, he's dead."

"One living person, Vic."

"You don't sound happy about it," he observed.

"I'm not," she said. "Because Webb won't be, either."

Chapter 10

Erin was right. As a precaution, she held her phone away from her ear after telling her commanding officer what she wanted.

"You want to do *what?*" Webb demanded. His voice echoed off the inside of Erin's Charger. Vic, seated next to her, winced and leaned away.

"I want to talk to Catherine Simmons, sir," she said, keeping her tone low and even. "Is she with you?"

"Of course she is," he said. "Which you already knew. Damn it, O'Reilly, I stepped out of the way so she wouldn't get hauled into this any further."

"Respectfully, sir, that's inaccurate. You stepped aside so your personal attachment wouldn't prejudice the case."

"Are you telling me you don't believe her statement?"

"No, sir."

"Then what possible good is this going to do?"

"Sir, I'd prefer to discuss that with Ms. Simmons, in person. Where is she, please?"

There was a pause, in which Erin heard an unusual noise. It took her a second to identify the sound of teeth grinding.

"Come to my place," Webb said at last. "You have the address?"

"It's in the computer," she said. "Brooklyn?"

"That's the one."

"Vic and I will be there ASAP. We're in the Bronx now, so it'll be a little while."

There was a beep in Erin's ear. "He hung up on me," she informed Vic.

"Aren't you glad you can't slam cell phones down?" he replied. "Jeez. We're going to Long Island again? We oughta hitch a ride on one of the Department's choppers, pick up some frequent-flier miles."

"I think you need to fly commercial to get those," Erin said, putting the car in gear. Rolf stuck his head between the seats, tongue hanging out. He, at least, loved car rides. They could do this all days as far as he was concerned.

Vic spent the drive down to Brooklyn on Erin's computer, looking up title deeds and comparing them with the police database.

"Looks like you're right," he said as they crossed the iconic Brooklyn Bridge. "All the guys who've bought property from Shady Acres have records. It's a bunch of drug dealers, extortionists, and violent thugs. I'm amazed Henderson didn't get killed sooner. Some of these guys, even I wouldn't want to get in a fight with them."

"And any one of them might've had a disagreement with our victim about the terms of their arrangement," Erin said. "So we've got a big suspect pool. All of them could have motive, and Henderson brought the means himself. That just leaves opportunity."

"Which is why you're trying to figure who knew his movements," Vic said. "But couldn't any of these guys have just tailed him to his love shack?"

"Yeah," she sighed. "But I'm counting on Henderson being paranoid. I think he would've noticed if he was being shadowed. Can you get the mugshots of all these guys?"

"Already got 'em."

"Send them to my phone," she said.

*　*　*

Webb's apartment was a second-floor unit in a row of three-story brick buildings on Dean Street. Erin, Vic, and Rolf climbed the worn, shabby stairs to a door whose paint was peeling.

"Y'know, this is exactly the sort of place I picture the Lieutenant living," Vic said, continuing his commentary on New York's residences. "Dreary, depressing, nothing but earth tones."

Erin ignored him and pushed the doorbell. Not hearing anything, she rapped on the wood with her knuckles.

Webb opened the door. He glowered at Erin. In response, she gave him a look she'd learned from Ian Thompson, staring just past his ear with a carefully neutral expression on her face.

"Okay, O'Reilly, come on in," he said gruffly, stepping back. Wisps of cigarette smoke trailed into the hallway past him.

The detectives found themselves in a sparsely furnished old Brooklyn apartment. Webb wasn't big on décor. The furniture looked to have come from secondhand sources. The sofa was better than the disreputable one in the Major Crimes break room, but not by much. In one corner of the living room sat a desk with Webb's laptop and a pair of framed pictures of smiling teenage girls; his daughters from his first marriage. An ancient cathode-ray television set, big and blocky, squatted across the room from the couch. On the couch was Catherine Simmons, her feet drawn up under her, a coffee cup and saucer in her hands. A blanket and pillow were piled at one end of the sofa, suggesting Webb had been telling the truth about sleeping there. On the battered coffee table in front of the couch was an ashtray, filled to overflowing.

"Nice place you got here, sir," Vic said. "It suits you."c

"Thanks for accommodating us," Erin said. "Ms. Simmons, I'm sorry to bother you again. I just have a couple of follow-up questions."

"Surely this could have been done over the phone," Catherine said.

"I have some pictures to show you," Erin said. "I thought it would be easier in person."

Catherine glanced at her ex-husband, who nodded slightly.

"All right," she said. "I don't know what help I can be, but..."

"You said you met Mr. Henderson at a real-estate seminar," Erin said, sitting on the far end of the couch from the other woman. Rolf settled on his haunches beside his partner, while Vic held up a wall with his shoulders and watched.

"That's right," Catherine said. "In California."

"So you were interested in getting into the business?" Erin asked.

"I thought... I thought it might be a good way to pick up some extra income."

"Can I get you anything, O'Reilly?" Webb asked. "Neshenko? A cup of coffee?"

"No thank you, sir," Erin said, keeping her attention focused on her interviewee. "Were you in business with Mr. Henderson, Ms. Simmons?"

"I didn't work for him," Catherine said.

"But did you work *with* him?"

"No. That is," she faltered, "he asked if I wanted to. I hadn't decided yet."

"What did you know about his business dealings?" Erin asked.

"Very little. I don't really know what he was up to."

"He must have given you some idea, if you flew all the way out here."

"Well, yes. He was interested in reclaiming ailing properties, making them profitable."

"You're a divorce attorney, isn't that correct, Ms. Simmons?"

"Yes."

"So you're well-practiced when it comes to reading contracts, that sort of thing?"

"I suppose so."

"Have you ever bought a house?"

Catherine blinked. "Yes. Of course. Harry and I bought a house together in Los Angeles. And I was looking to sell it."

"You loved that house," Webb said quietly. "You're the one who wanted it."

She looked up at him with a complicated expression on her face. "Yes, Harry, I did, when I thought we'd be raising a family in it. That place is too big for just me." She turned her attention back to Erin. "Why are you asking me about that?"

"You understand real-estate transactions," Erin said. "Like the one Henderson recently concluded in Brooklyn."

"I'm sure I don't know what you mean," Catherine said.

"I'd like to show you some pictures," Erin said, taking out her phone. "Please tell me if you recognize any of these men."

She leaned over and began scrolling through the mugshots Vic had sent her. However, she wasn't looking at the pictures. She was watching the woman's face, particularly her eyes.

Everybody had tells. People often thought of them as big, obvious gestures, like playing with your hair or biting your fingernails. The truth was more subtle. Recognition caused physical reactions in people, reactions that were extremely difficult to disguise. On the third picture, Erin saw what she was looking for. Catherine's pupils dilated slightly and her eyes went just a little too wide. Her breath sucked in and she went suddenly still.

"Ms. Simmons," Erin said softly. "Who is this man?"

"I don't know him," Catherine said.

"I need you to tell me the truth," Erin said.

"O'Reilly," Webb said in warning tones.

"Catherine," Erin said, deliberately shifting to a first-name basis. "This is important. Who is this?"

"I don't know his name," Catherine said. "I... I only saw him once. When Vern took me on a drive into... into another part of the city. He... they... had a conversation."

"What did they talk about?" Erin asked.

"Vern was selling a building to him. They were arguing... I mean, they were discussing the deal."

"Why did you say they were arguing? Were they angry?"

"The other man was."

Erin took the opportunity to glance at her phone. The picture on the screen, she saw without much surprise, was Clay Dodgson.

"What was he angry about?" she asked.

"The... the terms."

"The contract?"

Catherine shook her head.

"There was another part of the agreement?" Erin asked. "Something that wasn't in the contract?"

Catherine nodded.

"Cath," Webb said. "What did you do?"

"Sir, please," Erin said, trying to silence him with her eyes.

Webb's mouth closed with an almost audible snap. Erin had the feeling that only his long experience as a police officer kept him still and quiet.

"Vern was dealing under the table," Erin continued. "But you knew that already."

"No one was getting hurt," Catherine said. "It was either him or somebody else, somebody worse. He was trying to help these people. Take care of them. That's what he said."

"Did you believe him?"

Catherine opened her mouth, but nothing came out. She swallowed and dropped her gaze to the coffee cup in her lap.

"I... I wanted to," she said. "It was just a little extra on the side. So the government wouldn't get a cut? So what. Everybody does it. Kickbacks are a part of lots of businesses. What was the harm?"

"Why don't we step down to the morgue and ask Henderson that?" Vic said.

"Neshenko!" The work cracked like a whip as it left Webb's mouth.

Catherine flinched and began to cry. Webb put out a hand toward her shoulder and paused. Indecision was written all over his face. Finally, he laid the hand on her. She leaned into it, putting her own hand over her face.

"I'm such an idiot," she sobbed. "I just thought... I thought... he seemed so *normal*. He talked about work and it was... it was just *work*. He didn't bring it home with him like... like you did, Harry."

"What are you talking about, Cath?" Webb said, startled. "I never told you any of the stuff I ran into on the Job. I never brought casework home."

"You didn't talk about it," she agreed. "But you carried it with you. You're... you're *dark*, Harry. And heavy. And being with you, it made the whole world seem that way. Is that how... how it looks to you?"

"I'm a cop, Cath. I run into murderers, terrorists, armed robbers, victims. When I see people, a lot of the time it's the worst day of their lives. For me? Just another Wednesday afternoon. Another day at the office. You get used to it."

She twisted under his hand and looked up at him with eyes that were suddenly furious, almost wild. "It changes you. Don't you dare say it doesn't. All that tragedy sticks to you. It's like when one of those big tankers runs aground and all that oil spills out into the ocean. It sticks to everything, this black, messy goo, and you can't swim in it. It chokes you. I was choking, Harry. That's why I had to get out."

Erin was watching Webb's face as his ex-wife said that. He had the look of a man who'd just been stabbed in the stomach. He didn't react outwardly, not much, but his complexion had gone waxy and his muscles were rigid. She wanted to grab Catherine Simmons and shake some sense into the woman. Didn't she see how much she was hurting him?

Grief, fear, and anger were selfish emotions. When one of those got a grip, it was hard to see other people's pain. Erin knew that. But she still wanted to smack her.

"I'm sorry, Cath," Webb said in a very low voice. "I guess we both did the best we knew how. I never wanted you to get hurt. If you're happier without me, then that's where you ought to be. I just wish..."

Catherine took hold of Webb's hand. Her eyes softened a little. "What?" she asked.

"I wish you hadn't come to New York," he said. "You should've stayed in LA. Cath, if this guy made you happy, I'd try to be happy for you, no matter what kind of ass I thought he was. But this man... he was a criminal, Cath. If you can't hack being with a cop, fine, but you can do so much better than him."

"I don't have much choice now, do I?" she shot back, her mouth twisting bitterly. "I can't very well build a future on Vern."

Webb didn't say anything.

"Catherine," Erin said. "Anything you can tell us about Vern's business dealings may help us. Did you know about his guns?"

"What guns?" she retorted. "I didn't think he had one until you people were talking about it at the house."

"Did you ever see his apartment?" Erin asked.

"I told you, I thought he lived in the house he brought me to."

"What did he want from you?"

Catherine stared at Erin. "What do you think?"

"I meant, in terms of his business."

"He needed more money."

"How much?" Vic asked.

"About a hundred."

"Just so we're clear," Erin said. "You mean a hundred thousand dollars?"

Catherine nodded.

"Bank transfer?" Webb asked. He'd recovered a little. Being in detective mode was helping.

"Cash."

"You didn't bring a hundred grand, cash, into Brooklyn, did you?" Vic was aghast at the thought.

"I'm not an idiot, Detective," Catherine said. "No, I'm not carrying a suitcase full of money around with me. I didn't even have it. Yet."

"That's why you're selling the house," Webb said softly.

"I assume you knew what Vern wanted the money for?" Erin asked.

"He had a surefire prospect," she said. "But he needed to make some payments to... to a couple of guys. The cash was a sort of deposit."

"What guys?" Erin asked. When Catherine just looked at her, she set her jaw, reminded herself to treat this like any interrogation, and kept pushing. "Don't expect us to believe you'd hand over that kind of money without doing your due diligence. You're a lawyer, for God's sake. What was the property? Who owns it?"

"It's a place in Brooklyn," Catherine faltered, shrinking away from Erin.

"It's okay, Cath," Webb said. He sat down on the couch on the other side of her from Erin and held her hand. "Have you been there?"

"Yes. It's a brick house with a big garage. There's some sort of automobile shop in it."

"What's the address?" Webb asked.

"On 48th," she said. "I don't remember the number. I know about where it is, and I'd recognize it if I saw it. Vern had plans for making it profitable."

"I'll bet he did," Vic muttered.

"That's pretty close to Dodgson's neighborhood," Erin said. "You think he owns that building, too?"

"Probably," Vic said. "But he might have someone else fronting for him."

"Catherine, would you be okay with going for a drive with us?" Erin asked. "Just to point out the building?"

She nodded. "If you want. But what good is it going to do? Harry, I just want to go home."

"The fastest way home is on the other side of this mess," Webb said. "I promise, the moment it's over, I'll take you to the airport myself."

"All right." Catherine took the cup and saucer off her lap. Somehow she'd managed not to spill any coffee on herself. She set them carefully on Webb's battered, stained coffee table. "Harry, you really need some better furniture."

"When I get around to it," Webb said.

"What if you meet a nice girl?" Catherine asked, managing a weak, watery smile. "Would you bring her back to a place like this?"

"I think my days of picking up badge bunnies in bars are over," Webb said, returning the smile wearily. "Last time I tried, it didn't go so well."

"There's a story there," Vic said, glancing at Erin with a raised eyebrow.

"Maybe we can swap life stories later, Neshenko," Webb said. "Much later. We've got work to do."

Chapter 11

At Vic's suggestion, they swung by a sandwich shop to grab a quick lunch. Erin had a Reuben, Vic got a BLT, and Webb went with ham and cheese. Rolf ended up with a few pieces of corned beef from Erin's sandwich.

"I'm not hungry," Catherine said.

"You sure?" Vic said. "It's on the Department's dime. Just save your receipt."

She shook her head and turned back to the car.

They were in two vehicles, Erin and Vic in the Charger, Webb and Catherine in the Lieutenant's beat-up old rust-bucket. Rolf's compartment made it impossible to fit four people and one large K-9 in Erin's ride. Webb had his phone on speaker so the others could hear him and Catherine as they cruised down 48th.

"I think it was a little further," Catherine said. "But I'm not sure. Maybe it was back the other way?"

Vic muted Erin's phone. "Five bucks says we don't find the place," he offered.

Erin didn't think it was a good bet, but she knew it would cheer Vic up, so she said, "I'll take some of that action."

"We're just gonna drive around Brooklyn until we get sick of it," he predicted. "That's assuming this place even exists."

"I think she was telling the truth," Erin said.

"*Now* she was, you mean. She started off lying, leaving stuff out. I don't trust this chick."

"Who said anything about trust?" she said. "We're just following up a lead. Don't make it personal."

"What the hell planet are you living on, Erin? This is plenty personal. You saw Webb back there."

"He's still doing his job," she said.

"He's doing the job on her, that's for sure."

"Vic! You're damn lucky we're only listening, not transmitting."

"Shh," he said. "They're talking."

"...on the next block, I think," Catherine was saying. "Yes. There it is. That one on the right!"

"Norton's Body Work?" Webb asked.

"That's the one."

"Okay, folks," Webb said. "We'll park here." His car pulled to the curb and stopped. Erin parked behind him and the detectives spilled out onto the street. Rolf was eager for action, tail swishing back and forth. Catherine climbed out of the passenger side of Webb's vehicle.

"You can wait in the car," Webb said to her.

She shook her head. "I'm coming along," she said.

He looked like he wanted to argue, but he just sighed. "Okay, Cath. But if there's any trouble, get behind Vic."

"Why him?" she asked.

"I'll protect you," Vic said.

"He's the biggest," Webb said. "He'll provide the best cover, soak up the most bullets."

"That's not exactly what I meant," Vic said.

Erin, meanwhile, was looking over the property in question. It was an old red-brick structure, three stories tall, a bay window over the front door. A big garage was attached to the front of the house, a faded sign proclaiming it to be Norton's Body Work. It had probably been a very nice house when it was built, but that had been a long time ago. Now the bricks were chipped and battered, one pane of the bay window was covered by a piece of plywood, and the yard was overgrown with weeds and covered with litter. Erin bet there was enough leftover nicotine in the massive piles of cigarette butts to keep even a smoker like Webb happy for a day or two.

The garage door was raised about halfway. It was impossible to see more than a few feet into the interior. The house's windows—those not boarded up—were covered by curtains.

"What do you think?" Webb asked the others.

"Meth house," Vic said. "Absolutely. Every half hour you spend in there will strip a year off your life. They'll have to tear the whole thing down."

"Could be," Erin said. "Or it could just be lousy housekeeping. I don't think anyone lives here."

"Let's have a look," Webb said. He pointed to the sign over the garage. "That's a place of business and it's normal business hours. We can walk right in, warrant or no warrant."

"I thought you weren't involved in this investigation," Vic said.

"I still outrank you, Neshenko," Webb said. "I want you and O'Reilly to go in and see what's what. I'll wait out here with Cath."

"Whatever you say, sir," Vic said.

Erin ducked under the door and stood up carefully. In auto shops it paid to watch your head. Rolf easily scooted in beside her, not even needing to crouch. She saw exactly what she would have expected in any auto body shop: tools, machinery, and cars fading into shadow. The only light was the daylight filtering under the door.

"Hello?" she called. "Anyone here?"

Vic squeezed his broad-shouldered body in behind her. "Yo!" he said loudly. "This is the NYPD! Come on out! We want to talk to you!"

"Real subtle, Vic," she said more quietly.

"I don't want to get shot by some idiot homeowner who's got the wrong idea," he said. "Besides, nobody's home."

Erin nodded. "You got your flashlight?"

"I'm prepared, just like they teach you in Boy Scouts," he said, flicking on a big, heavy Maglite.

"You were a Boy Scout?"

"Scout's honor."

"Which doesn't mean a thing if you weren't," she pointed out. Then she raised her voice again. "Anybody in here, we're detectives. We're not looking for trouble."

"No need to look for it," Vic muttered. "We brought plenty of our own." He played the beam of his flashlight around the garage.

"Doesn't look like a drug lab," she said. In the middle of the garage was a Lexus sedan, on a hoist a couple feet off the floor. The car had been partially disassembled.

"No, it doesn't," Vic said. "Looks like a chop shop to me."

"How can you tell?" she asked.

"That car's too nice for this neighborhood," he said. "Body shops usually fix dented panels, broken windows, that kind of thing. But this car's bodywork is perfect. Take a look inside."

He stepped in close and shone the light through the gap where the driver's door had been. The dashboard was a mess of trailing wires.

"They yanked the radio," Erin said.

"Yeah," Vic said. "And see the steering column? The plastic's been pulled off, around the ignition."

"Hot-wired," she said. "You're right, Vic. This car is stolen."

Rolf didn't care about cars, but he was sticking close to Erin. Her attention was focused on the Lexus, while he watched and waited for something more interesting to happen.

The Shepherd's sudden growl was Erin's only warning.

She'd worked with Rolf for more than four years. They'd trained together, fought side by side, slept in the same bed, eaten the same food. She knew that growl. Adrenaline spiking, she started to turn, reaching for her gun.

"Vic, look—" she started to say.

There was a breathy whistle, followed by a meaty clank. Vic, in the process of reacting to Erin, grunted and fell against the side of the sedan, sliding toward the ground. His flashlight spun out of his hand and clattered across the concrete. The spinning beam gave things a weird strobe-light quality, like a nightmare disco.

Erin caught a glimpse of a vaguely human shape in the process of swinging something at her. She ducked, hearing that whistling sound again, and a metal bar whipped over her head close enough to feel. Her movement jammed her gun against her hip and she couldn't get it clear of the holster. She improvised, spinning on her heel and sweeping her other foot at ankle height. Her toe hooked behind the guy's leg and he went over backward.

"*Fass!*" she snapped, but the "bite" order was a moot point by the time she got it out. Rolf wasn't about to stand there like a chump while his partner got in a fight. He was already lunging at the falling man. By the time the guy hit the floor, Rolf's teeth were clamped on his arm.

Somebody screamed. Erin knew it wasn't her and was pretty sure it wasn't Vic. She whipped her Glock out of its holster and trained it on the struggling shapes, but she wasn't about to shoot into a scuffle that had her dog in it.

"Stop fighting!" she shouted, but the man on the floor was operating on instincts older than language. He didn't have a prayer of winning a wrestling match with ninety pounds of pissed-off German Shepherd, but he was giving it his best shot.

The flashlight finally fetched up against a toolbox. Erin reached it in three running strides, snatched it up just behind the lens, reversed her grip, and stepped back toward the fight.

Rolf was on top, but just as Erin got there, the guy under him made a supreme effort and rolled over on top of the dog. The K-9 held onto his arm with an unbreakable grip, so all the man accomplished was bringing his head up as a clear, clean target.

Erin brought Vic's flashlight down on the back of the guy's skull. There was another heavy thud, the flashlight went out with an electric sizzle of protest, and the goon went limp.

"*Pust,*" Erin said.

Rolf immediately let go and wriggled out from under the man. Erin couldn't see his face, but she could hear him panting and she knew he was giving his best triumphant grin.

"You okay, Vic?" she called.

"Yeah," he groaned. "Son of a bitch cold-cocked me. Where is he? I'm gonna kick his ass."

"Rolf got him and I busted your flashlight on his head. I think he's out cold."

"Then wake him up so I can kick his ass."

"No can do, sorry. Regulations."

Webb's voice came from the direction of the entrance. "What the hell is going on in there?"

"Better call in some backup, sir," Erin called back. "We've got one in custody. Call a bus while you're at it. I think I hit him pretty hard."

* * *

"You know, Vic, I always thought you had a thick skull," Erin said. "But this confirms it."

Vic, sitting on the ambulance's rear fender, rubbed the back of his head. He stared at his bloodstained fingertips.

"Can't believe I let that bastard sneak up on me," he muttered.

"Good thing Rolf was more alert than either of us," she said, glancing past Vic into the interior of the rescue vehicle. Their perp was handcuffed to a stretcher, a Patrol officer watching him while an EMT worked on his wounded head.

Rolf, lying on the pavement at Erin's feet, looked up and wagged his tail. His mouth was stuffed with his favorite rubber Kong toy. It made a wet squeaking noise as his jaws flexed.

"And a good thing he didn't have a gun," Vic grumbled.

Webb waved them over to Erin's Charger, which was now at the center of a cluster of police cars. Catherine was standing next to the car. As Erin and Vic approached, Webb's ex-wife raised a hand to her mouth. She awkwardly puffed on a cigarette, then doubled over coughing.

"I thought you hated smoking," Vic, ever the master of tact, observed.

"I heard... it calms... the nerves," she managed to get out between coughs.

"I've got an ID on our guy," Webb said, pointing to Erin's onboard computer screen. A mugshot of a man glared back. He definitely looked like the guy they had in the ambulance.

"Leroy Grant," Erin read off the screen.

"Priors for GTA, ADW, and Aggravated Assault," Webb said.

"You're as bad as the US Government, using all those abbreviations," Catherine said. She'd gotten her breathing under control and was trying to decide whether to take another stab at picking up a potentially deadly habit.

"They stand for Grand Theft Auto and Assault with a Deadly Weapon," Erin explained. "You weren't kidding. Webb really didn't talk to you about work, did he?"

"Never," Catherine said. "He'd just come in and sit at the dinner table, all tired and grim."

"Like that?" Vic asked, pointing a thumb Webb's direction. "Nah, he always looks that way."

"Very funny, Neshenko," Webb said.

"Yes, exactly like that," Catherine said. "Honestly, Harry, I don't know why you like these things." She stared at the cigarette.

"Spend a week smoking them," he said. "Believe me, you'll forget how you managed without them."

"So who's Leroy Grant?" Erin asked. "He's a crook, obviously, but who does he work for? Who does he run with?"

"Known associates are the Dwyer brothers, Max and Charles," Webb said. "Also a guy with the charming street handle of Gasoline Young."

"Do we even want to know?" Erin asked, feeling like she already knew the answer.

"Gasoline's real name is Burton Darius Young," Webb said. "Apparently he runs, or used to run, a protection racket. If people didn't pay up, he'd grab them and stuff them in a barrel full of gasoline. Then he'd put out cigarettes in the gas until they coughed up the cash."

Catherine dropped the cigarette she'd been holding as if it had burned her. "That's horrible, Harry."

"The gas wouldn't ignite," Vic said. "Probably. The fumes are what ignite. I saw the guys on *Mythbusters* test that one. But you gotta have gigantic balls to try it."

"I wonder if the poor guy in the barrel knew that," Erin said.

"Wouldn't matter too much," Vic said. "If your skin gets covered with gas and you leave it on too long, the skin starts cracking. Eventually it'll peel right off. You wouldn't even have to light the bastard on fire. It'll kill you either way, just more slowly."

Catherine shuddered. "Do you have to talk about that?"

"You want to know about my world, Cath?" Webb asked. "You want to know what's behind this look on my face? This kind of thing. You can't have it both ways. You want me to communicate? Here I am, communicating. Are you going to get back on your high horse and tell me now you didn't want to know?"

"Don't be nasty, Harry," she said, turning away and walking a short distance along the boulevard.

"So what I'm hearing," Erin said, "is that our boy there hangs around some unpleasant people. But I didn't hear Clay Dodgson's name on that list."

"That's because he's not on the list," Webb said. "As far as the NYPD is concerned, these guys don't know each other."

"They'd have to, though," Vic said. "Same neighborhood, same line of work."

"Let's talk to him," Erin said. "See what he'll tell us."

"Four-letter words," Vic predicted.

"You saying you don't want to try?"

He smiled. "No, I'm fluent in profanity. It's my mother tongue."

"I don't want to know about your mother's tongue," Erin said, stepping back quickly just in case he decided to take exception.

"Up yours, O'Reilly," he said pleasantly. "Let's do this. Hey! Can I be good cop this time?"

"Do you know how?"

"Considering you sicced your dog on him and bashed him in the head with a flashlight—*my* flashlight, runs almost forty bucks, and if the Department won't pay for it, you will—I think you might have some trouble playing good cop."

"That's a good point," Erin admitted. "Okay, fine. We'll try it."

* * *

"Can we ask him a few questions?" Erin asked the EMT. They'd pulled him away from the ambulance.

"I guess so," he said. "We're going to want to take him to Community Hospital to get him checked out, though. He might have a subdural hematoma. Those things can sneak up on you and bam! Next thing you know you're dead."

"We don't want him to die," Erin said. "But we do need to talk to him. Is his mind clear?"

"I think so. He's been swearing a lot, ever since he came to. Told me to cram my IV tube right up my own ass."

"Told you so," Vic said.

Erin told Rolf to wait outside. The K-9 obediently settled himself on the boulevard. As long as he had his chew-toy, he was perfectly happy. Then the detectives climbed into the ambulance.

"Leroy Grant," Erin said. "You're in some deep shit, buddy."

"Suck my big one," was his predictable reply. He was a thin, wiry guy with buck teeth and wild hair, dressed in a grease-stained T-shirt and cargo pants.

"That's what the lifers are going to say to you in the prison showers, smartass," Erin said. "You're going down for the long haul."

He rattled the handcuffs against the stretcher. "You don't scare me, bitch. Take these things off me and we'll see who ends up on their knees."

"You had more than a fair shot at me a minute ago," she said. "Now I'm here, and you're flat on your back. If you're trying to impress me, you're doing a shit job of it."

"Leroy," Vic said. "I think we got off on the wrong foot. We weren't here for you, pal. We didn't even know about your little basement operation. And you know what? We don't really care about you. You're a little fish. You ever been fishing, Leroy? You know what happens to the little fish? They get thrown back in the pond to grow up. It's the big ones that go in the pan."

"You got a big fish to throw us?" Erin demanded. "So you don't have to spend the rest of your life looking over your shoulder at Riker's?"

"Bite me, bitch," Leroy said.

"No hard feelings, pal," Vic said. "You got a mean swing, but I'm fine. So let's not get mad. We just want to know what's going on with Vernon Henderson and Clay Dodgson."

"You shittin' me?" Leroy said. "I ain't got nothin' to say about that prick Dog. He's a shit son of a bitch. He ain't worth usin' to wipe my ass."

"So, not a friend of yours?" Vic asked, keeping his tone light, suggesting the whole thing was some kind of joke.

"Man dresses like a pimp, hangs out with dogs all the time. Ain't nobody his friend."

"Especially Gasoline Young," Vic said.

"I don't know what you're talkin' about, man."

"Oh, I just heard something," Vic said. "Word on the street is that there's bad blood between Gasoline and Dog. Maybe just words now, but I'm thinking some shit's gonna go down one of these days."

"What you care? Anybody take out Dog, they be doin' the world a solid," Leroy said.

"Not gonna argue with you there," Vic said. "I've talked to the man, and he's a stain on this city. You want to help wash that stain away?"

"What you mean?" Leroy asked, his eyes narrowing suspiciously.

"Tell us about Dog and Henderson," Vic said. "Then we can tell the DA this was just a misunderstanding. Maybe you didn't hear us identify ourselves as police. You thought we were robbers, you were just defending your business."

Erin thought that defense was unlikely to fly in a court of law, but crooks, as a rule, weren't especially bright, even ones who hadn't been recently hit on the head. She said nothing.

"I don't know what they was talkin' about," Leroy said. "Henderson? Man can talk to whoever he wants. Dumbass only knows how to talk. Man won't never shut up."

Erin suppressed a smile. Their perp had just admitted to knowing Henderson.

"Do you own this building, Leroy?" Vic asked.

"Huh? No, it belongs to some white boy. He lives in, like, Midtown or somewhere. I just pay rent."

"But you could've owned it," Vic said. "You were going to buy it from Henderson."

"Who told you that, man?"

"It's all over the street, pal," Vic said. "I heard it was a pretty sweet deal, too."

"I dunno who you listenin' to, but that deal wasn't so sweet," Leroy said. "Man wanted a percentage, even after the sale. Like a mortgage or some shit, only worse. It's like them toll roads in Jersey. They say they gonna just leave the toll booths till they pay for the road, right? 'Cept they just leave 'em there. You ever heard of a toll booth getting' closed down? Hell no!"

"I hear you," Vic said. "Henderson was gonna put the squeeze on you, huh?"

"And I didn't have no choice, neither!" Leroy said indignantly. "He talked to that other white boy, the one owns the place. I been livin' here ten years, man. My momma lived here, 'fore she died. This my house, man! And it's his way or the highway, right?"

"That sounds like a raw deal," Vic agreed.

"You're telling me you were getting screwed here?" Erin demanded, leaning over the stretcher. "I don't buy it for a second. You bushwhacked a couple of cops, loser. And you're running a damn chop shop. You want me to think you're a victim? Bullshit!"

"Hey, Erin, take it easy," Vic said.

"Erin?" Leroy repeated. A strange look came into his face, one Erin hadn't seen on many perps. "That your name, lady?"

"Yeah," she said. "Erin O'Reilly. I'm with Major Crimes. You know what assaulting a cop is? It's a pretty damn major crime."

He wasn't listening to anything after the name. His face had gone suddenly pale. "Listen, lady," he said, speaking very quickly. "I didn't mean nothin' when I said that shit earlier, right? I didn't mean no disrespect or nothin.' You gotta understand, I didn't know who you was."

Vic gave Erin a sidelong glance and raised an eyebrow. The interview had just gone in a completely unexpected direction.

"So what've you got to say for yourself?" Erin asked, forcing her face to stay firm and threatening even though she was confused. Why should it matter what her name was? Maybe he'd known her dad in his Patrol days. But no. Sean O'Reilly had been a tough, fair street cop, but he was hardly legendary. Besides, it was a common last name. There had to be a dozen O'Reillys in the NYPD.

"My boys and me, it's just small-time shit," Leroy said, almost babbling now. "We ain't never stepped on nobody else's turf, 'cept maybe Dog's. We ain't got no beef with your people."

Then she did understand. He was talking about the O'Malleys. Word really had gotten around, at least some neighborhoods. She'd have to talk to Carlyle about that, find out what the hell people were saying. Leroy was looking at her like he expected her to bite his throat or something.

"You were pissed off at Henderson," she said. "So you followed him to the house, right?"

"What house?" Leroy looked as confused now as Erin felt, but considerably more frightened.

"You saw him with the woman," Erin went on. "You waited until he was downstairs alone. Then you knocked on the door."

"I ain't never follow that man!" Leroy protested. "I don't even know where he sleep! You gotta believe me!"

"Then who was looking for him?" Vic asked more gently. "One of your buddies, maybe? The Dwyers, or Gasoline?"

"Maybe Gasoline, he hated that guy," Leroy said. "Yeah, talk to Gasoline. He tell you everything you need to know! I ain't done nothin' wrong! I won't say nothin' to nobody!"

"Where is he?" Erin demanded.

"Upstairs! Sleeping! He up all night, lady!"

"Upstairs?" Erin repeated. "You mean in this house?"

Leroy nodded frantically.

Erin spun on her heel and jumped down from the ambulance. She snagged the Patrol officer who was loitering nearby.

"The house!" she snapped. "Has it been cleared?"

"I don't know, ma'am," the startled cop said. "I think Sarge was just going in with a couple of guys."

Erin looked past him. She saw the front door of the house standing open. Vic hopped out of the ambulance and landed heavily beside her.

"Shit," Erin breathed. They'd been too busy with other things. Now they had a tip a dangerous felon was in the house. He'd had plenty of time to wake up and run for it, or dig in for a last stand. She started running toward the house. Rolf, picking up on her energy, bounded to his feet and followed, still carrying his beloved toy in his mouth.

"Look out!" she shouted. "You got one inside!"

Erin was halfway to the door when the explosion ripped through the building.

Chapter 12

Rolf was a trained explosive-detection K-9, so before becoming his handler, Erin had gone through a basic course to learn about bombs. Most bombs were dirty, messy things when they blew up. Just like how fires in the real world were mostly smoke, explosions were mostly dust and debris. To get a really cinematic fireball, special-effects people liked to use gasoline. It burned hot, fast, and relatively clean, and created exactly the sort of spectacular blast that was coming straight at Erin, blossoming like the petals of some hellish flower.

There was no time to get out of the way. She just let her legs collapse under her and face-planted on the sidewalk. A wave of intense, searing heat rolled across her back. She tried to shout "*Aus!*" so Rolf would know to get down, but her voice was drowned out by the furnace-roar of the blast.

Then it was over, leaving an oily, chemical smell in its wake. Erin cautiously raised her head. The house was built on a terrace, which had probably saved her life. She'd been a couple steps short of the top and the main force of the explosion had skimmed just over her. Bits of the weedy lawn were on fire. Her ears were ringing. Her forehead stung. She put a hand up to her face. Her fingers came away bloody where the concrete had scraped her.

"Erin!"

There was Vic, sitting on his ass. He'd tumbled over backward and looked basically okay. He levered himself upright.

"Come on!" he shouted. "Our guys are in there!"

A cold, wet thing poked Erin's ear. She turned and saw Rolf, flat on his belly, nosing at her. He seemed only lightly singed, thanks to his low profile. She got to her knees and put a hand on the dog's head. What was Vic talking about?

She looked back at the house, expecting to see nothing but wreckage. To her surprise, the building appeared largely intact. The windows were completely gone, and the interior appeared to be on fire, but the brickwork was still solid. Vic was already on his way in.

Several uniformed officers were running toward the house from the street. The EMTs were right behind them, medical bags in hand. One of the medics veered toward her. She waved him off impatiently and made herself stand up. Stumbling only a little, she jogged toward the smoldering house.

The interior was dark and full of smoke. Erin wished she hadn't broken Vic's flashlight. "*Such!*" she ordered Rolf. Even with the smells of the explosion, the dog could find people easier than she could. She drew her gun but made sure to keep her finger outside the trigger guard. If they weren't careful, the cops were liable to shoot one another by accident.

A flash of memory stabbed her like a knife to the brain. She flashed back to a burning movie theater, a badly damaged young man throwing Molotov cocktails and shooting at her. Then there was the restaurant in Little Italy, full of fire, smoke, and dead mobsters. For a second, all she could do was stand there, reeling, right on the doorstep.

The pressure of Rolf at the end of his leash jerked her back into the present. Damn it, she wasn't supposed to crack under pressure. She couldn't afford to. People were counting on her.

She tried to shrug off the memories and plunged inside. "Vic!" she shouted. "Where are you?"

"Upstairs!" he called back. Then he said the two words every cop feared. "Officer down!"

Heart in her mouth, Erin raced up the stairs. She found Vic in the upstairs hallway, bent over a prone figure. The man was moving, which was good as far as it went. Erin didn't know how he could possibly be alive after what had just happened.

One of the EMTs was right behind her. He dropped to one knee and went to work.

"Others," the wounded officer mumbled.

"What others?" Vic asked, putting his head close to the guy's ear.

"Willis... Nunez."

"There's two others in here?" Vic asked.

"Two," the officer confirmed. He coughed and sagged back.

Erin took a quick look around. Things were on fire, but not as many as might have been expected. The blast had been so quick and violent, it had almost blown itself out in the process of exploding. She could hear sirens on the way, accompanied by the deep-throated horns of fire trucks.

"*Such*," Erin said to Rolf again. The K-9 started sniffing, casting about for other people. He was trained in search-and-rescue as well as explosives. He should be able to find bodies, whether living or dead.

The dog snuffled up and down the hallway for a moment. Then he tensed and pulled into the bedroom at the end of the hall. Erin followed. The smell of burnt fuel was even stronger here, coupled with an oddly mouth-watering barbecue odor. She was no arson investigator, but she guessed the blast had originated here. She also had a pretty good idea what she was going to find. She saw a bent, twisted piece of curved metal, probably part of a fuel drum. Behind it sprawled a man, or what was left of him. He was face down, which was a mercy. His body was actually on fire, little flames licking at his hair and clothes. It was hard to tell, but she could see this guy wasn't wearing NYPD blue.

"Got a body here! 10-54B!" she yelled, indicating a burn victim in need of an ambulance. That was optimistic. This guy was on a one-way trip to the morgue.

"Good boy, Rolf," she said, giving him a quick scratch behind the ears. "*Sei brav. Such!*"

With that, he was off, looking for more. By the time they'd cleared most of the upstairs, Erin heard firefighters entering the ground floor.

"We got a live one down here!" one of the firemen shouted from below.

Rolf paid no attention to the humans. He was busy doing his job. He snuffled his way into the upstairs bathroom and sniffed at the tub. He scratched and whined

Erin peered in and saw a man huddled there. He was dressed as an NYPD Patrol officer. He didn't move.

"Officer down!" she shouted as loudly as she could. She sucked in a breath to keep shouting, inhaled a cloud of smoke, and collapsed against the doorframe, choking and gasping.

Two firemen were there in seconds. They gave the downed man a quick once-over and slapped an oxygen mask on him.

"He's out cold," one of them said. "But he's breathing. Looks like he just conked his head on the tub. Probably fell over backwards when the explosion went off. Lucky bastard. Let's get him in a collar. Then the medics can shift him outside."

"Good boy, Rolf," Erin managed to wheeze.

The K-9 looked up and her and wagged his tail anxiously. He knew he was a good boy, but he was worried about her.

"You okay, ma'am?" one of the firefighters asked.

"Me? I'm fine."

"You're bleeding." He pointed to her face.

Erin nodded. "You should see the other guy," she said. Then she laughed weakly.

"We've got this," the other firefighter said. "If you want to get some fresh air?"

She correctly interpreted this to mean that she was just getting in the way now, so she took Rolf outside. Even more police and fire vehicles were arriving. The street had turned into a traffic jam spangled with flashing emergency lights.

She walked slowly away from the smoking house, taking deep breaths of clean air. She reached into her pocket for Rolf's Kong toy to reward him for an excellent search.

Her pocket was empty.

Then she remembered. "Where'd you drop it?" she asked Rolf.

He cocked his head. That wasn't one of the commands he knew.

"Where's your toy?" she asked.

That got a response. He knew that one. The Shepherd bounded joyfully into the yard, pounced, and came up with his hard rubber chew-toy. He'd probably dropped it when the explosion had happened. He pranced back to his partner, tail wagging so hard his hindquarters were swinging from side to side. His jaws worked the rubber. Drool trailed from his jowls. Life was as good as it could possibly be.

Someone was shouting down by the ambulance. Erin knew that voice. It was Webb. He sounded pissed. She drifted that direction, not because she wanted to, but because it was her job. Rolf followed, still chewing.

"What do you mean, you don't know?" Webb demanded.

The Patrol officer in front of him spread his hands helplessly. "Sir, the house blew up!" he said.

"I know that," Webb said grimly. "What I don't know is what happened to the man who was handcuffed to that stretcher. The man you were supposed to be guarding. You had one job, *one job*."

"He was cuffed!" the cop protested. "I only looked away for a minute!"

"What's going on, sir?" Erin asked.

"See for yourself," Webb said, indicating the ambulance. "We've got plenty of room for our injured officers, thanks to this idiot who decided to rubberneck while he was on the clock."

The stretcher was empty. A handcuff bracelet dangled from one side of it. Leroy Grant was gone.

* * *

"You searched this loser before you stuffed him in an ambulance, right?" Webb demanded.

Erin nodded absently, but she wasn't really listening. Of course she'd searched Grant when they'd arrested him. Even rookies knew the stories about perps who'd smuggled cuff keys, lockpicks, knives, or even guns into lockup. But that wasn't the point. The point was, Grant had been on the run for at least a few minutes. He had a head injury, but she had to assume his legs worked just fine.

"We got his car keys," she said. "From his pocket. But he's a car thief."

"So we have to assume he'll try to steal or jack a new ride," Webb agreed.

"Rolf can track him as long as he's on foot," she said, climbing into the ambulance and grabbing the stretcher. She wrestled it out, dropping it to the pavement with a loud clatter. Webb winced. That was probably an expensive piece of hospital equipment she was banging around.

"Rolf!" she said.

He dropped his toy and sprang to attention.

She scooped up the Kong ball and shoved the slimy thing into her pocket. Then she pointed to the bed of the stretcher.

"*Such!*"

With a single sniff, the K-9 was off and running. Erin sprinted to keep up. The dog was at the very end of his leash, lunging ahead, throwing his shoulders into the motion. Grant's smell was very fresh. Fear and stress made a man's body odor stronger and more distinctive. The fugitive might as well have used a paint-roller to lay a bright line showing the path he'd taken.

Erin briefly considered letting Rolf run loose, but the street was full of cars. She didn't want him getting run over by some idiot motorist. So she poured on what speed she could, running flat-out along 48th. She was a little light-headed, whether from the knock to her own head or from breathing smoke and fumes, but she ignored the feeling.

They raced to the next intersection and crossed under an elevated train track. That brought back another unwelcome memory, of an ambush and firefight under the tracks in Little Odessa. New York was a city of layers, everything piled on top of itself. Her brain was the same way. Memories just got added to the stack, one laid over another.

Rolf made for the shop on the far corner. Pedestrians stopped and pointed at them. On her own, Erin might have asked if they'd seen a guy running this way, but Rolf rendered that unnecessary. He ran to the shop door, went up on his hind legs, and scrabbled at the handle. Even as Erin got there, the dog's weight pushed the door open and he lunged inside.

It was a florist. The heavy smell of blossoms and pollen hit Erin like a wave of perfume. A startled young man, holding a single red rose, hopped awkwardly back, tripped on a big flowerpot, and went over backwards, tipping the pot. Cut flowers cascaded onto the floor.

"Hey!" the woman behind the counter shouted in an unmistakable Brooklyn accent. "Ya can't bring that mutt in here! And your friend's an asshole!"

"NYPD!" Erin gasped, snatching the shield from her belt and holding it up. Rolf jerked to a stop but kept tugging on the leash in the direction of the store's back room.

"That way," the shopkeeper said. "Jerk went right over my counter. Broke that vase there. I want him arrested!"

"Copy that," Erin said. She ran around the counter and shoved the door open. She and Rolf ran across a concrete room filled with floral tools and blooms. They hit the rear exit running and tumbled into an alley. Twenty running strides brought them to a chain-link fence with a privacy screen. Rolf threw himself at it, scrambling with all four paws, doing his best to run right up the fence.

Erin saw a coil of barbed wire along the top and opened her mouth to tell him to stop, but he was too quick. By the time she'd sucked in enough breath to call, the dog was up and over. By some miracle he didn't snag on the wire.

She let go of the leash, not by choice. It was either that or dislocate her shoulder when the ninety-pound dog jumped down the other side. She didn't relish the thought of going over the fence, but didn't have another good option. She jumped, grabbed the top railing, and put a foot over it. She grabbed hold of the wire between two of the barbs and pushed it down, flattening it as much as she could. Then she rolled sideways and let herself drop.

Fabric caught and tore. She felt several sharp metal points drag across her shoulders. Her pants were sturdier than her blouse, but something still jabbed her in the thigh. But she fell free, leaving a swatch of cloth hanging on the fence like a flag.

Rolf was almost out of sight, dashing across what looked like a preschool playground. They were a little too late for recess, thank God, and the playground was empty. That meant no chance of pint-sized hostages. Erin ran after her dog, who was still going strong. She could feel the sting of the barbed-wire scratches and sweat, or maybe blood, trickling down her back.

Erin trailed the K-9 down a short driveway toward a big yellow school bus. Rolf angled toward the front of the bus and leaped at the door, barking. Even as he did, the big diesel engine roared to life. The bus started to roll.

"Oh, no, you don't," Erin muttered. She dug deep and found a little more. The bus was picking up speed, but all that metal took time to get going. She made a running jump at the back of the vehicle. She slammed into the emergency exit, felt herself slipping, and caught the handle with a desperate grab. Even as she did, the bus swung out of the drive onto the street. The inertia nearly flung her off the back of the bus, but she hung on. In a quick backward glance, she saw Rolf behind the bus now, paws flying, tongue flapping out the side of his mouth. A human couldn't possibly have kept up, but a German Shepherd could run thirty miles an hour.

Erin found the release lever for the door. This wasn't the best idea she'd ever had, since the door swung outward, but her other option was to let go, and they were doing better than thirty now. Hitting blacktop at that speed would really ruin her day. Rolf was falling behind, still running hard.

She sucked in a breath and pulled the lever. The latch gave and the door tried to swing her into space. She threw one leg around the edge and found the fender with her toes. Still holding onto the door, she hauled herself up and in.

She landed hard on her knees in the bus's aisle. Up front, she saw Grant's face in the rearview mirror, staring right at her. His eyes looked enormous.

Erin stalked up the aisle toward him, unholstering her Glock while she tried to catch her breath. Grant ran a red light, drawing frantic horns and screeching tires. She heard the shriek of metal on metal as at least two cars ran into each other. The bus swerved. She caught herself on the nearest seatback. Then she took two more long strides and pointed her gun at Grant's head.

"Stop this bus," she said. "Right now."

"You gonna shoot me while I'm driving?" he asked. "What happens to you then?"

"I'll take my chances," she said grimly.

The look in her eyes convinced him. He pulled over and stopped the bus.

"Hands on the steering wheel," she said. "Leroy Grant, you're under arrest for grand theft auto, reckless endangerment, fleeing a crime scene, resisting arrest, vandalism, and a shitload of moving violations. You have the right to remain silent..."

She was interrupted by a scratching at the bus door. There was Rolf, on his hind legs, trying to get in. She pulled the lever to open the door. The Shepherd bounded up the steps to meet his partner. His tongue was hanging enormously down his face and his tail was wagging, but he looked confused. Erin never got to the bad guys ahead of him. Something had gone very wrong in his world.

"You okay, lady?" Grant asked.

Erin followed his eyes and saw several gaping holes in her blouse. A lot more skin was showing than she usually let out while she was on the clock, and some of it was oozing blood.

But embarrassment wasn't something she was prepared to bother with just then.

"Worry about yourself, dumbass," she said. Fortunately, they'd used Vic's cuffs when they'd collared Grant earlier and hers were still on her belt. She took them out and slapped the bracelets on his wrists.

"I'll be watching this time, Houdini," she added. "So don't get any more bright ideas."

Chapter 13

By the time Erin got back to the crime scene, things were starting to calm down. The injured officers had been taken away, the Patrol cops had established a perimeter, and the CSU van had arrived. Erin and Rolf had hitched a ride with a pair of uniforms who'd responded to Grant's vehicular mayhem. They left Grant in the back of the squad car after telling the two Patrol officers to keep a particularly close eye on him.

They found Vic and Webb loitering next to Erin's Charger. Catherine was there, too, standing a little ways off from Webb. Vic was sitting in the open passenger side of the car. When Erin approached, he started slowly clapping his hands.

"We've been listening on the 'net," Webb said, indicating the police-band radio. "It sounds like you had some excitement, but you got the guy."

"And left a trail of destruction in your wake," Vic added. "Playing demolition derby in the middle of Brooklyn with a school bus. I gotta say, I'm impressed."

"I wasn't driving the bus," Erin said.

"Details were a little sketchy," Webb said. "Do I understand you caught a guy in a bus? On foot?"

"Erin doesn't skip leg day," Vic said, grinning. "Never underestimate cardio."

"I made entry through the rear exit," she explained.

"Before he got moving?" Webb asked.

"After."

There was a moment's silence, broken by a low whistle from Vic.

"You car-surfed a bus through city traffic?" Webb asked, his eyebrows climbing his forehead.

She shrugged. "It seemed like a good idea at the time."

"You're lucky you weren't killed," Webb said.

"The important thing is, we got Grant," Erin said. "He's in the car back there."

"Wouldn't it be funny if he slipped his cuffs again?" Vic asked.

"Like that magician you arrested last year?" Webb asked.

Vic flushed and fell abruptly silent. He didn't like to be reminded of that incident.

"Uniforms are watching him this time," Erin said. "Carefully. So what's the deal here?"

"Skip Taylor's on his way to do the arson investigation," Webb said. "But preliminary indications are that some idiot lit a fifty-gallon drum of gasoline in an upstairs bedroom. He was probably trying to create a diversion while he ran for it. The bedroom window was open. But the gasoline must've had some vapor in the air and when he lit it, it went off right in his face. The poor son of a bitch did a somersault and wound up face down on the floor, burned to a crisp."

"And our guys?" she asked.

"Two of them were upstairs, one was downstairs when it happened. The downstairs guy was lucky. He was in the kitchen, out of the main line of the explosion. He got a little singed and I think he's got a burst eardrum, but he's more or less okay. The other two were in the upstairs hallway. The guy you found in the tub was lucky, too. When he went over backward, he knocked himself out but didn't take too much of the blast. He should be fine. The sergeant's the only one who's really hurt bad. He was holding the bedroom door and it shielded him a little. He's got serious burns, but he should pull through."

Erin let out a relieved breath. "So the only fatality was the guy who set it off?"

"Looks that way," Webb said. "It'll be a while before we get a positive ID. We're going to need dental records, for obvious reasons."

"His teeth are about the only thing left intact," Vic said, reentering the conversation. Catherine cringed and looked away.

"But we're guessing it's Gasoline Young," Webb finished.

"That seems likely," Erin said. "We still need to get Grant checked out by a doctor, just to make sure he doesn't keel over on us."

"Serve him right," Vic said. "He hijacked a school bus."

"Hotwired," she corrected. "Nobody was on board at the time."

"And you jumped on and took it back," he said. "Just answer me this. How many times have you seen the movie *Speed*?"

"Too many," she said.

"Well, O'Reilly, you're in charge of this investigation," Webb said. "What's your next move? I'd like to take Cath home."

"Yeah, that's fine," Erin said, thinking how weird it was to be signing off on Webb's actions. "We need to process Grant as soon as a doc okays it. And we'll need to go over the evidence from this place once CSU finishes. Then we need to find out who the hell killed Henderson."

"That's more of a mission statement than a plan," Vic said.

"You got any ideas?" she shot back.

"Yeah," he said. "I want to talk to Faith Copeland again."

"You want to make time with the pretty girl," Erin said. "Why didn't I see that coming?"

"She knows something," he said.

"How do you figure?"

"She was married to the guy. She knew about his paranoia, his guns. She knew he flipped the building she was living in. I think she's got more on Henderson than she let on."

Erin nodded. "That's a good thought. You feeling okay?"

"Me?" Vic looked surprised. "I'm the picture of health."

"I'm surprised they haven't put you on the cover of a fitness magazine," Erin deadpanned. "You've got at least eighty percent of a good-looking face. I was talking about the knock on the head you got."

"That's seventy-nine percent more than most," he said. "Don't worry about me. I got a hard skull. You want me to call her in to the Eight?"

"No, let's go to her," Erin said. "It'll be a few hours before they clear Grant to talk to us, and even longer until CSU wraps things up here. We've got some time. I was just thinking how much I wanted to drive all the way to the Bronx. Again."

"She's not in the Bronx anymore," Vic reminded her. "She's right here in Brooklyn."

"Oh, right." In all the excitement, Erin had forgotten. "Then what are we waiting for?"

* * *

"Faith's place looks better than the Lieutenant's," Vic said.

"It does," Erin agreed.

Faith Copeland's apartment was in an upscale complex on Leonard Street, a world away from the seedy tenement she'd grown up in. It was all glass and metal, postmodern and swanky.

Vic nodded. "Faith looks better than the Lieutenant, too."

"That's not hard," Erin said.

He snickered. "You know, that Simmons lady isn't half bad. I mean, if she wasn't the Lieutenant's ex, I'd think about hitting that. How'd she end up with a guy like him?"

"Vic, I have no idea."

"I mean, you gotta wonder. Has he always been the sad sack he is now? And if so, she must've known that about him when they hooked up. Why'd they get married in the first place?"

"Look," she said. "Maybe I could've been a relationship counselor. But I became a cop. So I'd rather do the job I was hired to do and not worry about my commanding officer's love life. Or absence thereof."

"Copy that," he said, grinning.

There was no guarantee their target would be home. If she wasn't there, they'd try her place of work. But when they buzzed her from the lobby, her voice came on the intercom right away.

"Hey, c'mon up," she said, before they could say anything. "I've been waiting for you." The lock clicked open. Erin and Vic shrugged to each other and went in, Rolf at Erin's hip. They got on the elevator and rode up to the sixth floor.

"What do you suppose the rent runs on a place like this?" Vic asked.

"Three or four grand, I guess," Erin said. "Even in Brooklyn, this is a nice joint. A little out of our price range."

"You think her job pays this well?"

"Maybe. What do you think?"

"I think where there's money, there's assholes. The more money, the more assholes."

"That's deep, Vic. Really profound."

"I'm a simple guy with a simple philosophy."

Vic knocked on the door of Apartment 629. After a moment, Faith's voice filtered through the door.

"It's unlocked, hon."

"Hon?" Vic mouthed to Erin.

She shook her head. "Vic," she began, but he was already opening the door.

Faith stood in the entryway, wearing a very short silk robe. It was open at the neck, showing a generous preview of her very attractive body. Her legs were long, shapely, and bare.

There was an awkward pause. Faith's eyes went very wide, then narrowed dangerously. Vic was trying not to be too obvious about staring at her legs.

"Ms. Copeland," Erin said. "We're not who you were expecting. Obviously. You remember us, I guess?"

"Yeah, the cops," she said, recovering her poise. "Tell your partner to pick his jaw up before he trips over it. And don't drool all over my tile."

"Rolf doesn't drool, ma'am," Erin said.

"I wasn't talkin' about the dog."

That made Erin smile. "I'm sorry to bother you, Ms. Copeland, especially when you're expecting company. This doesn't need to be a long visit. We just need to ask you a few follow-up questions about your ex-husband. Can we come in?"

Faith wanted to say no, Erin could see it in her eyes, but the woman nodded. "Sure. Just don't get too comfy."

"Copy that," Vic said.

They went into the living room, which was very soft. The upholstery had a velour surface, the carpet was thick and deep, and Faith had a lot of throw pillows. The hostess curled into an armchair, leaving Vic and Erin to settle into a very deep, very soft couch. Erin wondered whether she'd be able to climb out of it without assistance.

"So what do you want?" Faith asked, getting right to the point.

"I grew up on Long Island," Erin said. "Vic, too."

"That so?" Faith was unimpressed. "Brooklyn?"

"Queens. Vic's from Brighton Beach."

"Little Odessa," Vic said.

"Ain't that nice," Faith said.

"Wasn't as nice as here," Vic said. "What's this rent set you back?"

"Why you wanna know?"

"I was thinking maybe I'd retire here when I hit my twenty and collect my pension," he said in a flat deadpan.

"Seems a little pricy," Erin said. "You've done well for yourself."

"I did all right out of the divorce."

"You soaked him for everything you could," she said, giving Faith a smile of shared female victory.

"Damn right. He had it comin' to him, the lousy bastard."

"That's funny," Erin said. "See, most of Vern's income was off the books. He was hiding it. I'm a little surprised he'd declare those assets to a divorce court."

Faith said nothing.

"I'm sure you got paid by Vern," Erin went on. "But I don't think it was anything official. I think you told him you had dirt on him that you'd spill if he didn't pay up."

"Sounds to me like you're accusin' me of a crime," Faith said. "You got some nerve, comin' into my home and accusin' me like that. You got a problem with a sister makin' good? Is that it?"

"We can run your financial history," Erin said, keeping her tone calm and quiet. "Do you think we'll find anything irregular?"

"There ain't nothin' illegal in a man givin' a woman money."

"That depends on the situation. So Vern was giving you a payout. Not a one-time thing. Monthly cash payments?"

"What's it matter? He's dead now, ain't he? I wouldn't have killed him if he was doin' what you say. So what's your point?"

"I don't care about your arrangement with Henderson," Erin said. "Like you say, he's dead. Whatever he was giving you, that's over now. What I want to know is what you had on him."

"Why you think I had anything?"

"That's how blackmail works," Vic said.

"That's an ugly word," Erin said, and just like that, they fell back on their usual good cop, bad cop dynamic. "Sounds to me like a business arrangement. But he wouldn't have just been giving you money for nothing. So what was it? There's no reason not to tell us, Faith. It's not like that information is doing you any good now."

"He was workin' with bangers," Faith said.

"Yeah, we know," Vic said. "We know all about Kenny Parker."

Faith started at the name.

"And we know about Clay Dodgson," Erin added. "And Gasoline Young."

"Then you know everything," Faith said, and the look on her face was relief. "I shoulda just called the cops on him when we split. That lousy bastard. He talked about how he was gonna rebuild neighborhoods, but he didn't wanna change nothin' at all. He just wanted to run things, take everything he could, keep it all the same."

"That's why he got the guns, isn't it?" Erin said. "For protection against those guys?"

"That's what he said," Faith said. "Like he even knew how to use 'em. He was the sorta guy who'd just buy the biggest piece he could find, just so's he'd feel big, right?"

"I hear you," Vic said. "I run into a lot of those guys on the range. Big gun, little dick, right?"

Faith glanced at Vic's holstered sidearm and back at him and raised a speculative eyebrow. Then she burst out laughing.

"You got that right," she said. "But he was scared, too. See, he'd been just grabbing up these places wherever he could. But gangs are political, right? They got their own turf. And they don't like the guys next door. It's like the Middle East or some shit. And he'd been steppin' across some of those lines, gettin' some of these guys mad at each other."

"Gasoline Young and Dog Dodgson," Erin said. "Their turf is right next to each other."

"Yeah, those two. And they was both nasty pieces of work, right? You can't work with both of 'em at the same time."

"Gasoline Young is dead," Erin said. "Blew himself up earlier today."

"Serves him right," Faith said coldly.

"Do you think he might have killed Vern?"

Faith shrugged. "Could be. Or Dog coulda done it. What's it matter? These losers are always popping each other."

Her intercom buzzed. She got out of her chair. "That's my company. You wanna take off? You're crampin' my style."

"Of course, ma'am," Erin said. She pried herself out of the sofa's clinging embrace, turned, and extended a hand to help Vic up. "Thanks for your cooperation."

"Have a nice day," Vic said, giving her a slightly suggestive smile.

"I plan to. Now get outta here."

Chapter 14

"It's got to be one of those two," Erin said. "Dodgson or Young."

"And Young's dead, so that leaves Dodgson," Vic said.

Erin paused in the apartment lobby. "Vic, just because somebody's dead doesn't mean he wasn't a murderer."

"Yeah, but we can't arrest a dead guy. And I really want to arrest somebody."

"You already arrested Grant."

"But he got away and you got to arrest him again. That didn't count."

"Poor Vic. And you didn't even get to score with the person of interest."

"Knock it off, O'Reilly. I know better than to screw around on the clock."

"Except with that Russian girl."

"How many times do I have to say it? I didn't know she was with the Mob! You, on the other hand... Geez. How did it happen, anyway?"

"How did what happen?" They were outside now, next to Erin's car. Rolf was watching them, head cocked, trying to figure out what the humans were talking about.

"You know what I mean. You and Carlyle. I know what you're doing now. Was it always about that?"

Erin glanced quickly around to make sure no one was nearby. This was a dangerous subject. "Vic, we shouldn't be talking about this," she said.

"I'm not telling anybody anything," he said. "What the hell do you think, I'm gonna get a cop killed by running my mouth? But I dare you to tell me you were always trying to turn him. What happened between the two of you?"

"Well, Vic, it's like this. Boys and girls have different body parts. And when a boy and a girl like each other a whole lot... maybe you should ask your parents about it. They can explain how the whole thing works."

"I just don't know what you see in him." Vic shook his head in disgust. "He's a criminal. You *know* he's a criminal. Hell, and a terrorist. Where's your patriotism?"

"It's not like he was with Al Qaeda or anything. The IRA... the Troubles were complicated, Vic. You're not Irish. I don't expect you to get it."

"Right. Because I'm too dumb to understand. I'm just the big guy who kicks down doors."

"I love him, Vic."

"Yeah, I know. What I'm trying to figure out is why. I thought you were smarter than that."

"Love isn't smart. And he understands me. Hell, he trusts me more than any man I've ever known. He never tells me a lie. *Never*. How many guys can say that?"

"Lots of guys say it. That's one of our best lies."

"I tried dating civilians. It never worked out. They don't understand the world we live in. And we don't want them to.

Look at Catherine and Webb, for crying out loud. She complains he doesn't tell her anything, and the moment he does, she freaks out. You think I want to come home at the end of the day and just sit at the table staring at each other? I can talk to Carlyle. About anything. And he can help. He's helped us crack more than one case."

"I know you trust him. But you shouldn't. He's gonna screw you one of these days. And I don't mean in the good way. Shit, Erin, I'm trying to help you here."

"I know, Vic. I've got older brothers, remember? Junior and Michael were always trying to make sure my boyfriends were good enough for me."

He cracked a slight smile. "Were they ever?"

"Hell no. Nobody's good enough for an O'Reilly girl. You don't have a sister, do you?"

"Nope. Just a kid brother. Total screwup. He's out west somewhere, last I heard. Probably getting in trouble."

"Do you ever want to get hitched, Vic?"

He blinked. "You're thinking of *marrying* this guy?"

"I don't know." Erin looked away. "We can't. Not now. There's too much going on. Maybe... once this whole thing is over."

"It'll never be over." Vic lowered his voice almost to a whisper. "I know what you're doing. You're taking down the O'Malleys. But do you really think you'll get all of them? Somebody always slips through, and you don't need me to tell you, these guys got long memories. The two of you will be looking over your shoulders the rest of your damn lives. You're living in a fairy tale, a crazy dream. Wake up! You want my advice, get what you want and walk away."

It was Erin's turn to look disgusted. "Typical male relationship advice."

"What the hell is that supposed to mean? The hell with getting a gangster. Maybe you need to find yourself a woman, if you hate men so much."

"That's not what makes a girl like girls," she said. "It's about love, not hate."

"I'm not gonna talk you out of this, am I?"

"Not a chance, Vic."

"You know how it ends, right? Divorce or a funeral."

"That's how marriage always ends," she said. "Let's go back to the Eightball. If Grant hasn't been delivered yet, we can at least get started on the DD-5s."

*   *   *

Grant wasn't there when they arrived. Erin called the hospital to get an update and eventually got through to the doctor.

"He's got some swelling in the brain," the doctor explained. "We're going to drill a hole to relieve the pressure. It's a good thing you got him in when you did. This sort of injury can result in permanent brain damage or death."

"He didn't make it easy," Erin said.

"That's probably why he's cuffed to the bed with one of your officers hovering over him," the doctor said dryly. "We're going to keep him overnight for observation. Assuming his condition stabilizes, we'll release him into your custody tomorrow."

"They're keeping our guy at the hospital," Erin told Vic after hanging up.

"Shit, Erin, how hard did you hit him?"

"I broke your flashlight on his head. What do you think?"

"I think I don't want you cold-cocking me. Do you think he knows anything?"

"I think he knows about the beef between his gang and Dodgson. What do you think our chances of picking up the others are?"

"You mean his KAs?" Vic asked, turning to his computer. "That'd be the Dwyer brothers. Max and Charles, otherwise known as Tiny and Scooter."

"I'm guessing Tiny's an ironic nickname?"

"He's six-four and weighs about three-fifty," Vic said.

"Three hundred fifty pounds?" Erin repeated.

"Yeah. Shouldn't be hard to find. And I don't think he'll run as fast as Grant did. Take a look at his last mug shot."

"That's a large man," Erin said after looking.

"Yeah. And it doesn't look like muscle."

"What about Scooter?"

"On average, they're a normal-sized guy," Vic said. Scooter was thin to the point of emaciation. He grinned nervously in his mugshot, as if he was embarrassed. Several of his teeth were missing and the remaining ones were badly discolored.

"Meth head?" Erin guessed.

"That's what he was busted for," Vic said. "These aren't muscle guys, Erin. How about we put out the call to the Seven-Oh to scoop 'em up?"

"You don't want to be in on it?" she asked. "How uncharacteristically lazy of you."

"I'm just sick of driving to Brooklyn all the time. But you want me there, I'm there." He jumped to his feet and started for the stairs.

"Hold it," Erin said. "Is this just a plan to get out of doing your Fives?"

"No..." he said unconvincingly.

She smiled and waved him on. "Go. I'll handle the arrest paperwork. It was my collar anyway."

She went down to the locker room and grabbed a spare shirt to replace her shredded blouse. Then she settled into the familiar work of departmental paperwork. Detectives spent an awful lot of time filling out forms and typing in data. The Job worked out to about eighty percent office work, nineteen percent dealing with terrible people and situations, and one percent sheer, heart-pounding excitement and terror. She'd had her excitement for the day. Now it was back to the grind.

With Vic and Webb gone, Major Crimes felt empty and hollow. Rolf was her only companion and the Shepherd, recognizing the familiar tedium of office work, had curled into a ball, tucked his snout under his tail, and gone to sleep. Erin envied him. Now that the adrenaline from the chase was wearing off, she was tired. She checked the clock. It was a little after three.

The clock's hands crawled. She didn't hear from Vic. Finally, a little after five, she finished most of her paperwork and decided to call it a day. She logged off her computer and got to her feet.

Rolf was instantly awake and on his paws, wagging and excited. The end of the day meant another walk and supper to follow. He was ready.

* * *

Alcoholics *needed* a drink. Erin only *wanted* one. At least that was what she told herself. But living above a pub could be a sore temptation for an Irishwoman, especially when she had an effectively limitless supply of top-shelf whiskey. But she'd earned it today. She walked through the after-work crowd at the Barley Corner to the bar, where she found her boyfriend enjoying a pint with his best mate.

"Erin, love!" Corky exclaimed, bouncing up to give her a quick kiss on the cheek. "If you're looking for a grand time, you've come to the right place."

"You're not what I'm looking for, Corky," she said, disengaging but smiling. Corky was a scoundrel, but it was almost impossible not to be at least a little charmed by him.

"Ah, that's all right, love," he said, grinning. "I've a hot date later this evening."

"A gentleman doesn't discuss such things," Carlyle said. "Particularly in front of ladies."

"That's why I never hear about your exploits," Corky said, "while you're stuck listening to mine. You're a gentleman. I've never claimed to be."

"Who is she, and what story did you tell her?" Erin asked.

He gave her a wounded look. "I've never yet taken a lass under false pretenses. If they want to believe something about me, that's their affair, but I'm precisely what I appear to be."

"Get you something, Erin?" the bartender asked, gliding over to them.

"The usual, Danny," she said. "Better make it a double." A glass of Glen D whiskey accordingly appeared in front of her.

"A trying day, I imagine?" Carlyle asked.

"I had some trouble catching a bus," she said.

"That doesn't sound so bad."

"It'll probably be on the evening news."

He raised an eyebrow. "I hope nobody was hurt."

"Nothing that won't heal," she said. "Say, Corky, I've got a question for you."

"Grand," Corky said. "I was just thinking it's been some time since a copper interrogated me. Would you be wanting to use your bracelets, love?"

"My handcuffs are already spoken for."

"If you're needed another pair, I know a lad. A lass, actually."

"Would these handcuffs be fur-lined?"

"Leopard-print. How did you know?"

"Lucky guess. I'll pass."

"You're prejudiced, love. I imagine your bracelets have been around wrists like hers more than once."

"Stop it, Corky."

"Stop what?"

"Making sense. I'm not drunk enough for that."

He laughed. "Then you'd best fire ahead with your question, so we can get down to the drinking."

"What do you think of marriage?"

He was in the act of taking a sip of Guinness. He spit the mouthful clear across the bar, narrowly missing Danny. Carlyle patted his friend on the back while Corky choked and spluttered.

"I think you took him off his guard, darling," Carlyle said, smiling.

"I'm in favor of the institution," Corky said when he had his breathing back under control.

"Really?" Erin asked. "I wouldn't have thought so."

"Oh aye. If not for marriage, where would we get all the discontented, unsatisfied housewives?"

"This hot date of yours wouldn't happen to be married, would she?" Erin asked, her police instincts hopping on board Corky's train of thought.

"If she is, it's her business," he said cheerfully. "I'm only committing adultery if I'm the one who's married."

"You've got an interesting perspective on morality," she said.

"Morality's not nearly so important as integrity," Corky replied.

"What's the difference?" Erin asked.

"Integrity's about being the man you appear to be," Carlyle said quietly. "There's many a lad in the Life with integrity, but you'd hardly call them moral."

"That wasn't really my question anyway," Erin said. "What I was asking was whether you'd ever see yourself marrying someone."

"Perish the thought!" Corky said. He found the notion disquieting enough to require half his remaining Guinness.

"But if you did find someone," she persisted. "Would it be a girl in the Life?"

"There's no girl alive would have me," he said.

"You've had plenty of lovers," she argued.

"And not a one wanted me to stay," Corky said, his face serious for once. "Nay, love, I'm the lad the lasses go to for a grand time, for an adventure. The boring, reliable ones are the ones they go home to." Then he smiled again. "But I do show them a grand time, that's certain, and someone has to. I'll let you know how it goes with my sweet colleen tonight. I'll have some grand tales for you when next we meet."

"You don't have to on my account," Erin said. But the works skated right past Corky, who'd downed the rest of his drink and was on his way out the door.

"Is he ever going to grow up?" she asked Carlyle after the other Irishman had gone.

"I'd not hold my breath," Carlyle said. "He's pushing fifty. I think if he was going to, he'd have done it by now. Is marriage on your mind then, darling?"

"Yeah. I keep seeing all these screwed-up relationships. I guess I'm wondering if it's worth it."

"Nothing worth doing is easy," he reminded her.

"Copy that." Erin looked into her glass of whiskey. If there were answers at the bottom, she couldn't see them.

Chapter 15

Erin arrived at the Eightball the next morning to find Major Crimes dark and empty. While Rolf circled, preparing his bed next to her desk, she went into the break room to get a cup of coffee. A terrible snorting, tearing sound met her in the doorway. She recoiled. Then her brain identified the noise as the sort of snore a man might make when his nose had been broken more than once. She was therefore unsurprised to find Vic sprawled out on the disreputable couch, one leg trailing on the floor, mouth open. His cheek was swollen and bruised. She saw freshly-scabbed abrasions on the knuckles of his right hand.

"Oh, Vic," she said quietly. "What did you do now?"

Getting no answer, she turned to the coffee machine and poured herself a cup. She added a dash of creamer and stirred.

"You should see the other guy," Vic muttered.

Erin spun around, nearly spilling her coffee. Vic's eyes were still closed and he was lying just the way he had been.

"What other guy?" she asked.

Vic grunted and did an awkward sit-up on the couch, pivoting to face forward. His hair was buzz-cut close to his scalp, so he didn't look as disheveled as most guys who'd just spent the night on a couch, but he did look tired. He rubbed red-rimmed eyes and squinted up at her.

"Tiny Dwyer," he said.

"I thought he was a slob," she said. "Out of shape."

"Guy's stronger than he looks," Vic said. "And he's *big*. Got him downstairs in lockup, along with his tweaked-out brother, plus Leroy Grant. A couple Patrol guys from the Seven-Oh dropped Grant off at zero dark something-or-other."

"How'd you find the Dwyers?" she asked.

"Tipoff from a guy I know in Little Odessa. He knew a meth house on 50th where Scooter liked to score. I grabbed two Patrol units and dropped in."

"Meth houses are dangerous, Vic."

"I was more worried about the tweakers than what was in the walls," he said. "But you're right. They had a whole lab in the basement. Someone's gonna have to tear down that whole house, and they better be wearing hazmat gear when they do. Not my problem. Here's what happens. I find Scooter upstairs, strung out on a nasty-ass couch."

"Sort of like I found you," Erin said.

Vic smiled sourly. "Yeah, pretty much. I grab him no problem, but then who comes through the door but his big brother. Tiny chucks one of the Patrol guys clean out the window before he knows what's going on."

"Out an upstairs window? Is he okay?"

"Yeah. Turns out, that window looks over the garage. Lucky bastard lands on the roof, doesn't even get a bruise. But the other Patrol guy and I don't know that. The uniform goes for his gun, but Tiny stiff-arms him into a doorframe and he goes down. So I shove Scooter into his brother and they get tangled up. That buys me a couple seconds. I put a hard right on Tiny's jaw." Vic rubbed his knuckles. "He gets dizzy and I follow up with a left in the gut. My fist goes in, I swear, up to the elbow. It's like punching a beanbag chair. I'm wondering if I'm ever gonna get my hand back, or if I'm gonna have to get a shovel and dig for it. Tiny yells something and clocks me in the face. So I grab the back of his head with my right hand and give him my forehead right in the jaw. Hurts both of us, but he sits down hard and I'm still up.

"While I'm standing there clearing my head, the Patrol dude comes up on one elbow. He's got his Taser out and he lets Tiny have it center mass. Tiny gives a squeal. Then he tries to get up and the uni gives him another jolt. That knocks the fight out of him.

"Scooter makes a run for it, but I just put out a foot, he trips over it, and that's the end of it."

"Sounds fun," Erin said.

"By the time I got them processed, it was getting pretty late," Vic said. "So I figured I wouldn't bother going home. I crashed on the couch and here I am."

"Sounds like we've got Tiny dead to rights for assaulting an officer," she said. "And drug charges on his little brother."

"Yeah," Vic said. "We found felony weight of meth in his pockets."

"So we've got leverage. Let's find out what they know. Did they lawyer up yet?"

"I haven't given them the chance. Didn't put them in Interrogation yet. I thought the high and mighty Detective Second Grade might want first crack at them."

"Okay, let's take a run at them and see what happens."

"I'm gonna be bad cop this time, huh?" Vic said.

Erin gave him a wry smile. "You beat them up and arrested them. Yeah, I'm thinking good cop may not be the best fit for you."

* * *

They tried Scooter first, on Erin's principle that the best way to get at a gang was through its weakest member. Scooter Dwyer was a classic meth head. The moment she stepped into the interrogation room, Erin smelled the distinctive, foul aroma of a tweaker. It was mostly bad breath and rotting teeth, with an undertone of BO and chemicals. His face was twitchy and his pupils were dilated like the entrances to subway tunnels. He wasn't just thin, he was practically skeletal.

"Max Dwyer, AKA Scooter," Erin said, taking a seat opposite him and trying not to lean away. "I'm hoping you can help me with something."

Scooter didn't say no. He didn't say anything. His eyes jittered from Erin to Vic and back again.

"What do you know about Vernon Henderson?" she asked.

Scooter didn't react.

"Hey, numbnuts!" Vic shouted, banging his hand on the table. "Answer the lady's question!"

Scooter jumped and twitched, giving Vic a wide-eyed, frightened look. But he seemed a little more awake and alert than he'd been a second before.

"Vernon Henderson," Erin repeated, deliberately using a calm, steady tone to contrast with Vic's outburst.

"What 'bout him?" Scooter mumbled.

"He was selling his chop shop to Gasoline Young," Erin said.

"How you know that?"

"In exchange, Gasoline would give him a piece of the action," she went on. "What was the percentage? Ten? Twenty?"

"I didn't have nothin' to do with that," Scooter said.

"If he was taking more than fifteen, he was ripping you off," Erin said.

"Course he was rippin' Gasoline off! That's why he was pissed!"

"Gasoline was pissed at Henderson?" Erin asked.

"Yeah. But that ain't nothin' special. Everybody hated that boy."

"Did Gasoline talk to him?"

"I don't have to tell you shit, police lady."

"No, you don't," Erin said. "Of course, that's between you and your brother."

"Tiny? What's he got to do with anything?"

"Tiny's looking at five to fifteen for assaulting a cop," she said. "He tossed a police officer out a window. Your brother looks after you, Scooter. He was trying to protect you. Do you want him to go down for fighting for you?"

Scooter shifted uncomfortably. "You leave my brother outta this."

"I'd like to help him," Erin said. "I bet you would, too. How'd you like to pay him back for all the jams he's gotten you out of?"

She knew she had him. His eyes filled with unexpected tears. She reflected, not for the first time, that even hardened street criminals and junkies loved their families. Using a man's brother against him was a dirty trick, but detectives had to play dirty. Besides, it was true. His cooperation might help Tiny, at least a little.

"Tell me about Gasoline and Henderson," she said. "Did they talk about their business disagreement?"

"Gasoline was gonna. Don't know if he did. Was gonna straighten that jerk out."

"His usual way?" Erin asked. "Barrel of gas? Cigarettes?"

"Hey, don't nobody get hurt when he do that. The gas don't light, see?"

"Yeah, we know," Vic said. "Just fun and games. A little prank, right?"

"Yeah!" Scooter said, eager to please. "Hell, we all laugh about it after."

"That's what the barrel upstairs was for," Erin said, thinking of the explosion. "Gasoline was getting ready to see Henderson."

"Yeah, he was gonna go get him last night," Scooter said.

"Wait a minute," Erin said. "He hadn't talked to Henderson yet?"

"Naw, he was getting' everything ready. We was all gonna go get him, but this big boy come in and get me and Tiny first." Scooter indicated Vic.

"Did you know Henderson was working with Dog Dodgson?" Erin asked.

"We heard," Scooter said. "That's another thing Gasoline was gonna discuss."

"But he hadn't gotten around to it?"

"Naw, lady, I told you that! Henderson, he called Gasoline, couple days ago. They set up, like, a meeting."

That was news to Erin. She sat forward. "Henderson set a meeting?"

"Yeah. For last night. Talk to Gasoline, lady. He'll tell you."

"I'm talking to you right now," she said, thinking it would be a little difficult to get Gasoline Young's attention. He was in the morgue and not very talkative. "This is important, Scooter. Who else was he meeting with?"

"He said he had to sort out some other shit first, with some other boy."

"Dodgson?"

"Maybe. I didn't talk to him. I just heard."

"What's the bad blood between you guys and Dodgson?"

Scooter shrugged. "He's takin' stuff over. He wants Leroy's shop too. Leroy, he don't wanna give it to him. You know how it is."

"Dog wants the shop?"

"Yeah."

"Do you mean he wants to own it?"

"That's what I said."

"Dodgson's in the real estate business?" she asked.

Scooter shrugged. "Maybe. I dunno. That ain't my thing."

*   *   *

"That was fun," Vic said. "Let's go get Dodgson."

"Soon," Erin said. "I want to talk to Grant one more time before we go."

"Okay," Vic said. "You want to be good cop again?"

"No, I bashed him in the head, remember? And then I ran him down when he tried to escape. I don't think he and I are going to get along great. You be good cop."

"Copy that."

"Vic? Be nice."

"I'm nice."

"You are not."

"Zofia thinks I'm nice."

"Zofia's an idiot."

"Take that back!"

"She's seeing you. Voluntarily."

Vic couldn't quite hide his smile. "Okay, point. But she's only an idiot about me."

Leroy Grant was in Interrogation Room 2. He had a bandage around his head and looked like he was feeling pretty lousy. When he saw Erin, he groaned.

"Aw man, not you again."

"You think I forgot about you, Leroy?" Erin sat down opposite him. Grant tried to scoot his chair away, but it was bolted to the floor and didn't budge.

"We got good news for you," Vic said. "Thanks to your warning about your buddy, no cops died when the house blew up. I'm glad you've decided to cooperate. This whole thing's going to go a lot easier."

"Whoa, nobody said nothin' about cooperating," Grant said.

"Then I guess this is going to go the other way," Erin growled. She put her hands on the edge of the table and glared across it. "You can always go down as Gasoline's accomplice. That means attempted murder of police officers. Plus the bus you stole, the accidents you caused, and the fact that you bent a tire iron on this guy's thick skull. You're looking at a whole lot of years, kiddo."

"What my partner's trying to say," Vic interjected, "is that's your worst-case scenario. But it's not gonna come to that. You've been a big help already, Leroy, and if you can just help us with one more little thing, I can get the accessory charges dropped."

Grant looked at Vic, then back at Erin. "Man, my head hurts," he said.

"I heard they drilled a hole in it," Erin said without much sympathy.

"We know Gasoline was going to snatch Henderson and stuff him in a barrel," Vic said.

"Who told you that?" Grant demanded.

"And we know Dog Dodgson wanted your shop," Vic went on.

Grant stared at him, mouth open.

"But you didn't own your shop," Vic said. "Did you?"

The prisoner shook his head. "Look, you gotta understand, I didn't have nothin' to do with what Gasoline was planning. I mean, I told him the gas barrel thing was over the line. It was just a matter of time before he screwed up and burned some dude. I said we didn't need to grab him. We could have somebody else sort it out for us."

"Dodgson?" Vic asked quietly.

"Gasoline didn't want that," Grant said. "He hates that son of a bitch. Hell, I hate him. But this was business, right? So who cares? So when I talked to Dog, I told him he needed to talk to Henderson, not me. 'Cause Henderson's name is the one on the deed, at least till we settle up. He wants the shop, he gotta talk to the man."

"That's what you told Dodgson?" Erin asked.

"Yeah. So I guess that's what he did."

Bingo, Erin thought. "Did Young know you were talking to Dodgson?" she asked.

"Hell no. And you better not tell him."

"Young's dead, dumbass," Erin said. "That explosion you heard was him blowing his own head off with his own damn gasoline, just like you said was going to happen."

"Aw, man," Grant said, putting his head in his hands. "That bites so hard."

"Thanks for the help, Leroy," Vic said. "Don't worry, this whole thing's almost over."

* * *

"Dodgson's our guy," Erin said as soon as the door to the interrogation room closed behind them. "He's got to be."

"Yeah," Vic said. "But how do we prove it?"

"We've got Grant and Scooter's testimony," she said. "That should get us a warrant from Ferris."

Judge Ferris was the oldest man on the New York City bench. He had a soft spot for the police in general and the Major Crimes squad in particular, so they could expect a little latitude from him. Erin accordingly got on the phone. In the twenty-first century, a judge could issue a warrant without even getting out of his favorite armchair. This suited Ferris fine, and a few minutes after Erin had explained the situation, search warrants for Dodgson's home and place of business were sailing across the ether into Erin's computer.

Five minutes after that, Erin, Vic, and Rolf had piled into her Charger and were on their way to Brooklyn yet again.

"You gonna tell me not to pick a fight with him again?" Vic asked.

"If he comes quietly, yeah, don't pick a fight," she said. "But if he doesn't, feel free to kick his ass."

Chapter 16

They got to JAWZ in the late afternoon. Erin, Vic, and Rolf climbing out of the car and stood on the sidewalk, looking at the door while they put on their vests. Rolf had his K-9 body armor strapped around him. He was excited, his tongue hanging out and his tail swishing eagerly. The vest meant he was working, and work was *fun*.

"You think maybe we ought to get ESU?" Erin asked.

"What for?" Vic replied. "It's one punk and a few mutts."

"It's the mutts I'm worried about," she said.

"Relax. They're in cages. Besides, if one of them gets out, the ESU boys would blow his furry little head off, and that'd give you nightmares."

Erin shuddered. "Thanks for that image. Let's try not to shoot any dogs, okay?"

"I try not to shoot people, too," he said. "But I do carry a gun."

"Right," she said, rolling her eyes. "Let's go."

They were greeted by the expected cacophony of barking from the kennels, Dobermans throwing themselves against the chain links. Everywhere Erin looked she saw bared fangs and wild, frantic eyes. But she didn't feel fear. She felt pity for these poor animals, coupled with anger at the man who'd molded them this way. She'd known several Dobies in her life. All of them had been sweet-natured, friendly dogs. Vic was right. Bringing a bunch of keyed-up, armed to the teeth ESU doorkickers into a place like this was a recipe for dead dogs.

They walked quickly to the office door. Erin thought about knocking, but knew the barking had already alerted whoever was inside, so she just opened the door.

Clay Dodgson and a pair of young street toughs were in the middle of the room, looking expectantly at the door. One of the punks had his hand on something stuffed down the front of his pants, and Erin would've bet it wasn't the equipment God had given him.

"Easy there, guys," she said, her own hand dropping to the butt of her Glock. Vic already had his Sig-Sauer in hand, the barrel of the pistol pointed at the floor.

"Detective O'Reilly," Dodgson said. "And her pair of guard dogs."

"There's a little bitch in this room all right," Vic said. "But I'm looking at it."

"I wasn't expecting to see you again so soon," Dodgson said. "Did you forget something the last time you were here? Or did you change your mind about purchasing one of my dogs?"

"I'm here to execute a search warrant," Erin said. She produced the warrant out of her pocket, using only her left hand, the one with Rolf's leash looped to the wrist. This was no time for her gun hand to be busy.

"Search warrant?" Dodgson echoed. "For what?"

"I'm looking for a pistol which was used in a homicide," she said. "You're a suspect."

"We'll get outta your way," said one of the punks. They started for the door.

"Hold it," Vic said. The barrel of his Sig rose so it was pointed in the vicinity of the guys' kneecaps. "Hands where I can see them. Now."

One of the two glanced at Dodgson. Erin recognized the look. He was seeking instructions. Erin saw the flicker in Dodgson's eyes and the fractional nod of his head.

Shit. She thought the word but didn't have time to say it before everyone started moving at once.

The office was a terrible place for a fight. It was way too small for five people, let alone three dogs, and made of nothing but hard surfaces. It was like a bar fight in a suburban bathroom. When the action started, only a couple of feet separated the different sides. Knives and nightsticks would've been more useful than guns.

"Gun!" Vic shouted, which was a waste of breath. Everybody already knew one of the punks was packing. Erin saw the man in front of her whip a revolver out of his trousers. She dropped the warrant and grabbed his wrist with her left hand. She shoved the hand to the side, pushing the pistol barrel out of line as the punk pulled the trigger. The sound of the shot, in that confined concrete room, was deafening.

To her left, Erin saw Vic moving out of the corner of her eye. He was trying to take aim at the other punk, but the kid was too close and the two of them went into a clinch, muscles straining. Dodgson, behind his buddies, dropped to one knee and temporarily out of Erin's line of sight.

She cleared her Glock, still holding her opponent's gun hand, and tried to bring up the barrel. There just wasn't room between their close-pressed bodies. Then the kid snatched at her gun with his free hand, wrapping his fingers around the slide.

"*Fass!*" Erin grunted. Rolf sprang up. His jaws snapped shut on her opponent's forearm, just behind her own hand. As the K-

9 bit, Erin glanced down along her gunsight and fired. The bullet went almost straight down, punched a hole in the top of the kid's sneaker, and went clean through his foot into the concrete floor.

With a bullet hole in his foot and a ninety-pound dog chewing on his arm, the guy dropped his own gun and collapsed screaming. Erin left Rolf on that guy, controlling the suspect through jaw pressure, and spun to help Vic.

Vic was about six inches taller than the guy he was facing and spent a lot more time at the gym. Dodgson's guy was doing his best, but he had about as much chance of winning an arm-wrestling match with Vic as he did of tipping over the Statue of Liberty. Vic grunted with effort, picked the goon clean off the floor, and heaved the struggling man at Dodgson's desk. The guy skidded across the top of the desk, clearing everything off it, and slammed into the wall. He dropped in a limp heap to the floor behind Dodgson's chair, which slowly rotated in his wake.

"Love! Hate! Kill!" Dodgson shouted.

For just a second, Erin had no idea what he was talking about. Then she remembered the names of Dodgson's personal pair of attack dogs.

There was a blur of black and brown motion. Then, with unbelievable speed, one of the Dobermans was on her. Erin stumbled back, reflexively throwing up an arm in front of her face as she caught a confused glimpse of wide, snapping jaws.

Her arm probably saved her life. Police K-9s were trained to bite a perp's arm, to immobilize a suspect. Clay Dodgson's dogs were trained to kill. The Dobie went for Erin's throat, but she barely got her arm in the way, her forearm pushing the dog's chest back just a little. The jaws clicked shut less than an inch from her cheek as she fell over backward, the dog on top of her. She hit the wall just beside the door, her head slamming concrete hard enough that stars flashed across her vision, and ended up in an awkward sitting position, the Doberman scrabbling at her with its claws.

Even then, Erin didn't want to shoot the dog. She fended it off with her left hand, grabbed at its collar, and missed. It snapped at her again, teeth tearing at her shoulder. By good luck it caught the Kevlar shoulder-strap of her vest and momentarily snagged its fangs. She heard Vic swearing and knew he was having similar problems with the other dog.

She had no choice. She shoved the muzzle of her Glock into the Doberman's belly and pulled the trigger.

Nothing happened.

A little scrambled by the blow to the back of her head, Erin had no idea why the gun hadn't fired. Stupidly, she pulled the trigger again, then a third time. The gun still didn't fire. The Doberman freed its teeth from the Kevlar and made another try for her face. Saliva sprayed into her eyes. She smelled foul, meaty breath and strained her left arm, trying to keep the teeth away.

Rolf hit the Doberman from the side with every ounce of muscle in his hefty frame. The Shepherd gave a terrific snarl and sank his teeth into the other dog. Suddenly, the pressure on Erin's chest was gone. The two dogs went over and over each other in a snapping, growling ball of fur and fangs.

Erin started to get up and felt a wave of dizziness. She must've hit her head harder than she'd thought. She saw the guy she and Rolf had wounded lying a short distance away. He was curled in a ball, cradling his arm and whimpering. He was out of the fight. A little to one side, Vic was wrestling with Love, or maybe Hate. It wasn't immediately clear who was winning. Dodgson was nowhere in sight. The office door was open.

She had to get up. Her partners needed her. But her legs felt wobbly. She thought she might throw up. She lifted her Glock and worked the slide, thinking the gun might have jammed somehow. A spent shell casing popped out and spun through the air, brass shining brightly under the harsh light from the ceiling bulb. She steadied the pistol across her knee and took aim at the struggling dogs, waiting for a clear shot.

The Doberman squealed suddenly, a high-pitched, terrible sound. Rolf was on top now. He had the other dog by the scruff of the neck and gave a vigorous shake. The Dobie's teeth rattled and it yelped helplessly.

"*Pust!*" Erin ordered, sighting on the Doberman's body.

Rolf obediently released the other dog and sprang back. At that moment, Vic yelled. Erin saw the Doberman had the big Russian's left hand in its jaws. The teeth had sunk in to the gumline. Big drops of blood were falling to the floor.

"*Fass!*" Erin snapped, pointing at Vic's opponent. She kept her gun on the first dog, but that Doberman was done. It lay panting on its side, tongue flopping weakly.

Rolf lunged and bit. He wasn't trained to fight other dogs and didn't really know what to go for, but instincts older than the K-9 guided him. He got hold of the Doberman just under the ear. Rolf's jaws flexed. There was an audible crackling sound and, with an incredibly forceful oath, Vic pulled his hand free. The Doberman went down with Rolf holding its head in his mouth. All the K-9 had to do was bite down a little harder and that would've been it for the dog.

Rolf twisted so he could see Erin. His hackles were raised as high as she'd ever seen them, but his tail was wagging enthusiastically and he cocked his head quizzically. Even with a mouthful of Doberman, it was such an unexpectedly cute expression that she felt a smile forming.

"Dodgson?" Vic asked Erin.

She tilted her head toward the door. Vic nodded and started to push through it.

He slammed it again. Less than a second later, something hit the other side of the door.

"Son of a bitch opened the cages," he explained, leaning against the door and forcing it to latch. "Hallways full of dogs. God damn it." He looked down at his hand. Blood continued to drip down.

Erin finally managed to stand up, cursing her own weakness. On her feet, she felt marginally better. There was only the one door, and if what Vic was saying was true, about a dozen berserk attack dogs were between them and the exit. They might manage it, but only by shooting their way out.

"Window," she said, looking at the small, wire-reinforced pane near the ceiling.

"Maybe," Vic said doubtfully. "Not sure I can fit, and you look a little shaky."

"I'm fine," she growled. It was neither more nor less true than when she usually said it.

"Okay," he said. Then he raised his Sig-Sauer and put three bullets through the window. The glass shattered, held in place only by the wire frame. Vic reversed the gun and used the butt to break out the fragments.

Erin considered the dogs and suspects. "What about them?" she asked.

"I've got them," Vic said. He set his pistol down on the desk and cupped his hands. "I'll call backup. Go!"

Erin put one foot in Vic's hands. He flinched a little as she put her weight on the injured hand, but he gritted his teeth and lifted and she stepped up. It was a tight squeeze with her vest on, but she made it through the window. Vic was right, he never would have fit. She came out in a recessed niche in a back alley. She hoisted herself out and started jogging toward the front of the building.

If Dodgson hadn't been such a snappy dresser, she might have had trouble picking him out. As it was, she saw the distinctive white coat and fedora half a block down the street, moving at a run.

Erin's blood was up. She wanted nothing more than to go after him on foot, run him the hell down, but her Charger was right there. She opened the door, slid into the driver's seat, and started the engine. Against her instincts, she didn't stomp the accelerator. She didn't want any roar of the engine or squeal of the tires to warn him. Instead, she just drove along the street, nice and easy.

Dodgson came to an intersection and stepped off the sidewalk, jogging into the street. That was the moment Erin had been waiting for. She gunned the motor and sent the Charger into an angled skid, just as if she'd meant to cut off another car.

The police car screeched to a halt right in front of the fleeing gangster. Dodgson, taken completely by surprise, couldn't turn or stop fast enough. He hit the hood of the car and doubled over. By the time he recovered, Erin was out of the car with her Glock aimed at him.

"Clay Dodgson," she said. "You're under arrest. I think you know why."

"Holy shit," Dodgson said quietly. "You really are what they say. Where the hell did you come from?"

"Queens," she said. She heard sirens, already close and coming closer. In New York, backup was rarely far away. She turned Dodgson to put his hands against the car and started frisking him. She hoped the adrenaline would hold out a little longer. She had the feeling once it wore off, she was going to go down hard.

Chapter 17

A pair of Patrol officers arrived a minute or two later. Erin saw two more squad cars pull up in front of JAWZ, four uniforms spilling out and drawing weapons. One of the officers started toward the door, the other three covering him.

"Oh, no," Erin said under her breath. Then, louder, "All officers responding to Neshenko's 10-13! Don't go inside! Tell them!"

One of the uniforms at Erin's location gave her a questioning look. "Why not?" he asked.

She lunged back into her Charger, snatched up her radio handset, and shouted, "All units outside JAWZ, stand back! Do not make entry!"

Even as she said it, she saw the patrolman start to open the door. He paused with it cracked a couple of inches. Then he stumbled back as something hit the door from the other side. He fell on his ass and scrambled away.

"Ah, Dispatch," an unnaturally calm voice said over the radio. "This is Sergeant Hickman, Six Baker Delta, responding to Neshenko's 10-13. We've got an Animal Control situation. It appears we have, ah, multiple hostile canines interdicting us. Please advise."

"Neutralize the threat," Dispatch said at once. "Use any necessary force."

"Belay that!" Erin snapped into her handset.

"Ah, identify yourself, please," Hickman said.

"This is Detective O'Reilly," she said. "That's my partner in there, and I'm telling you not to shoot those dogs."

"Please advise as to your partner's status," Hickman said.

"He's fine," she said. "He's got a minor bite, but he's not in danger. He's barricaded in the back room. He's got my K-9 with him and four in custody, two humans and two dogs."

"Say again, O'Reilly," Dispatch said. "Did you say Neshenko has dogs in custody?"

"Affirmative," Erin said. She turned to the Patrol officers near her. They were standing watching Dodgson, uncertainty on their faces. "You two, keep this man. He tried to kill a cop, so watch him."

"Copy that, O'Reilly," one of the uniforms said. He grabbed Dodgson and started moving him toward their squad car.

Erin climbed back into her Charger, did an illegal U-turn, and drove back to JAWZ the wrong way. It wasn't dangerous; the police cars outside the kennel had blocked oncoming traffic. But she knew it would've made her dad cringe. Sean O'Reilly believed in following the rules of the road.

She parked and got out to find the four officers discussing their options.

"What happens if you Tase a dog?" one of them asked.

"I've seen it done," Erin said. "It just pisses him off."

"How about pepper spray?" another asked.

"Does anybody have any?" the first one asked.

No one did.

"So why did you ask?" the first cop demanded.

The second cop shrugged. "I just thought, you know..."

"Those are vicious bastards in there," the third cop said. "I say we take them down."

"No," Erin snapped. "They're abuse victims who don't know any better."

"Then what do you suggest, Detective?" he shot back.

"I'll call a vet and get some trank pills," she said. "And someone who knows the area, go to the nearest grocery store and get about five pounds of hamburger."

There was an emergency vet clinic just a few minutes away. A vet tech arrived in answer to Erin's call, bringing a bottle of powerful canine tranquilizers. By the time the vet got there, one of the cops had already fetched the requested raw meat. Meanwhile, Erin had gone to the alley window and told Vic what was going on.

"I'll just wait here, then," Vic said. "It's not like I'm bleeding or anything."

"Quit being such a crybaby," she said. "Like you've never been bitten before."

"Hell, I've been bitten by drunken assholes," Vic said. "Human teeth are worse. But I think I should maybe get a Band-Aid or something."

"The dogs okay?"

"Yours or Dodgson's?"

"Both."

"The Dobermans are pretty dinged up, but I think they'll live. Your boy's fine. He's got them under control. All he's gotta do is look at 'em and they lie down flat and wag their tails. I don't think there's any doubt who's big dog in this room."

Once they had the medicine and meat, Erin mixed the tranquilizers in with the ground beef. Then it was just a question of cracking the door just enough to toss in the meat, one handful at a time. The ferocious barking gradually diminished as one dog after another gulped down the drugged meat, got woozy, lay down, and took a nap. Soon, ten Dobermans lay sprawled on the hallway floor. Then the police carefully entered and got the dogs penned back in their kennels.

"Good trick," Vic said when he emerged from the back room, pushing a handcuffed perp in front of him. The other one, the guy Erin had shot in the foot, couldn't stand up and would have to be carried out.

"Old burglar's trick," she explained. "For dealing with guard dogs."

"What if they hadn't been hungry?" one of the uniforms asked.

"Dodgson was using them as attack dogs," she said. "I think he kept them hungry all the time. Look at them. You can see their ribs. Makes them more vicious."

Erin hadn't wanted to show it, but she'd been worried about Rolf. However, when she saw her K-9, she had to smother a laugh. Rolf was standing proudly over Love and Hate. The two Dobermans slunk around him, utterly cowed and submissive, their stumpy tails wagging ingratiatingly. Both Dodgson's dogs were, as Vic had said, obviously beaten up, particularly the one whose head the Shepherd had bitten. That dog's jaw was visibly askew and probably broken. Erin handed them over to the vet tech, who gave them some sedative and agreed to take them back to the emergency clinic.

Rolf's own injuries were relatively minor. He had some scratches from the other dogs' claws on his haunches, and a couple of shallow gashes on his face, but if he was in pain, he didn't show it. Still, Erin knew he should get checked out. She decided to take him to her usual vet instead of the emergency clinic, since he wasn't in immediate danger.

After that, it was a matter of turning over the scene to CSU, arranging for the prisoners to be transported to Precinct 70 for overnight lockup, and taking Vic to the hospital. Rolf curled up in the back of the Charger and, after licking some of his lacerations, went to sleep. Erin was feeling pretty tired herself and her head throbbed mercilessly.

"Why didn't you just shoot the damn dogs?" Vic asked as she drove.

"There was no need," she said. "I wouldn't kill any animal just for being in the way." She paused. "Not even a human."

Vic chuckled. "No, I meant the first two. Love and Hate."

"Oh. I tried, actually, when I got jumped. But when I was wrestling with Dodgson's sidekick, he grabbed my gun by the slide. It didn't cycle properly when I fired, so I didn't have a live round chambered, and there was no chance to fix it until Rolf had already tackled the dog."

Vic nodded. "Okay, that makes sense."

"Why didn't you?" Erin asked after a moment.

"Why didn't I what?"

"Shoot the dog that was trying to rip your throat out."

Vic stared at his hand. It was still oozing blood from several punctures. "You know, I never really thought about it," he said.

"Bullshit. You had the gun in your hand."

"Okay, maybe I like dogs more than I used to. Even ones that are trying to kill me. I blame you. And the mutt, of course."

"That mutt saved our asses."

He nodded. "I guess maybe he did. You think CSU will find anything?"

Erin shrugged. "I hope so. We've got Dodgson dead to rights on a bunch of other charges, whatever happens. Maybe we can flip one of his goons. How's the hand?"

"How do you think? It hurts like hell. I'll never play the piano again."

"You play the piano?"

"I thought maybe I'd learn one of these days."

"Good thing it's your left hand."

"Yeah. I did that on purpose, you know. Fed him my unimportant appendages first."

"That's what I like about you, Vic. You're always so considerate."

"Bite me, O'Reilly."

"I don't think I should. You might have rabies."

"Isn't that only a problem if I bite you?"

"It goes both ways. But most people don't go around biting rabid raccoons, so it doesn't come up often."

"I was just thinking I needed a new hobby."

"Biting rabid raccoons? It'll never catch on."

* * *

After an hour and a half at the hospital, they were back in Erin's car and headed back to Manhattan, Vic's hand looking like a drunken patchwork quilt from eight stitched-up punctures. Rolf was still snoozing. The tip of his tongue stuck out the front of his muzzle.

"He looks like I feel," Vic said. "With the shit they put in these pain pills, it's no wonder America's got a narcotics problem. Please remain in your seats and fasten your seatbelts, prepare for takeoff. I am flying!"

"And that's why I'm behind the wheel and you're in the passenger seat," Erin said. She'd had her head looked at, resulting in a diagnosis of a minor concussion.

"Excuse me, Stewardess, I'd like a vodka martini," Vic said. "Shaken, stirred, however you want."

"Once we're off the clock, you can drink whatever you want," she said. "But I think maybe you shouldn't mix booze with Percocet."

"You sound just like my mom."

"Your mom's right."

"I just got in a fistfight with a Doberman. Cut me some slack."

"Yes, you did. The Dobie tried to eat your fist."

"You live over a bar, right?"

"Yeah." Erin was suddenly suspicious. "Why?"

"Okay, you know what? The hell with it. Let's have a drink once we clock out. We've earned it. My treat."

"My boyfriend's the pub owner. I drink for free."

"Oh. Your treat, then. Bring the mutt."

"I don't care how stoned you are, Vic, I'm not giving Rolf booze."

"He's earned it too. That bad boy took down two attack Dobermans single-handed. Dobermen? Single-pawed?"

"Alcohol is poisonous to dogs."

"It's poisonous to people, too. You gonna let a little thing like that stop you?"

"Yeah, Vic. I am. Because I want Rolf to live a long, full life."

"Does that mean I shouldn't drink either?"

"No, you drink whatever you want. The sooner you kick off, the better for everybody."

He grinned. "No such luck, Erin. I'm the hardest son of a bitch to kill in the entire NYPD. Got the scars to prove it. You wanna see 'em?"

"Maybe later."

* * *

It would've been nice to just hop into the Eightball, sign a couple of forms, and leave, but Erin and Vic both had a lot of paperwork to fill out. In addition to the ubiquitous DD-5s, they had arrest reports, use-of-force reports, and all the other rigmarole of police work. Since Erin had fired her weapon, she had to turn it in, even though nobody had died. Ballistics would verify what everybody already knew, which was that her bullet had gone through the suspect's foot at close range. She was lucky it hadn't ricocheted off the concrete. The spent round could have gone almost anywhere in that room. Then there was initial evidence to catalogue and preliminary reports to write up for Lieutenant Webb and Captain Holliday. Erin also had to explain to Holliday why she was acting as lead investigator, just in case any question came up regarding Webb and his conduct.

The bottom line was, by the time they finally finished up, it was after suppertime and Erin's headache was worse than before. Vic's initial Percocet high had mostly dissipated.

"See you tomorrow, I guess," Erin said, standing up and jingling Rolf's leash. The K-9, having rested for several hours, had his second wind. He was already up and wagging.

"What the hell are you talking about?" Vic replied. "We're getting that drink. Come on."

"You want to go to the Barley Corner," she said in a flat voice.

"Why not? Gotta see what all the fuss is about."

"You've been there before. You got in a fight last time, remember?"

"I know. But I'm feeling full of love for all humanity tonight." He paused. "And maybe still a little stoned."

"Okay," Erin sighed. "It's a free country. Just remember, the situation with these guys is a little delicate."

"I understand operational security, Erin. Just a drink, I promise. I won't get into it with any gangsters."

Chapter 18

"This was a bad idea," Erin said the moment they walked into the Barley Corner.

"How come?" Vic asked.

"Mickey's here," she said. The big O'Malley enforcer was hard to miss. He was sitting with a couple of his goons at a table covered with empty beer bottles and shot glasses.

"Screw him," Vic said. "I came for a drink. No lowlife chucklehead is gonna scare me off."

It was too late anyway. Mickey had already seen them. He gave Erin a cold stare out of his pale, almost colorless eyes. Without changing expression, he raised the bottle in his hand in a silent salute.

"I get it, you hate that meathead," Vic said as they walked toward the bar. "So what? He's dumb muscle, just some washed-up ex-boxer. There's gotta be a thousand like him in this city."

Erin shook her head. "He's dangerous, Vic. You know some of the stuff he's done."

"Yeah," Vic said. They both knew Mickey had committed at least one murder they could tie him to, though it might not be enough for a conviction. "But hell, anyone can kill. That doesn't make him special."

She couldn't explain it to him, the sense of deep physical unease Mickey Connor instilled in her. Maybe it was because Vic was a man and couldn't feel the sexual threat that emanated off the former prizefighter. Mickey was a rapist who got off on pain. He'd tried to kill Erin once and very nearly succeeded. She knew, from personal experience, what he could do with his bare hands.

"Forget about him," she told Vic, wishing she could. As they approached the bar, the mismatched pair of Corky and Carlyle stood up to greet them.

"Erin, it's a pleasure as always," Carlyle said. "And Detective Neshenko. What'll you be drinking? It's on the house, if that doesn't trouble your conscience."

"Free booze doesn't bother me tonight," Vic said. He raised a hand to the bartender. "Can you get me a Stoli?"

"And a Glen D, straight up," Erin said.

"Coming right up," Danny said.

While the bartender got their drinks, Vic and Corky eyeballed one another. Corky drew out the staring contest for several seconds with an uncharacteristically serious look on his face. Then, just as the tension was becoming unbearable, he winked.

"Corcoran," Vic growled.

"One and the same," Corky said cheerfully. "Come, lad, you're not too proud to drink with me. We've something in common, the two of us."

"Yeah?" Vic asked suspiciously.

"Oh aye. We'd both do near anything for this sweet colleen," he said, indicating Erin with a tilt of his head. "Though we get precious little in return. We're like brothers to her, you ken, and she'll never shower us with her charms."

Vic clearly had no idea whether to even be angry at Corky's words. He opened his mouth and closed it again.

"Here you go," Danny said, sliding two glasses across the bar. "Anything else?"

"Yeah," Vic said. "I'm hungry. Can I get two bacon cheeseburgers? One with fries, one without, hold the onions and tomato."

"Can do," Danny said.

"Make it three," Erin said. "Fries for me, too."

Corky emptied his own shot glass and licked his lips. "Ah, that's grand. I can scarce believe I've settled on the wrong side of the ocean from that wee Scottish glen where they work this magic."

"So, how was your hot date?" Erin couldn't resist asking.

"A mite confusing," Corky said. "She's a fine ride, no doubt of that, but I've not gotten the chance to climb into the saddle, if you take my meaning."

Erin raised an eyebrow. "That's not like you, Corky. You usually put the moves on a girl pretty fast."

"Aye, and she was up for it," he said. "But she wasn't quite certain, I think, and with a particular type of lass, that means you won't be going all in."

"Maybe because she's married?" Erin suggested.

Corky waved the idea aside. "Half the lasses I've known were married, love."

Vic rolled his eyes and snorted loudly.

"You don't believe me?" Corky asked.

"I believe you," Vic said. "I just don't like you."

"Honesty," Corky said, grinning good-naturedly. "But I don't fault you for it. Maybe you've never known just how sweet and grateful an unsatisfied wife can be when you show her what she's been missing. I tell you, those shy Catholic lasses can be the best."

"Okay, Corky, I'm sorry I asked," Erin said.

"No apology needed," he said. "Besides, I'm seeing her again. In fact, I'd best be off. She'll have just put her wee ones down for the night. Ta, love." He pushed off from the bar and headed for the door.

"I hope you're not badly injured," Carlyle said to Vic, glancing down at his stitched-together hand.

"You should see the other guy," Vic said.

"We got in a dogfight," Erin explained. "All three of us."

Rolf, at Erin's feet, gave Carlyle a cool look that suggested subduing a pair of vicious attack dogs was nothing worth mentioning.

Erin felt Vic tense beside her. She turned her head and dropped her hand instinctively to her waist, only to feel nothing. Her Glock was back at the station, awaiting ballistics testing. She saw Mickey getting to his feet. But the enforcer wasn't even looking at them. He was on his way out, flanked by his goons.

She let out a silent sigh of relief and saw Vic relax, too. She realized that, in spite of his words, he'd been keeping a wary eye on Mickey.

"Here you go, Erin," Danny said, setting a plate in front of her. "And here you are," he added, giving Vic his two very large burgers and generous plate of fries.

"Are you really going to eat all that?" she asked.

"Of course not," Vic said. "I'm thanking my partner for helping me out."

"But I've got one," she said.

"Wasn't talking about you," he said. Then he took one of the burgers, hopped down from the bar stool, and took a knee, offering the sandwich to Rolf.

The K-9 couldn't believe it. He turned questioning eyes toward Erin. He didn't budge. His tail didn't even wag. But a slow droplet of drool gradually trickled from his jowl. He really, really wanted the hamburger.

She laughed. "Fine. Have it your way. Okay, Rolf. Go on."

The Shepherd opened his jaws and tore a big mouthful off the burger. He chewed twice, swallowed, and came back for more. Vic, not wanting more holes in his hand, set the remains of the food carefully on the floor and stood up. Rolf finished the burger, licked the floorboards a couple of times, and looked up at Vic. Now his tail was wagging. He was still drooling.

"I gotta find a girl who looks at me that way," Vic commented.

*   *   *

Erin still had a headache the following morning. It felt like a bad hangover, so she decided to go with the usual Irish remedy. A shot of whiskey made for acceptable hair of the dog. The pain retreated to a bearable distance. Of course, she wasn't allowed to drink on duty, but taking the shot an hour before work meant it would have time to work its way out of her system.

She arrived in Major Crimes to find Webb waiting for her. The Lieutenant was sitting at his desk, slowly twirling an unlit cigarette between his fingers.

"Sir," she said.

He stood up, tucked the cigarette behind his ear, and approached with his hand outstretched. Erin, a little confused, shook with him.

"Good work, O'Reilly," he said. "How are you feeling?"

"Just fine, sir." The headache was still there, pulsing at the back of her skull, but she wouldn't admit that. "Are you back on the clock?"

"Affirmative," Webb said. "It looks like the case is about wrapped up."

"How do you figure, sir?"

"According to CSU, the revolver you took off that guy at Dodgson's kennel is a match for the bullets that killed Henderson."

"I'm guessing Dodgson did the shooting," she said.

"You can ask him, but you might get further talking to the guy who was holding the gun."

She nodded. "Is he still in the hospital?"

"No, he got lucky, relatively speaking. Your bullet broke one of the bones in his foot, but they pinned it back together and put a cast on him. He's downstairs."

"What's his name, anyway?"

"Omar Banks. He's got a nice, thick jacket. If we pin the shooting on him, he goes down for life."

"Sounds like good leverage to me. You want to sit in?"

"I'll watch from the gallery," he said. "You've got this."

* * *

"That ain't my gun," were the first words out of Omar Banks's mouth when Erin put a photo of the revolver in front of him.

"That's funny," she said. "Because you tried to kill me with it yesterday."

He tried a weak smile. "Hey, baby, I didn't mean nothin' by that. Just business, you feel me?"

"Business," she repeated. "Who gave you the gun?"

He sat back and shook his head.

"Omar, look at me," she said. "Take a good, long look, because this could be the last time you look at a woman without a sheet of Plexiglas in the way. You tried, but you didn't hurt me. But that pistol was used in a homicide, so unless you can convince me it belongs to someone else, you're going down for Murder One. You know what that means."

"Hey, I didn't kill nobody!"

"Convince me," she repeated.

He licked his lips. "Look, this boy ain't nobody to mess with."

"Neither am I," she growled. "What's word on the street about Erin O'Reilly?"

Banks's smile disappeared completely. "Yeah, I heard of you," he said.

"What'd you hear?"

He said in a low voice, "I got no beef with you, lady. Look, I needed a piece, okay? So I got this one from my boss."

"Clay Dodgson?"

"Yeah."

"Where'd he get it? Tell me, or you go upstate and get old staring at four concrete walls."

"He told me he took it off this loser, thought he was a gangster. See, Dog was in business with this guy. Dog bought this apartment, but he had to pay, like, a cut of everything that was goin' down."

"I know about the deal," she said. "In exchange for the title, he had to pay Vernon Henderson for the privilege of running illegal businesses."

Banks looked relieved. "You know about that? No problem, then. Thing is, Dog didn't like the terms of the deal. But he thought the plan was solid. So he figured he'd get in on the action, try it himself. So he wanted this other piece of property."

"Leroy Grant's chop shop," she said.

Banks nodded. Finding out how much Erin already knew made him even more talkative. That was often the case with interrogations. If they didn't think they were giving up new information, most crooks figured, what was the harm in confirming what the cops knew?

"So Dog talked to Leroy," he went on. "But Leroy didn't own the place. That Henderson boy did. And Dog wanted to talk to him, renegotiate, like. He wanted to be an equal partner, fifty-fifty. Woulda been a good deal, I gotta say. He shoulda taken it."

"How did they meet?" Erin asked.

"Ving and me, we was followin' him around."

"Who's Ving?"

"Irving Niles. That other boy who was with us yesterday."

"Okay, go on."

"This boy, Henderson, he was real twitchy around his pad. He had, like, army guns and shit. I saw in his window once, he's got this crazy big gun in his hands. So we figure, we go in to talk to him there, it's gonna turn into World War Three or some shit. But then he goes to this other house, and he shacks up with some babe. We tell Dog, he figures it's his best chance to talk sense with the man. So I bring him to that house. Ving and me. Ving drives. And Dog goes in to talk to him, alone."

"Alone? He didn't bring Love and Hate?"

"You kidding? You saw what they're like. This wasn't supposed to be a fight. That was the whole point. Dog wanted him for a business partner, he wasn't tryin' to intimidate him or nothin' like that. So he goes in, Ving and me, we're waitin' in the car. We got no idea what's goin' on in there. Then we see these flashes through the curtains and we hear the shots."

"How many?" This was a test to verify the information.

"Three. Then Dog comes back out. He's pissed off, he's holding that piece, that one right there." Banks pointed to the photo. "He can't believe this shit. He tells Ving to drive and we get the hell out of there. He says this dumbass got mad, threw down on him. Says the loser was wearin' a bathrobe, but he still got a piece in his pocket. So Dog says it's, like, self-defense. Not even murder, you feel me? And he gives me the piece, 'cause I'm in need of one."

Erin nodded. "I understand. What happened after that?"

"Nothin' much. We went home."

That was the way it went, Erin thought. A meeting went sideways, a guy got murdered, the survivors went home afterward and went on with their lives. What a crazy world, and it was *her* world now. Even the best guys in Carlyle's circle, guys like Ian Thompson, could kill on a moment's notice. And they slept just fine afterward.

"What were you doing at JAWZ last night?" she asked.

"We heard something went down at the chop shop. Saw it on the news. We were talkin' about what to do about the territory. We heard Gasoline Young got smoked."

"Smoked himself," she said. "He tried to light a barrel of gas and it blew up in his face."

"Damn." Banks drew the word out into three long syllables.

"We'll need a statement," she told him, producing a legal pad and pen. "I just need you to write down what you told me. Then I can tell the DA you cooperated. And you're sure Dodgson wasn't intending to kill Henderson?"

"Geez, lady, if you're gonna kill someone, you bring your own piece, you don't use his."

"Yeah, I know," she said, thinking that cops and crooks often thought along the same lines.

Chapter 19

"Self-defense," Webb said. "The funny thing is, that's almost true."

They'd put Banks in Holding and had gone back up to Major Crimes to write up the case. Rolf was lying next to Erin's desk, staring at her with his chin between his paws.

"That'll be up to Dodgson's lawyer," Erin said. "Looks like we've got him dead to rights."

"The murder weapon and at least one witness? Yeah. He's lunchmeat. And it's about time. I'm sick and tired of this." Webb rubbed the bridge of his nose.

"Sir? Where's Catherine Simmons?"

"On her way to the airport. I called her a cab as soon as Banks started talking."

"Already?"

"She's got no reason to stay," he said. "We've got her statement. If we need anything else for the trial, we can get it then. But this case won't go to trial. Dodgson will plead out, probably try to get it knocked down to manslaughter. It won't be Murder One anyway, not with him taking Henderson's own gun."

"That isn't quite what I meant, sir." Erin looked at her commanding officer. "Didn't you want to see her off?"

Webb's eyes were very tired. "I don't think that'd be good for anybody," he said. "She didn't want to see me in the first place. The only reason she called me was because she needed help. I helped. Now she's gone."

"She's not the only person whose feelings matter here," Erin argued. "How long were you married to her?"

"Five years, give or take. But what's the difference? Last time I left town, now it's her turn. She doesn't want me. Why would she?"

"You're a hell of a cop, sir," she said. "And a damn good man. If she doesn't see it, that's her problem and she doesn't deserve you."

A thin smile creased Webb's face. "Did you ever notice how partners rub off on each other, O'Reilly? You're a regular attack dog when it comes to protecting your people."

"Damn right. Anyway, sir, self-pity isn't covered in the Patrol Guide."

"You sure about that?"

"I'm sure of one thing, sir."

"What's that?"

"Love's too valuable to spend on someone who won't give it back."

He nodded. "You know, for a while, I thought you were one of those people who believed in love conquering all."

"I still believe that," she said. "But both people have to believe it."

He gave her a long, thoughtful look. "I'm older than you," he said. "And I've had more experience in things going wrong. So let me give you a little advice. I'm no shining example, but I can be a cautionary tale. Things are going to go sideways. It's inevitable. Life is a shitstorm and you're bound to get some on you. When you do, even if you both love one another, someone's going to get hurt."

"I know that," she said.

He held up a hand. "I wasn't finished. When you get hurt, you find out what you're made of. You also find out what the other person's made of. The Job erodes us, Erin. It eats away at the edges of us. Either the people we love can stand by us, or they can't. And if they do, they pay the price, too. If I were Cath, I'd walk away from me. I'd never date a detective, much less marry one."

"You saying we should all be celibate?" she asked, half-jokingly.

Webb sighed. "I don't know what I'm saying. I guess I just want you to pay attention. Keep your eyes open. Because sooner or later, everything the world gives us has to be paid for. At least your man understands that."

Erin had never asked Webb what he thought of Carlyle since he'd found out about their relationship. She hadn't dared. She still didn't, but she looked the question at him silently, letting him read it in her eyes. She had no doubt the experienced interrogator knew exactly what she was thinking.

"I know he loves you," Webb said. "A man doesn't take a bullet for a woman he's not sure of. Is he worth it?"

"Worth what?" she asked.

"That's the problem," he said. "Love is open-heart surgery. You never know the price until the bill comes due. So I guess that's the real question. Is he worth anything? Everything?"

"Only one way to find out," Erin said. "You think I'm an idiot?"

"I know you're no idiot. You're smarter than Neshenko, and he's smarter than he lets people think he is. This was never about being smart. It's about being reckless. And remember, sometimes someone else pays for our sins. Cath sure as hell paid for mine. It's not fair, but it's the way things work."

"So you're telling me to be careful?"

"I'm just following the Classical tradition. The old soothsayer tells the truth, but the young lovers never listen."

"We're not that young. You think this is a tragedy?"

"Life's always a tragedy," Webb said. "Or it's such a dark comedy, there's no difference. In the end, everybody cries or everybody laughs, and I never had much sense of humor."

"That's a lousy way to live, if you ask me," Erin said. "Christ, what gets you up in the morning?"

He smiled again. "There's tobacco. And coffee. And a little hair of the dog, to fight off the hangover."

"You're a real glass-half-empty guy, you know that, sir?"

"At least I've got a glass and there's something in it. I've been doing some thinking while I was on the bench. I think I've got a couple innings left before I hit the showers. You're not getting rid of me yet, O'Reilly."

"That's a relief, sir."

"What, you don't want to be a Lieutenant?"

"It's not that, sir. I'm just ready for someone else to be giving Vic orders for a while."

Webb chuckled quietly. "Fair enough. Fine work, Detective. Let's get the rest of these reports filed, and then we can pack up the evidence and let the DA's office take over. And if we're lucky, the next one won't hit quite so close to home."

Erin thought of Carlyle, bleeding on her living room carpet, and shuddered. "Copy that, sir," she said.

Keep reading after the sneak peek to enjoy a special
bonus.

Pinot Noir

A Harry Webb Story

Here's a sneak peek from Book 15: Punch Drunk

Coming 3/28/22

The buzz of the phone cut through Erin O'Reilly's sleep, invading her dreams like a mosquito crawling into her ear. She shook her head, rolled over, and fumbled for the phone. It kept insistently buzzing, vibrating its way toward the edge of the nightstand. She caught it just before it passed the tipping point and lifted it to look at the caller ID.

The phone screen cast a green glow on her face. The name on it was SHELLEY. That meant her sister-in-law's cell phone. And the clock at the top of the screen read 1:52.

The bottom dropped out of Erin's stomach and she was suddenly awake and scared. She'd thought the call would be from work, a Patrol unit stumbling across a body. But murder was an everyday part of the Job and nothing to get excited about. A call from a family member at two in the morning meant trouble.

She glanced to one side and saw an unoccupied pillow, the bed half-made, its fine silk sheets smooth and empty. Carlyle, her boyfriend, must not have come up yet. That wasn't unusual. Pub owners and gangsters tended to live by night, and Carlyle was both. He was probably hanging out with other Irish Mob associates at the bar downstairs.

At the foot of the bed, a pair of anxious eyes reflected the phone's light in flashes of greenish white. Rolf, had also been roused by the phone. Now the German Shepherd K-9 was watching her, head tilted to one side, wondering what was happening.

Erin took a breath and thumbed the phone. "Hello?" she said.

Her imagination filled the silence on the line with a whole parade of horrors, waking nightmares with names like cancer, car crash, and heart attack. Names danced through her head. Michelle wouldn't be calling about Erin's mom or dad, would she? Shelley's husband, Sean Junior, maybe? Or one of the kids? Dear God, Erin thought, not Anna or Patrick. Please, not them.

"Erin?" The voice was distorted. Maybe they had a bad connection. It sounded a little like Michelle.

"Shelley? Is that you?"

"Erin, I... I didn't mean to wake you up. I'm sorry."

"I'm up now, Shelley," Erin said, throwing the sheets down to her waist and sitting up. "What's the matter? Is everyone okay? Junior? The kids?"

"They're... fine," Michelle said. Erin heard a really strange sound, a rapid-fire clicking that she couldn't identify.

"Are you okay, Shelley? Talk to me. Are you hurt?"

"Can... can I see you? Will you be up for a little while?"

"I'm hardly going to go back to sleep now," Erin said, fatigue and worry making her voice sharper than she meant it to be. "Do you need me to come over?"

"No, I... oh, I'd better not come to your place. Can we meet at that coffee shop? The one just down the block from you?"

"Java Passion?"

"That's the one."

"Sure." Erin flicked on the bedside lamp. She pivoted and stood up, walking to the closet to get a pair of pants. "Are you driving from your house?" Michelle lived in a Midtown brownstone, about twenty minutes away.

Michelle hesitated. "No," she said, her voice still sounding odd. "I'm close by. I can be there in five minutes."

"Give me ten," Erin said. "I have to get dressed. Shelley, are you okay? Look, if you're in some sort of trouble, I can help, but I need to know. If it's an emergency, you'd better call 911. Are you in danger?"

"I don't..." Michelle started to say. Then she cut herself off and that strange clicking sound came again. "I'll explain when I see you." Then, with a beep, the call disconnected.

Erin stared at her phone. That call had been as unlike Michelle as any conversation she could remember. Her sister-in-law was bright, vivacious, warm, and cheerful. And she never just hung up on someone.

Erin dressed as quickly as she could, just a T-shirt and jeans over her underwear. It was June, the New York weather was mild, and this was a late-night meeting. She didn't have to bother with makeup or fancy hairstyles. She pulled her hair back into a plain ponytail. She slipped her feet into her everyday shoes, a good, sensible pair which cheated her height up to five-foot-eight. Then she opened the nightstand drawer and took out her shield and her guns; her service sidearm, the Glock nine-millimeter, went on her belt and her backup piece, a snub-nosed .38 revolver, clipped to her right ankle. Both guns had saved her life before. It wasn't that she was expecting that sort of trouble. The weapons were just part of her wardrobe, as much as her shoes or phone.

She clipped the gold NYPD shield to her belt beside her holster. As she closed the drawer, she saw Rolf again. The Shepherd was standing now, tail waving uncertainly. He loved Erin's morning ritual of dressing and arming, because it meant they were going to work. Work was the best thing in the world. But he could tell she was worried, and that confused him.

"*Komm*," she said, speaking the command in the language he'd been trained to obey by his Bavarian breeders. That one word got him moving. He pranced beside her, wagging more enthusiastically. He was ready. Maybe there'd be bad guys to chase. If he was really lucky, maybe he'd get to bite one and be told what a good, brave boy he was. And then he'd get his rubber Kong ball and life would be great.

Erin opened the door at the bottom of the apartment's stairs. A flood of voices washed over her, the loud, happy chatter of a late-night public house. She stepped into the back of the Barley Corner's main room. The place was packed. She thanked God, and good building contractors, for the soundproofing that insulated the upstairs apartment. She couldn't see him in the crowd, but she knew Carlyle would be at the bar in his place of honor.

She threaded her way over, keeping Rolf close on his leash. She found the silver-haired Irishman engaged in conversation with a pair of rough-looking guys. She recognized one of them, so knew they were with the Teamsters Union.

"Hey, Wayne," she said by way of greeting. "How's the Beast?"

Wayne's face lit up. A big, burly trucker, he'd given Erin a ride back to New York as a favor once, a favor she'd repaid by keeping him out of jail. The Beast was his truck, his pride and joy.

"She's running like a champ," he said. "How're you, miss? Share a drink with us?"

Carlyle had gotten to his feet when he saw her, only a hint of hitch in the motion. He'd almost completely recovered from the bullet that had nearly killed him earlier that spring, but some of his muscles hadn't quite gotten their old tone back. He gave her a quick, sharp glance. He didn't miss much.

"What brings you down, darling?" he asked in his Belfast brogue.

"I need to step out for a little. Got some family business."

"All well?" he asked, his face growing more concerned. Like Erin, he knew that family news in the wee hours was rarely good.

"I think so. I'll just be down the street. I should be back in an hour, at the most." She gave him a quick kiss on the cheek, marveling on the inside. Just a couple of months ago, she wouldn't have dared show any affection for him in public. But now their relationship was known both to the NYPD and the underworld. It wasn't that they weren't deceiving anyone. It was more that the deception had shifted onto new ground.

"I think I'll wait up for you," he said with a smile. "The night's young yet."

"The drink will have to wait," she said to Wayne. "Business first."

"Always," he agreed pleasantly. "Catch you later, Miss O'Reilly."

As she and Rolf walked toward the front door, she caught Wayne's words to Carlyle.

"—a lucky guy," he was saying. "I know guys would kill for a girl like that."

She smiled. What woman didn't want to hear herself described that way? She nodded a greeting to Caitlin, one of the Corner's waitresses, on the way out. The perky redhead grinned and waved to her. At least some folks seemed to be having a good night.

* * *

The night air, pleasantly cool, finished clearing Erin's head. The coffee shop was just a couple of storefronts down from the Barley Corner. She let Rolf sniff some things and cock a leg at an alley entrance. As long as they were up, they might as well get a little walk out of it.

Java Passion was open twenty-four hours a day, but at this ungodly hour, not too many patrons were there. Most of them appeared to be taking advantage of the coffee shop's free Wi-Fi and were concentrating on their laptops. But one customer, a tall, striking, dark-haired woman, was standing at the front window, a cup of coffee in one hand, the other wrapped around her own elbow. The cup was shaking. As Erin walked up to her, a little coffee sloshed over the brim.

"Hey, Shelley," Erin said.

Michelle O'Reilly nodded jerkily. "Thanks for coming," she said. Her eyes were puffy and bloodshot, like she'd been crying.

Erin put a hand on Michelle's shoulder. Her sister-in-law was trembling like a live electric wire. "Let's sit down," she said.

"Do you want to get something?" Michelle asked, cocking her head toward the front counter.

"No, thanks." In truth, Erin could've used a cup of something hot, or better yet a shot of whiskey, to steady her nerves. But she had an odd feeling like Michelle might vanish if she turned her back, maybe bolt and run. She heard that clicking sound once more, and finally recognized what it was. Michelle's jaw was clenched so tight, her teeth were chattering.

They sat at a table along the side wall. No one paid them any attention. Rolf, his ambitions for an early workday thwarted, settled at Erin's feet with a sigh and closed his eyes. Michelle clutched her coffee cup in both hands, drawing comfort from the heat. She stared at her own hands.

Erin was an experienced cop. She'd done dozens of interrogations. If Michelle had been a suspect in her interrogation room, Erin would've recognized all the "guilty" signs. Shifty body language, lack of eye contact, nervous tension.

She reached out and gently touched the back of Michelle's hand. "Hey, sis," she said. "What's wrong?"

"I think I screwed up," Michelle said. "Big time."

Erin's stomach made a flip-flop. "What do you mean?"

"Erin, I'm an only child," Michelle said. "You know that. One of the things... one of the things about... Sean is his big, tight family. You... you've always made me feel like I belong. With you."

"Of course," Erin said. "It doesn't matter if you're born one of us or if you marry in. You're an O'Reilly."

"I think of you like my sister," Michelle said.

"That's because you are," Erin said. That earned her a weak, watery smile and the briefest bit of eye contact.

"Thanks. So I'm asking... I'm begging you. Don't tell Sean what I'm going to tell you."

A cold feeling crept through Erin's midsection. "Shelley, he's your husband, and he's my brother."

"Promise!" Michelle snapped with sudden, brittle energy.

"Okay, okay," Erin said. "I promise." But even as she said it, she wondered what she was getting herself into.

"He's working tonight," Michelle said. That wasn't unusual. Sean O'Reilly Junior was a trauma surgeon at Bellevue Hospital and often worked the late shift in the emergency room.

"Okay," Erin said again.

"I... I wasn't at home," Michelle said softly.

"Where are the kids?" Erin asked. She was surprised when Michelle flinched at the question.

"Home. In bed. Asleep."

"You got a sitter, right?"

"Of course I did! Sam Perkins, from up the street. She's home from college for the summer and she's used to late hours."

"Shelley? Where were you?"

"I went to a dance club," Michelle said.

"Which one?"

"What does it matter? Stop being a cop for one second, Erin!"

"Okay, sorry. Old habits. Just tell me what you want to."

"I went out dancing. And I... I wasn't alone."

Erin swallowed. "I'm guessing you're not talking about one of your girlfriends."

Michelle shook her head.

"A guy you know?" Erin asked.

A nod.

"What happened?"

"We danced and had a few drinks," Michelle said. "Then he... he asked if I wanted to go back to his place. With him."

"Shelley," Erin said softly. She didn't even know what she was trying to say. Surprise, anger at the betrayal of her brother, concern, all of it jumbled together in her head.

"We got there and he... we went up to his apartment. And he made us cocktails, and we sat down on his couch, and we were talking and then... then we weren't..." Michelle's eyes filled with tears. One of them started rolling down her cheek. She didn't seem to notice it.

A part of Erin wanted to reach out and touch Michelle, to give her some comfort, but she sat back and watched. Now she was feeling a kind of clinical detachment, and that disturbed her. She liked Michelle. Hell, she *loved* her. But this was her brother's wife, talking about having an affair. What was she supposed to do with that information? And she'd been sworn to secrecy. Under the detachment, she felt a rising anger. How dare Shelley make her promise to keep something like this a secret?

"He was... he was really... it was..." Michelle faltered and didn't seem to know what to say.

"I hope it was worth it," Erin said grimly.

"No. It wasn't. I mean, it was good, at first. But I got scared. I haven't... I mean, not with any other guy. Not since Sean. So I panicked. I pushed him away. We didn't... you know. Not all the way. And I grabbed my... my shirt and things. And I got out of there."

Erin sagged back in her chair. "So you didn't go to bed with him?"

Michelle shook her head. "But I was going to," she said miserably. "I thought I wanted to. I *did* want to. But there, on his couch, I heard Anna's voice, like she was talking to me. And I thought, how am I going to explain this to her? Isn't that weird? I should've been thinking about Sean. Oh God, Erin, I'm the worst wife in the world."

"Think of this as a wake-up call," Erin said. "Whatever's gone wrong between the two of you, get to work on it. Make it right. I love you, Shelley, and I don't want to see your marriage blow up over some stupid bullshit you and Junior weren't willing to fix. That goes for him, too."

"You're not going to tell him," Michelle said. "Are you? You promised."

"I'm not going to tell him," Erin said. "Because you are."

"Are you crazy?" Michelle was horrified. "He'd kill me! And it'd wreck him. It'd break his heart."

Erin looked at her. "Are you worried more about protecting him? Or yourself?"

Michelle's eyes slid away again. "You're right. I'm such an idiot. I just wanted an adventure. Some excitement. To feel like a *woman* again. You don't know what it's like. And up until I freaked out, everything was just incredible, Erin. This guy... he's something else."

Erin nodded. "I get it, Shelley. But we don't get to do everything we want."

"You did. You got your bad boy."

"Yeah, and he got shot in the middle of my goddamned living room!" Erin snapped. "Both of us almost died, Shelley. So yeah," she went on in a lower voice. "I got him. But it wasn't easy and we've paid for it every step of the way. Because actions have consequences and love doesn't change that. You know how many bodies I stand over who were killed by people they loved?"

Michelle's shoulders shook and she started to cry again.

"Hey," Erin said, and now she did put out a hand. "I didn't mean to go all self-righteous on you. It'll be okay. You went right up to the edge, but you didn't step over it, and that's something. Your family is what you thought of. That's what's important. So think of them again. Do what you have to for them. There's nothing I wouldn't do for my family."

She thought of something Carlyle had once told her, hearing his angry, tormented voice in her memory. *When it comes to the people I love, there's no bloody line!* Where was her own line? She hadn't found out yet, and for that she was grateful.

"I should go home," Michelle said, once she had her waterworks back under control. "I told Sam I'd be there half an hour ago. She's going to be worried."

"Just slip her an extra twenty for the overtime," Erin suggested, getting to her feet. "She'll be fine."

"Thanks for listening," Michelle said as they walked out of the shop. "You're a good sister. And you're right. I'm not going to lose my family."

She put her arms around Erin and gave her a tight, fierce hug that had desperation in it. Erin returned the embrace. As she did, she saw a parked car across the street suddenly start up and angle into the road. Two men were in it, the driver and a big, bulky guy in the passenger seat. It was too dark to see their faces. A jolt of irrational alarm shot through her and she pulled back from Michelle, dropping her hand to the butt of her Glock. But the car just drove into the night, of course. It wasn't an assassin, it was just a couple of guys going home after a late night. Erin felt foolish.

"Goodnight, Shelley," she said. But she didn't think either of them would be getting any more sleep that night.

Ready for more?

Join Steven Henry's author email list
for the latest on new releases, upcoming books and
series, behind-the-scenes details, events, and more.

Be the first to know about new releases in the Erin
O'Reilly Mysteries by signing up at
tinyurl.com/StevenHenryEmail

Now keep reading to enjoy

Pinot Noir
A Harry Webb Story

PINOT NOIR

The Erin O'Reilly Mysteries

A Harry Webb Story

*Don't underestimate
a man with nothing
to lose*

USA TODAY BEST-SELLING AUTHOR

Steven Henry

Pinot Noir

A Harry Webb Story

Steven Henry

Clickworks Press • Baltimore, MD

First publication: Clickworks Press, 2021
Release: CWP-EORHW1-INT-P.IS-1.0

Sign up for updates, deals, and exclusive sneak peeks at clickworkspress.com/join.

Pinot Noir

A red wine, mainly associated with the Burgundy region of France. The name comes from the French words for "pine" and "black." The grapes are now found, among other places, in South Africa, Australia, New Zealand, Oregon, and California.

A young Pinot noir has aromas of red fruit such as cherries, raspberries, and strawberries. As the wine ages, it acquires a more complex bouquet. Master Sommelier Madeline Triffon calls Pinot "Sex in a glass."

Chapter 1

The weather was cold for a Los Angeles November; forty degrees, and raining. It was the kind of damp chill that slipped in under your clothes and just wouldn't leave, like a mean hangover.

Harry Webb was already a little drunk when he got to the bar, intending to get drunker. He wasn't sure he was under the legal limit, but that evening, he just didn't care. He took a final drag on his cigarette, dropped it to the pavement, and walked across the parking lot through the rain, flipping up the collar of his trench coat and hunching his shoulders under his hat.

It would've been hard for a stranger to tell Webb had been drinking. He could walk a straight line, he didn't slur his words, he could even hold a steady gun if he had to. But he could feel the alcohol insulating him, a layer of numbness under his rain-soaked coat.

He pushed through the front door, scuffed his shoes on the

mat, and walked to the bar. The bartender came over with a smile.

"Hey, Detective! How's it going, my man?" The barkeep was a little Latino guy who was working on a mustache, with minimal success.

"Low and slow, Manny," Webb said. "Low and slow. Gimme a beer and a shot."

"Usual, coming right up," Manny said. He poured a shot of Jim Beam and a glass of Corona. Manny knew Webb's brands and knew he preferred the cheap, everyday drinks. Webb wasn't a top-shelf kind of guy.

Webb tossed down the bourbon in one go. The burn felt nice in his throat, fighting it out with the chill of the rain. He chased it with a sip of beer, letting his breath out in a slow sigh.

"Excuse me."

If dark, melted honey had a voice, it would sound like that. Throaty, husky, sweet. Webb pivoted on his stool to see who'd spoken.

She was tall, long-legged, done up in the style of classic Hollywood: black hair spilling in endless waves across bare shoulders, spaghetti-strap black dress that clung to her in all the right places, lipstick the color of bright arterial blood. Eyes so dark they looked black in the dim-lit bar. Skin like... well, like nothing Webb had seen in a good long while. And she was looking at him, talking to him.

"Help you, ma'am?" he asked gruffly.

"I don't mean to intrude, but I couldn't help overhearing," she said. "He called you 'Detective.' Are you, by any chance, a policeman?"

"That's right, ma'am." He could see she wasn't wearing a wedding ring, but to call her "miss" just didn't fit. He couldn't guess her age. She might've been anything from twenty-five through forty. Here in La-La Land, home of the plastic surgeons of the stars, a woman could look like anything she wanted.

She extended a long-fingered, graceful hand, the nails painted deep crimson. "Maureen Sinclair, Detective. And you are...?"

"Harry Webb, Ms. Sinclair." He took her hand and gave it what he hoped was a brief, professional shake. Despite the chill and her bare shoulders, her hand was warm.

"Maureen, please.... Harry." She withdrew her fingers in a slow, almost teasing way. Webb's palm tingled.

"What can I do for you, Maureen?"

"Well, when I heard you were a detective, I simply had to introduce myself."

Oh, great, Webb thought. A badge bunny. But he couldn't quite make himself believe it. She was too put-together. The cop-chasers he'd known were younger, tending toward tattoos, piercings, and a wild outlook on life.

"And what is it you do, Maureen?"

"Show business, of course," she said, giving him the sort of slow-smoldering look he remembered from old black-and-white movies. "Everyone plays a part, Harry, wherever you're from and wherever you're going. In Hollywood we're just more honest about it."

"You been in anything I'd have seen?"

"Well, I don't know about that," she said, giving him an appraising look. "What is it you like to watch?"

"I don't get to the movies much. I'm working most of the time."

"Pity." She uncrossed her legs, turned toward him, and re-crossed them. She was wearing black silk stockings and stiletto-heeled shoes. Something about the curve of her calf made the roof of Webb's mouth go dry. "You know what they say about all work and no play, don't you, Harry?"

"I'm as dull as they come," he replied.

"Oh, I doubt that. You must have all kinds of stories to tell."

He shook his head. "People don't want to hear about real police work."

"Nonsense. It must be a thrill." She raised a finger to Manny. "Red wine, please. Pinot noir, there's a dear. Thank you so much."

"Why do you need a detective, Maureen?" Webb asked.

"Well, Harry, I seem to have gotten myself into a somewhat awkward situation," she said. "I do hope you might be able to help a girl in trouble."

"You can call the police." Why the hell was he trying to talk her out of this? He heard his second, soon-to-be-ex-wife's voice in his head.

"You push people away, Harry. I try to get close and you push me away. Watch out. If you're so determined to be alone, one of these days you'll wake up and that's just what you'll be."

"It's a... personal matter," Maureen said. "I really don't want my dirty undergarments aired in public. Surely you understand."

"Well, Maureen, I'm not a private eye. I work for the city of Los Angeles. But if you need the services of a private firm, I can recommend a good guy. A lot of retired cops go into the private sector and I know a few of them. You need to be careful of some of those fellas, but I can point you in the right direction."

"Why don't we just keep it between the two of us, for now?"

Manny put the glass of wine in front of Maureen. In that dim-lit bar it was a red as dark as an eight-ball hemorrhage. She raised it to her lips, paused, and tilted it slightly his direction.

"To new acquaintance," she purred.

Webb acknowledged the toast with a tip of his beer glass. He took a swallow of Corona. She delicately tasted the Pinot noir, running the tip of her tongue slowly along her upper lip.

"So, what's the problem?" he asked.

"I seem to have gotten myself entangled with a rather unpleasant fellow. He's also in the movie business. After all, who isn't, in Hollywood? In any event, we were engaged in making a film together some time ago. In the course of its production we worked... somewhat closely. He believed our relationship extended beyond the professional. He's not the sort of man who will take no for an answer. He's been quite persistent. At first, I'll admit, I was flattered. Then I was annoyed. Now I'm beginning to be alarmed. I wouldn't want to think he was capable of... violence, but I can no longer discount the possibility."

"Maureen, you definitely need to go through police channels," Webb said. "You can get a restraining order, get some protection from him."

"Are those particularly effective, in your experience?"

Webb wanted to say yes, but he knew better. Restraining orders could intimidate weak bullies, and they could punish stalkers, but the punishment tended to come after they'd acted. If a man was really dangerous, he'd walk right through a court order.

"I can't arrest him if he hasn't broken the law."

"But you could talk to him, couldn't you? Just talk, let him know you're in my corner, that you're my... champion." She trailed her fingers down the back of his hand, sending another pleasant thrill down his spine to a part of him that was as far from conscious thought as it was possible to get.

"I don't know," Webb said. This was the sort of thing that got cops in trouble. And something about this woman made him just a little edgy, in spite of the alcohol swaddling his detective's mind. She really was out of his league. He knew he wasn't a very handsome man; forty was in his rear-view, and when he looked in the mirror, the lean, mean Patrol cop he'd once been was a distant memory. He was going bald and growing a gut, and that was just the way things went.

"I'd be ever so grateful," she added, leaning in and almost whispering the words beside his ear. He felt the warmth of her breath. Her body, her voice, everything promised without speaking words.

It'd been a long time since he'd responded to a woman this way. His marriage, finally disintegrating, had been falling apart for months. Years, probably. Maybe ever since it had started. His wife, an attorney, had pursued her own life and career, and they'd become just two people who happened to share the same house. Not that he'd keep the house. To be specific, his soon-to-be-ex-wife was a *divorce* attorney. He was screwed.

What the hell did he have to lose? His marriage? Already lost. His health? On its way down the drain whatever he did. His career? He wasn't even sure he cared about the LAPD anymore. He'd come to hate Los Angeles. It was a superficial, fake, glitzy crust covering rot and desperation, like makeup layered on the face of a middle-aged streetwalker.

"Why don't I buy the next one," he said, "and you can tell me about this guy."

* * *

According to Maureen, her admirer was named Terry Volkman. He was an aspiring actor with a few minor credits, one of the countless dreamers who came to La-La Land. Now he made ends meet between acting gigs by helping out on film sets, doing gofer chores, bringing coffee, that sort of thing. She described him as having a face like a gerbil: a long nose, protruding ears, and beady little eyes. He favored a ratty little mustache.

"Has he tried to contact you?" Webb asked. "Recently?"

"Oh yes. Telephone calls, until I blocked his number. He sends me letters, even attempts poetry."

"Did you keep the letters?"

"Well, no. You have to understand, I find Terry physically repulsive, and thinking about him is quite uncomfortable. I've thrown away several unopened, once I began to recognize his handwriting on the envelopes. But I may have one or two lying about."

"That's good. Keep them. We may need them as evidence, if he doesn't scare off easily."

"Surely you can handle someone like Terry. I swear, he's not half the man you are." She looked him up and down with frank appraisal.

"I don't go picking fights," Webb said. "Every fight has at least one loser. Sometimes no one wins."

"I didn't imagine you to be a philosopher," she said. "But then, you'd have to be intelligent to make detective. What other secrets are you hiding?"

"One and a half divorces, two kids, and a messy legal settlement coming up." The words slipped out before he was fully aware of them. The two shots of Jim Beam soaking through his stomach lining might have something to do with it. He wasn't usually this open, especially with someone he'd just met.

"Oh dear," Maureen said, putting a hand up to his cheek. "No wonder you've got all those worry lines on your face. You're carrying the weight of the world around with you. But I expect I could smooth some of those lines away. Why don't we discuss what's to be done somewhere a little more discreet?"

She slithered—there was no other word for it—off the barstool. Her coat was on the counter next to her. Webb picked it up and held it for her.

"A gentleman," she said, slipping her arms into the sleeves. "Another pleasant surprise."

As they walked to the door, Maureen snaked her right arm around Webb's left, which made him feel like Clark Gable in the golden age of Hollywood. He felt like he was holding a winning lottery ticket and was on his way to cash it in. Outside, the drizzling rain was still falling, making halos of fine mist around the streetlights. The neon sign in the bar window buzzed.

"I'm not sure I'm good to drive," Webb said. "I've had a few drinks."

"Oh, that's all right," she said. "My car is parked close by. I can give you a ride. And I promise, it'll be one you won't forget. Mine is the red one in the second row, you see?"

He saw it. Maureen drove a red Mazda Miata MX-5 convertible. It was a sporty, flirty little roadster. The top, of course, was up, given the conditions.

Maureen reached into her purse for her keys. As she did, Webb caught movement out of the corner of his eye. Someone was coming out from between the parked cars. It was a little guy, no raincoat. He looked bedraggled and unkempt, almost like a street person.

"Maureen?"

The little guy said her name hesitantly, like he was afraid to be right.

Maureen shrank against Webb's side. Suddenly, all her seductive warmth evaporated. Now she seemed scared, helpless. "It's him," she whispered. "Terry."

"Okay, buddy," Webb said. "I don't know what you want, but the lady doesn't want to talk to you. I suggest you keep right on walking."

"Maureen, you're with... him?" Terry asked. He'd come closer, under the misty globe of one of the streetlights. His face really did uncommonly resemble a gerbil's. He blinked his beady eyes and wiped at the rain on his face. Or maybe it was tears. He looked like he'd been crying.

"Yeah, she's with me," Webb said, using the flat, no-nonsense voice he'd learned years ago working Patrol. "Take a hike, buddy. I'm LAPD, and more trouble than you can believe."

"How could you?" Terry exclaimed, his face twisting in sudden anger. "I love you, Maureen! You belong to me!"

"I don't belong to anyone but me," Maureen said. "You'll never have me."

"Then no one will!" Terry shouted.

Webb saw the look in Terry's eyes and suddenly knew what was going to happen, as clearly as if it was already done. Twenty years on the LAPD and he'd never been in a for-real gunfight, and now everything moved both very fast and very slow.

Terry's hand went behind his back and came out holding a shiny revolver. He began to raise the pistol to point at Webb and Maureen. Rainwater glistened on the barrel. It was a small gun, some unengaged part of Webb's brain absently noted. Probably a snub-nosed .38. Useless outside twenty-five yards, but lethal within ten.

All the cushioning alcohol seemed to instantly dissipate and Webb was thinking completely clearly. "Gun!" he shouted reflexively. He sidestepped in front of Maureen, shielding her with his body, and went for his service sidearm.

Most cops carried automatics these days, but Webb was

old-school. His gun was a grandfathered .38 Colt Detective Special revolver, a classic wheel-gun. It only held six shots, and it took forever to reload, but it would never jam or misfire. He hadn't spent much time on the range since leaving Patrol, so he was astonished how quickly he got his pistol out.

"No!" Terry screamed, but he was aiming the pistol as he said it, and Webb brought up his own gun, knowing that in spite of his quick draw he was just a little too slow. Webb saw the barrel of Terry's pistol staring right at him like the black eye of eternity.

Then Maureen screamed, and fire blossomed at the muzzle of Terry's revolver, and Webb didn't feel an impact, but that didn't mean anything, sometimes you got shot and didn't know it till later because of the adrenaline, and Webb pulled his own trigger and his .38 flared and jumped in his hand.

Terry jerked like he'd been hit with an electric shock. A look of stunned surprise came over his face. A dark spot appeared on the breast of his soaking wet white shirt. But he didn't fall down, and he didn't drop the gun, so Webb wrapped his left hand around his right to steady his aim and shot him again, center mass, exactly the way he'd been trained.

Terry Volkman went down as if his whole skeleton had liquefied, collapsing in a tumbling sprawl to the wet pavement. One leg folded beneath him. His arms flew out to either side. His pistol spun in the air, its wet chrome plating catching the light.

Webb was conscious of letting out his breath in a cloud of steam that drifted away, like the departing spirit of the man he'd just killed. He still felt no pain. He couldn't believe Terry had missed him, not at that range.

A sob came from behind him. He half-turned in time to catch Maureen with one arm as she clutched at him. He still held the smoking Colt in his other hand, though he knew he wouldn't need it. He'd seen many victims of firearms in his years with the LAPD and knew the look of a fatal shooting. Terry had been dead before his head hit the pavement.

Webb carefully holstered the gun and pulled out his phone. He'd call an ambulance, just to follow proper procedure. He'd also have to call his precinct captain.

Harry Webb no longer thought this was his lucky night. His winning lottery ticket had turned out to be one number off and was just a worthless scrap of paper.

Chapter 2

"How long have you been a cop, Harry?" Captain Lucano asked wearily.

"Too long, sir."

The two of them were sitting on the back bumper of an ambulance, watching the forensics guys going over the scene. The Captain was wearing a raincoat with LAPD emblazoned on it. He was holding a paper cup that had been full of coffee when he'd first gotten there. The rainwater was diluting it, second by second.

"This is your first shooting."

"Yeah."

"Was it your off-duty piece?"

"No, sir. My official sidearm."

"They give you a breathalyzer?"

"Yeah."

"What's it going to tell us?"

Webb sighed. "The truth. I'd had some drinks."

"Over the limit, you think?"

"I don't know, sir. I was off duty. I wasn't expecting to get in a gunfight."

It was Lucano's turn to sigh. "At least it was a white guy you shot."

Webb nodded. It wasn't the sort of remark a police captain would make anywhere near a reporter, but both of them knew the very last thing the LAPD needed was another minority kid getting blown away by a cop, no matter what color the cop's own skin might be.

"He drew on me," Webb said. "I ID'd myself, he fired, and I put him down. I don't know what the hell he was thinking."

"He was probably thinking he'd better get off the first shot. That's the best way to survive a gunfight. You didn't disturb the scene?"

"Of course not."

"Well, we've got the weapon, you have a witness who swears he fired first, and you're a good cop with a decent record," Lucano said. "It'll be a headache, and you may have to deal with those bastards from Internal Affairs, but sounds like you're in the clear."

Webb nodded and said nothing.

"You don't look happy," Lucano said.

"I just killed a guy, Captain. Should I be putting on my dancing shoes?"

Lucano put a hand on Webb's shoulder. "You didn't have a choice, Harry. It was you or him. This comes with the Job sometimes."

Maureen walked over to the ambulance. She stood in front of them, holding her coat closed with one hand. Her hair hung wet and bedraggled around her ears. Her face, even streaked by rain and tears, was still the loveliest thing Webb could imagine.

"Harry?" she said quietly.

"We shouldn't be talking," Webb said. "Not until after you've given your statement."

"I just finished," she said. "They're sending me home. I just wanted to say... thank you. You saved my life, and I'll never forget it."

"Just doing my job, Maureen. You're safe, that's the main thing."

Lucano and Webb had stood up when she arrived. Lucano offered his hand.

"Captain Lucano, LAPD," he said. "I'm sorry you were inconvenienced, ma'am. Please get in touch with my department if you need anything else. We have resources to help people who've been through experiences like yours."

"Thank you, Captain," she said, taking his hand. "But I'll be all right. It's sweet of you to offer, though." Webb felt a slight stab of irrational jealousy.

"Do they need anything else from you?" Webb asked her.

"They told me I'm free to go," she said. "How deep is the hot water you're in?"

"I have to stick around a while," Webb said. "Cross all the Ts. But I'll be fine."

"Well, I'm sure I'll see you again," she said. She held out her hand. Webb took it. She squeezed gently and pulled slowly away, her fingertips trailing along his, drawing out the contact. "I'm sorry this evening ended this way. I'm sure you were hoping for something more enjoyable."

"Story of my life," Webb said.

Maureen turned and walked away. She opened her car door, glanced over her shoulder at him, climbed in, and started the engine.

"That's quite a woman," Lucano observed.

"She is that," Webb agreed.

Maureen drove out of the parking lot. Her taillights dissolved into the rainy night. Webb watched her go and sighed again.

"Captain?" a voice asked behind them.

Lucano turned to face an evidence tech. The guy was holding a plastic baggie with Terry's revolver encased in it.

"What?" Lucano asked.

"Is this the gun he fired at you?" the tech asked Webb.

"Looks like it," Webb said. "I already identified it for the responding officers."

"What about it?" Lucano asked.

"It's loaded," the tech said. "One round fired, five still in the chamber. But..."

Webb felt a crawling coldness in his guts. "But what?"

"This gun's loaded with blanks."

Webb and Lucano looked at one another.

"You were wondering how he managed to miss at that range," Lucano said. He smiled grimly. "Maybe he didn't."

"You think this is funny, sir?" Webb demanded. "I just killed an unarmed man."

"No, you didn't. The law's clear on this. If he'd pointed a squirt gun at you, and it looked like the real thing, you'd have been justified in shooting."

"Yeah," Webb said. "But why'd he do it?"

Lucano shrugged. "There's no intelligence test for being a bad guy. I've seen it before. A guy runs into the cops, he pulls a pellet gun on them. What does he think is going to happen?

Maybe he hopes they'll run away. Maybe he's bluffing. Maybe
he's just tired of living and too much of a damn coward to take
care of things himself. But that's not your problem, Harry. We'll
have other detectives on this one. Kwon and Cox, probably.
You're on the bench this time."

*   *   *

On the bench. Webb liked a sports metaphor as much as
the next guy, but that was just depressing. Sitting on the
sidelines, watching your team and feeling about as useless as an
ashtray on a motorcycle. How many years until retirement? Too
many to feel as tired as he did.

Webb climbed the outdoor stairs to the second floor of the
cheap motel. He fumbled in his pockets for the room key. Of
course it had slid all the way to the bottom, under the rest of the
pocket litter. He pulled out a handful of crap and sifted through
his cigarette lighter, $1.35 in loose change, his car keys, an
unopened pack of nicotine gum, and a half-empty pack of
Camels. He finally found the key, an old-style actual key instead
of an electronic card, and stared at it in the harsh halogen lights.
Maybe he should loop the key onto the ring with the rest of
them.

He decided that would be even sadder than having it loose.
That would mean he was accepting all of it: the divorce, moving
out of the house, and that this piece of shit motel room would be
his home until he found somewhere else to hang his hat.

Webb unlocked the door and went inside. The room was
mostly empty. He'd been living out of his suitcase for the last
week. Most of his stuff was in a storage unit just off Interstate 5,
a place almost as depressing as this motel room. The room was
drab, smelled like a combination of stale cigarette smoke and

other peoples' feet, and the carpet was always slightly damp. This was the sort of place dreams went to die, the sort of room where they found washed-up has-been actors in the bathtub, their wrists slit, empty bottles of pills on the bathroom floor.

Webb hung up his trench coat and hat, both dripping wet, and went into the bathroom. He splashed water on his face and looked in the mirror. What he saw was a washed-up cop in his forties, heavier than he ought to be, bags under his eyes.

What the hell had Maureen Sinclair seen in him that attracted her? The shield? There were plenty of younger, hotter officers out there. Metro SWAT, with their bulging biceps and go-get-'em energy, should be more her thing. Maybe she liked older guys.

"Daddy issues, maybe," Webb said gloomily. He washed his hands and came out of the bathroom. He slumped down on the bed, kicked off his shoes, and stretched out his legs. He reached for his holster to put away his gun, then remembered he'd turned his .38 over to Internal Affairs.

There was a half-full bottle of Jim Beam on the nightstand. He took a slug from the bottle and stared at the wall. In most hotels there'd be a TV set, but not this one. Here, all he had to look at was a dreary watercolor print of some European city. Venice, probably. Maybe, if it kept raining, LA would flood just like Venice and they'd have to get around the freeways on gondolas. Then, if they were really lucky, the rain would keep falling and wash the whole damn city out into the Pacific.

Webb hauled out his phone and checked his email. Two messages from his divorce lawyer, two from his soon-to-be-ex-wife, nothing from his kids. He put the phone away without even opening the messages. God, but he was tired.

It was understandable. After all, he'd just killed a man. Killing a guy ought to take something out of you. It shouldn't be easy, something you did and then just went on with your day.

He loosened his necktie and removed it, hanging it over the bedside lamp. Then he unbuttoned his shirt and stripped down to his undershirt and boxers. He hadn't even gone to sleep and he already felt like he had a hangover. He lay back, covered his face with one arm, and closed his eyes.

Terry Volkman. What a loser. Of all the guys to kill, why did it have to be some schmuck of a failed actor with a prop gun?

A prop gun. Webb's eyes snapped open. What sort of idiot went to a confrontation packing a blank-loaded pistol?

The kind who was bluffing, obviously. But you didn't bluff by firing a blank at someone. That looked like an attack, not a threat, and was guaranteed to escalate things. Volkman had to have seen Webb drawing his own gun, had to have known what was going to happen. If you started shooting at a cop, the cop was damned well going to shoot back. And what had the kid said? He'd said no one would have Maureen. The sort of thing a guy would say when he was about to kill a girl, not get himself killed. Suicide by cop? No, that didn't scan.

Volkman hadn't acted like a guy who thought he was going to die. Webb had seen at least his fair share of death in his career. You couldn't be a cop in a city like LA for better than two decades without coming across plenty of bodies. He'd also seen people in the process of dying. Volkman had been... false. Theatrical, right up until the first bullet had punched into him. There was no other way to describe it.

Well, he'd been an actor, after all, and not a very good one. Maybe he'd been playing out some silly scene for himself, the scene where he got to be the big, tough guy. Webb had certainly seen macho posturing before.

Webb closed his eyes again. He was too tired for this. Besides, it wasn't his case. Lucano had been clear on that. All he had to worry about was the Internal Affairs probe. And even if his blood-alcohol level was high, he'd probably be okay. He hadn't been on duty, and Maureen had given her statement agreeing with his version of what had happened. It didn't matter that Volkman's gun hadn't fired real bullets. He'd fired a gun in the direction of a police officer. That was textbook justifiable force.

He drifted into an alcohol-numbed sleep, still turning what had happened over in his mind.

* * *

Six hours later Webb was awake, his headache worse than before, his mouth tasting like a wild turkey had been run over on the highway and crawled in there to die. The sun wasn't up yet, the heat unit in the motel was rattling sulkily, and he'd killed a man the previous night. If it hadn't been a bad dream.

He hauled his sorry ass out of bed and got in the shower. The water took so long to heat up that he gave up on it and showered cold. Then it got hot, so fast he practically scalded himself before he could scramble out.

He lit up his first cigarette of the day, which helped his mood but not the taste in his mouth. There was a 24-hour greasy spoon half a block from the motel. He found a shirt and pants that weren't too wrinkled and got dressed. Then he walked to the diner. It was still drizzling rain. His trench coat hadn't even dried out from the night before.

The waitress was a tired-looking, stringy-haired woman pushing forty. She'd probably come to Hollywood twenty years ago to be discovered, just like everybody. He nodded to her and sat at his usual table. She brought him a cup of coffee. It was terrible, but better than the tar they had at the police station.

His normal breakfast was heavy on bacon and eggs, but the thought of all that grease made his stomach do a somersault this morning. He went with oatmeal and brown sugar instead, with a blueberry muffin on the side. The muffin looked and tasted like it belonged in shrink-wrap in a gas station, its expiration date sometime next decade. The oatmeal sat in his belly like wet cement.

When he'd eaten all he could of his breakfast, he paid his bill and sat with another cup of coffee, thinking what to do. He was on administrative leave, of course. Standard procedure for a police officer who'd shot someone. That meant his normal duties were suspended, though he suspected his inbox would be piling up. He couldn't go home, and he was damned if he'd sit around his musty motel room all day.

He went out to his car and turned on the onboard computer. The first name he ran was Terry Volkman. Terrence Volkman, it turned out, had a record, but he wasn't a violent criminal. He'd been busted for a variety of sleazy lowlife stuff, strictly the purview of Vice. Pandering, solicitation, solicitation of a minor, unlicensed distribution of pornographic materials. Webb's lip curled. It didn't sound like Terry's death would be a great loss to society.

The weirdness of the situation ate at Webb. Volkman was a bottom-feeder, part of Hollywood's seedy underbelly. He'd never been involved in anything that would suggest he was capable of murder, or even of threatening it. Webb knew how abusers operated. They tended to start small, yelling at their partners, beating them with their fists, and gradually escalating to more violence. It was rare for a guy to snap and go from zero to sixty, grabbing a gun and going after a girl. Webb was a detective who believed in patterns, and Volkman's actions didn't fit into a pattern.

He looked up Maureen Sinclair, just to see what popped, and got nothing in the police database. No moving violations, no parking tickets, nothing. Nada. That was possible, but struck Webb as unlikely. Maureen seemed like a woman who liked to move on the wilder, darker side of the street. Could a woman be as comfortable there as she seemed to be, and leave no trace in the system?

Webb rubbed his face. What had Maureen's license plate number been? He couldn't remember. It'd been dark, he'd been a little drunk, a lot had been going on, but he still should've picked up on it. Maybe the detective Lucano had put in charge of the shooting had noted it. Unfortunately, he couldn't very well ask the guy. He'd just get told to shut up and enjoy his time off.

When all else failed, try the Internet. Webb looked up Volkman first. Maureen had said Terry had been involved in making movies with her. That would leave some sort of trace online. He went to an online movie database and typed in the name. Nothing.

That didn't make sense. Why would Maureen have lied about that? Without much hope, Webb tried looking up Maureen.

He finally got a hit. Several, in fact. An actress using the screen name Maureen Sinclair appeared in a whole series of movies. But these weren't the sort of movies you'd take the kids to. They had titles like *Hot Teacher 3* and *Intensive Care*.

Webb smiled at the thought of what Internal Affairs would think if they checked his computer's browser history and clicked on the first title. Maybe it was a coincidence, someone using the same stage name as Maureen. He found some images from the movie, fairly racy.

That was Maureen, all right. The girl of Webb's dreams was a porn movie actress. It was just like that song about the singer's high-school crush who turned into a centerfold. Which was now stuck in his head, of course.

"Na, na, na-na-na-na, na na na na na na-na-na-na-na..."

"God damned Hollywood," Webb muttered. He hated this town. He tried to bury his disgust and just be a detective. He lit another cigarette and kept looking.

He didn't see Volkman's name in the credits or his image in any of the production stills. Then again, Volkman might be the guy's real name, and Webb guessed nobody would want their birth name associated with a movie like this one.

Why was he gnawing on this anyway? Lucano had been extremely clear on the subject. This wasn't Webb's case. But it was his responsibility. He'd killed Terry Volkman. So the guy was a shit stain on humanity's diaper? That wasn't the point. The point was that Webb had enough baggage already. He wasn't about to carry around any doubts about the only man he'd ever killed.

Well, what else was he going to do with his unplanned day off? Webb looked up the name of the movie studio. Then he called his partner.

"Hey, Jimmy?"

"Harry! You okay, man?" Jim Gutierrez was a young, enthusiastic guy who'd made detective three months ago. He'd been paired with Webb on the principle that combining youthful exuberance with canny experience would bring good results. Webb wasn't sure about that. Gutierrez made him feel old and tired a lot of the time.

"Yeah, I'm fine."

"I heard about the thing at the bar last night. Damn! You got in an honest-to-God gunfight? Without me?"

"Wasn't that much of a fight, Jimmy. I was wondering if you could look something up for me. I can't be at the station right now."

"Oh, yeah, admin leave. The Cap told me about that. Hey, don't worry, man, I got you covered here. I'm taking care of all the paperwork on the Nuestro case, and I filed the fingerprints on that repository break-in, and—"

"That's great, Jimmy. I need an address on a movie studio."

"Huh? Movie studio? What for? We don't have anything running on any movie place right now."

"This is a personal thing."

"Oh... well, I guess, sure. What's the name of the studio?"

Webb looked at his computer screen. "Fantasy Feathers."

"What?"

"You need me to spell it for you?"

"No, I heard you, man. Just a second. Hey, you said this was personal? I don't want to pry, man, but you know what kind of movies this place makes?"

Webb sighed. "Yes, Jimmy. The address, please."

"Okay, man, I'm not judging. Hey, I know you're going through a rough spot with the missus here, and a man's got his needs."

"Jimmy. Focus."

"You got it, man." Gutierrez rattled off the address. "Hey, you want backup on this one? I know you're not on duty, and I still got stuff here, but I can make some time, you know?"

"Jimmy, if you're looking for an opportunity to score with skin-flick actresses, do it on your own time. This is work."

"I thought you said it was personal, man."

"It's that, too. Thanks, Jimmy."

"Hey, no problem, man. You just call me if—"

Webb hung up. Then he started the car.

Chapter 3

Movies were dreamlands, places people went to escape the dreary prisons of their everyday lives. Nothing took the glamour out of the movies faster than doing police work in Hollywood. Something Webb had quickly realized was that, for people who worked on films, movies *were* their dreary everyday prisons. He could only imagine how that played out for the folks who made skin flicks. He expected that took the glamour not only out of the silver screen, but out of sex, too. Nothing killed romance quicker than making it your job. He supposed someone would be glad to explain the difference between porno movies and prostitution, but he wasn't prepared to be convinced.

The Fantasy Feathers studio was a drab, square, dirty concrete building on a back film lot. The studio logo was small and looked to have been painted over another name. Webb saw only three cars in the parking lot and a big, heavyset guy standing outside the door. The guy was wearing a black shirt that said SECURITY.

Webb parked his Crown Vic and got out. The sun was just coming up, but it made no real difference. The rain had paused, sure, but the sky was gray overcast and the weather was chilly. Webb was glad of his shabby, slightly damp trench coat.

As he approached the door, the big guy shifted his weight slightly. It was a subtle and unmistakable sign Webb recognized from bar bouncers. *You wanna get through this door, buddy, you gotta get through me.*

"You look cold," Webb said. "I'm not going to have a problem with you, am I?"

"Yeah, well, drivin' that car, lookin' like you do, you're either a cop, a PI, or a debt collector," the big guy said. "So which is it? Then I'll know if we got a problem or not."

"LAPD," Webb said, showing his shield. "So, what's it going to be?"

The guy grunted. "Okay, go on in. Miz Winter oughta be in her office."

"Which is...?" Webb prompted.

"Second door on the left."

"Thanks. Out of curiosity, what would you have done if I'd turned out to be one of the other two?"

The big guy shrugged his massive shoulders. "Depends."

"You got many PIs and debt collectors coming by?"

Another shrug. "You'd have to talk to Miz Winter about that."

Webb went in and found himself in a dreary lobby. There was a desk for a secretary, but no one sitting behind it. One of the fluorescent bulbs in the ceiling was buzzing and flickering. The sound reminded him of the neon light at the bar and he shivered for a second, remembering. The magazine racks were empty. Even the potted plants were dying.

He went through the door on his left, into a short hallway, and found the second door. It said WINTER on the frosted glass. Webb knocked.

One of the last people he would have expected opened the door. She looked like a sweet old grandmother, sporting white, salon-curled hair, horn-rimmed glasses, and a conservative dress the color of robins' eggs. She looked like some distant relation of the Queen of England.

"Ms. Winter?" Webb asked.

"That's right, Detective."

Webb hadn't had his credentials in hand, but it didn't surprise him that she knew what he was. Put in your twenty years and the Job would leave its mark on you.

"Harry Webb, LAPD," he said, offering his hand.

"Samantha Winter," she said, taking his hand and smiling. "I'm sorry, you've caught me a little unprepared this morning. I wasn't expecting to see more people from your office today. It's good that I came in early. Come in, Detective."

"Doing some remodeling?" Webb asked, looking around her office. Cardboard boxes lay on the floor, the desk, and the chairs. There wasn't a good place for him to sit, so he stood to one side of the door.

"Packing up shop," she said. "Didn't your people tell you? My goodness, Detective Webb, you seem very uninformed, if you'll pardon my saying so."

"Ma'am, I'm with Robbery-Homicide," Webb said. "I don't know who came to see you yesterday, but I'm pretty sure it wasn't anyone from my department, unless they were talking to you about Terry Volkman."

Ms. Winter had been putting some knickknacks into the box on her desk. Now she paused and looked quizzically at him.

"No, Detective, your colleagues weren't from Robbery-Homicide. They were with Financial Crimes. I suppose the Los Angeles Police Department is rather compartmentalized, and you know what they say about bureaucracies."

"I know some of the things they say."

"Robert Heinlein said governments were three-quarters parasitic, the rest stupid fumbling."

"I think I read some Heinlein back in high school," Webb said. "I don't really remember. Something about space marines and aliens. But sounds like he knew what he was talking about. With government, I mean."

"People don't expect a woman in my job to read much," she said, smiling at him. "But then, people don't expect a woman to be in my job at all. Rather amusing, really, considering the weight of history and tradition. The bordello madam, after all, was a fixture of the frontier. One could argue all I've done is carry on a fine Gold Rush tradition."

"So you're running a whorehouse here?" Webb said, raising an eyebrow.

"I'm not running anything, Detective," she replied. "As I told you, Fantasy Feathers Studio is closed. We're packing up."

"Why?"

"Why does any business cease operation?"

"Because it loses money. You said guys from Financial Crimes were talking to you?"

Ms. Winter continued to smile, but the smile turned bitter. "Some of the studio's investors raised concerns about possible misappropriation of funds."

"Would you know anything about the money in question?"

"I'll tell you precisely what I told them. I make movies to make money. The money is tracked by my accountant. Any questions regarding that money will be best answered either by him, or by my attorney."

"That's impressive," Webb said. "Usually I have to accuse people of something before they lawyer up. You're sharper than most."

"When I was a girl," she said, "condescending men called me precocious. When I was a young woman, they called me feisty. Now that I'm an old woman, they say I've stayed remarkably sharp. I haven't changed, and neither have they."

"I guess you haven't met very many polite men in your line of work."

"But many condescending ones," she said brightly.

"Ma'am, I don't care what you do for a living. I'm investigating the death of Terry Volkman."

Ms. Winter blinked. "Death? Terry's dead?"

"Yes."

"Murdered?"

"No."

"But now I'm confused, Detective. You said you were with Robbery-Homicide. If he died of accident or illness, I don't see how it falls within your purview."

"How well did you know Mr. Volkman?"

"He was employed by my studio."

"Was?"

"As of yesterday, my studio has no employees. Even I no longer work here."

"Not even the guy with no neck you've got out front?"

"A contract worker, drawing a daily wage to keep out the riffraff. It seems he is not performing as advertised."

"What did Volkman do when he worked here?"

"Personal assistant."

"You know, I've never known exactly what that is."

"Glorified gofer."

"I didn't see his name on the movie credits."

"Detective, you won't see my name on the credits either, but I assure you, I presided over all this studio's films. This niche of the industry is one you don't often see listed on a resume. How did Mr. Volkman die?"

"I shot him last night."

There was a brief pause.

"Detective," she said, "I hope you won't think it impolite of me if I ask to see your police identification now."

Webb showed her his shield.

"It's funny," she said after examining it. "Police officers always show their badges, but how many people would really know the difference between a fake badge and the genuine article? I've made movies with police officers in them, and they show badges, but those badges are as false as the actors themselves. Why did you kill Mr. Volkman?"

"He pulled a gun on me and threatened to kill me."

"So you gunned him down?"

"That's probably what the papers will say. They like to use that phrase. Why do you think Volkman would draw on a cop?"

"I have no idea, Detective. Did he say anything to you?"

"He claimed it was about a girl."

"A particular girl?"

"Yes."

Ms. Winter waited, but Webb didn't add anything more. "I fear my business has the reputation of treating young women as something of a commodity," she said. "But they do have names."

"Yes, they do."

"But you won't tell me the name of this particular damsel?"

"Damsel?"

"It's a somewhat archaic word meaning a young woman."

"I know what it means, ma'am."

"An educated police officer. *Mirabile dictu.*"

"And you accused me of being condescending," Webb said, deadpan.

"*Touche*, Detective," she said with a light laugh. "It's unfortunate, however. I'd begun to hope you were here in the other half of your capacity."

"Meaning?"

"Robbery, rather than homicide."

"Have you been robbed, ma'am?"

"It's difficult to escape that conclusion. Should you find a spare one point five million dollars lying about, I would appreciate its return."

"You're missing one and a half million dollars?"

"Hence the appearance at my door of your accounting compatriots yesterday. I've gone over the numbers with my own accountant and it appears someone has, as the saying goes, cooked the books."

"And that's why you've had to close down."

"They say sex sells, Detective," Ms. Winter said, and suddenly he saw the lines of worry and weariness among her other wrinkles. "But in this Internet age of free downloads and webcams, it doesn't pay as well as it once did. This studio operated on a shoestring, and that string has now snapped. I'm sorry Mr. Volkman is deceased, but it makes very little difference to my situation here. It's been surprisingly pleasant chatting with you, but unless you have something to contribute to the resolution of my own problems, I fear our interview must terminate. I have a great many matters requiring my attention, and as I'm sure you've seen, I am not overburdened with staff."

"Thank you for your time, ma'am." Webb turned for the door. Then he paused, one hand on the knob. "Just one more question. What's Maureen Sinclair's real name?"

"Ah," Ms. Winter said. "I knew the girl in question had a name. Well, it sounds like the dear departed Terrence was batting much out of his league. Ms. Sinclair was one of our top performers."

"I believe it. Her name?"

"I'm afraid I can't reveal that without a court order. You understand, surely, the importance of preserving privacy in such personal matters."

Webb gritted his teeth. "Yes, ma'am. I do. Have a nice day."

*   *   *

Webb might not have a lead on Maureen, but Terry Volkman was definitely in the system. A paroled sex offender wasn't a hard guy to track down; Volkman was required to register his address within five days of taking up residence if he didn't want to go straight back to prison. Webb brought up an apartment on his computer, five miles from the studio. Volkman was listed as one of two occupants; the other was someone named Audrey Knowles.

Webb double-checked Knowles next. If you were going to knock on a criminal's door, it was always a good idea to know as much as possible about the people who lived there. If Knowles was likely to answer the door with a gun, or maybe a fire ax, he wanted advance warning.

Unsurprisingly, Knowles was also in the system. She'd packed a lot of experiences into her nineteen years. Drugs, prostitution, and burglary were the worst of it. She'd been in and out of juvenile facilities basically her whole life. Webb had two daughters from his first marriage, thirteen and fifteen years old, and the thought of half the things Knowles had been through made his flesh creep. But she didn't have anything violent in her jacket, and she was described as five foot one and a hundred pounds, so Webb figured he could handle her if she turned aggressive.

He pulled up to the apartment a few minutes later. The clouds were darker now, with more rain likely. Webb parked under a scraggly palm tree and checked out the building. It was two stories of battered stucco with a Mexican tile roof, pretty typical lower-income housing. Volkman's unit was the one around back, on the second floor. He climbed the outside staircase and knocked on the door.

After a few moments of waiting, two more knocks, and more waiting, he gave up. Obviously, no one was home. Knowles's parole sheet said she worked at a local tattoo parlor. Maybe he could catch her there. Webb turned and started down the stairs.

The click of the door latch behind him made him freeze. He turned back and saw a thin, pale face peering at him with bloodshot eyes.

"Ms. Knowles?" he said.

"Yeah?"

"I'm Detective Webb, LAPD." He held up his shield. "Could I talk to you for a moment?"

She looked him over. "Okay, I guess so."

The apartment was small, dirty, and Webb smelled a number of unpleasant odors. He recognized mildew, cheap cigarette smoke, and a faint smell of acidic vinegar. That wouldn't have meant much to most people, but to an experienced cop, it was the smell of recently-smoked heroin.

Audrey Knowles definitely looked like a junkie. She was very small and slightly built, with big, wide eyes. Her skin was pale on the surface but flushed underneath. She was twitchy and nervous, like a trapped bird. The apartment was very warm, so hot that Webb felt sweat starting on his forehead within a few moments of stepping inside. That explained Knowles's wardrobe choice of a thin tank top and pajama pants. The top showed bony shoulders covered with colorful tattoos.

"I had my meeting with my PO already this week," Knowles said. "Everything's cool with him."

If that was true, Webb thought, the parole officer wasn't doing his due diligence. The drug use alone was a major violation. He sighed.

"Ms. Knowles, I'm not here about your situation. I want to talk to you about Terry Volkman."

"Huh?"

"Terry Volkman. This is his address."

"Oh. Yeah." Knowles looked at Webb with eyes that were definitely somewhere along the road to dreamland. If she wasn't on a heroin nod, Webb had never seen one.

"What can you tell me about Terry?" he asked.

"Terry's cool. He treats me good."

She didn't know about Volkman's death. That made sense. She wasn't next of kin, and it had happened less than a day ago. The detectives on the case apparently hadn't gotten around to checking Volkman's apartment yet. Webb decided not to drop that info on Knowles just yet.

"You've been in some trouble in the past, Ms. Knowles," he said. "But things have been okay since you hooked up with Terry?"

"Yeah. I mean, he was going through a rough spot, but he's coming out of it fine. I mean, it's his big break, right?"

"Right," Webb said, although he had no idea what she was talking about. One of the best tricks in interviews was to make the subject think you already knew everything. That way they had no incentive to keep secrets. Then you just had to keep them talking.

"The thing he was involved in last night," Webb said, keeping as vague as possible, letting Knowles's drug-marinated brain fill in the gaps. "He told you about it?"

"Oh, yeah. Terry tells me everything." She giggled and leaned toward him conspiratorially. "I'm his number-one special girl. He says I'm absolutely just perfectly right."

"So you know all about Maureen?"

Knowles nodded.

"And it didn't bother you?" Webb asked.

"You kidding? That bitch? She ain't got nothing on me, not for Terry. For one thing, she is way, I mean way too old for him."

Terry Volkman's date of birth, according to his police file, made him thirty-eight years old, which was exactly twice Audrey Knowles's age. Webb felt his skin crawling again.

"So he didn't have a thing going with her?" Webb asked.

"No, that was just for show. You know, in the movies? That's never real. It never means anything."

"Yeah, it meant nothing," Webb agreed. He was really confused now. His head was hurting and he wanted a cigarette.

"So how'd it go?" she asked.

Webb had no idea how to answer that, because he didn't know what she was asking about. "What do you mean?" he asked, that last-resort hail Mary of questions.

"The shoot," she said, like he was an idiot. In fairness, Webb kind of felt like one.

"There was some shooting," he cautiously agreed.

"And it was a wrap? He got the part?"

"What part?"

"In the movie, dummy."

"The movie," Webb repeated.

"Yeah." Knowles had a dreamy smile on her face. "Terry always wanted it. To get out in front of the camera for real, that was what he always said."

"Terry was going to an audition?" Webb asked. "For a mainstream movie?"

"Yeah. He was super-duper excited about it. He was practicing his lines all yesterday, getting ready, getting in character. It was his first big screen test."

"What was the movie?" Webb asked.

"Oh, I... I forget the name." Knowles's eyes went unfocused. "It's one of those, like, heavy movies."

"Heavy?"

"Yeah. With all the, like, emotions and stuff. And dark, sad. Terry's gonna play this guy nobody understands, but he meets this girl, and he falls in love with her, but this other jerk takes her away from him. And he's all sad and alone, and he goes to get her back, but she won't take him, and everyone dies in the end. Like I said, heavy."

Webb nodded, but this wasn't helping him. He needed names, locations, concrete information he could follow up on. He also needed nicotine. "You're sure you don't know the title? What about the studio?"

Knowles shook her head. "You can just ask Terry. He'll be home soon, I think. What time is it?"

Webb checked his watch. "Quarter to nine."

"Cool. What day is it?"

"Thursday." *And the planet you're standing on is called Earth,* Webb silently added.

"Oh. I thought it was, maybe, Wednesday. But that was yesterday, I guess."

"Wednesday comes once a week," Webb said. "On average. What else can you remember about this screen test?"

"Well, I know some of his lines. I mean, how could I not? He was repeating them over and over again. Practicing different tones of voice, finding the character, you know? You want me to say them for you?"

"I'm good, thanks," Webb said. He'd had just about enough of this space cadet, and he really wanted that cigarette. "I'll just—"

Knowles wasn't listening to him. She stretched out her arms in a grotesque caricature of a lover and cried out, "How could you? Maureen, I love you! You belong to me!"

Webb felt goosebumps rise on his skin. "I don't belong to anyone but me," he said quietly. "You'll never have me."

"Then no one will!" Knowles proclaimed as theatrically as she could. She raised one hand and pointed her index finger at Webb, cocking her thumb, making her hand into a pistol.

The bottom dropped out of Webb's stomach. He'd played this scene, except it hadn't been a scene at all. Or if it had been, someone had forgotten to give him a script.

"So, did he get the role?" Knowles asked.

"He nailed it," Webb said. "Absolutely killed it."

Chapter 4

Webb went out to his car in a daze. He felt like the ground had been kicked out from under him. Maybe he was still drunk. That would make as much sense as anything. Maybe he'd wake up in Tijuana with the mother of all hangovers and this whole thing would turn out to have been a nightmare fueled by beer and cheap whiskey. He paused in the street, fished out a cigarette, and fumbled for his lighter.

"Webb? That you?"

He dropped the cigarette and cursed under his breath. Turning, he saw a couple of familiar faces attached to a pair of off-the-rack suits.

"Detective Kwon, Detective Cox," he said. Kwon was a very small man, five foot five and lightly built, who never seemed to put on weight. That might be because he seemed to live off black coffee; Webb could never remember seeing him eat anything. Cox, his partner, was an overweight hulk of a man.

Webb wondered if the motor pool maintenance guys could tell which car was theirs because of the uneven strain on the shocks.

"A remarkable coincidence," Kwon said. "Running into you here."

Cox pulled a pocket handkerchief and sneezed into it.

"You still believe in coincidence?" Webb asked. Kwon had been on the LAPD almost as long as Webb.

"No, Detective Webb, I do not."

"So you were jerking me around."

"I was ironically calling attention to the fact that our meeting here, outside the home of a person of interest in your officer-involved shooting, was not, and could not possibly be, a coincidence."

"Lot of big words in that sentence," Webb said. "You carry a backup dictionary in your ankle holster?"

Kwon didn't smile, but Cox did.

"Care to explain what you're doing here, Webb?" Cox asked.

"I was just in the neighborhood," Webb said. "Enjoying my unexpected day off."

"He was being facetious as well," Kwon said. "We know why you are here, Detective."

"Been following me? I know Internal Affairs would love to have you, but I didn't think they already did."

Cox scowled. "Screw you, Webb. I work for a living, and I don't snitch on other cops."

"What Detective Cox means," Kwon said, "is that while an independent line of inquiry brought us to the same location in which you find yourself, we know that you are here regarding the same business upon which we are embarked; namely, addressing the issue of why a motion picture assistant would threaten a police officer with a firearm loaded with blank cartridges."

"Did you brace that Audrey chick who lives with him?" Cox asked Webb.

"I crossed paths with a young woman who claimed to know Mr. Volkman," Webb said.

"An uncharitable observer might conclude you were attempting to influence testimony pertaining to an investigation in which you are a person of interest," Kwon said.

"Good thing we don't have any uncharitable observers," Webb said.

"We're the LAPD," Cox said. "Everybody's uncharitable to us."

"What Detective Cox is implying," Kwon said, "is that we must avoid even the appearance of impropriety. Caesar's wife must be beyond reproach."

"I don't think any wife is beyond reproach," Webb said. "If Caesar's was anything like mine, I'm sorry for the poor murdered bastard. She was probably screwing Brutus on the side."

Cox blinked. "Wait, who are we talking about? Who's been murdered? Who's Caesar?"

"Detective Webb is referring metaphorically to a cold case outside our jurisdiction," Kwon said. "A *very* cold case. It does not concern us at present."

"You guys should get yourselves an agent," Webb said. "It's a great act you've got going, except for one thing. I can never figure which of you is the straight man, and which one is just messing with the other guy."

Cox scratched his head and sneezed again.

"Was Ms. Knowles able to shed any light on the late events?" Kwon asked.

"She said it was show business," Webb said.

"Show business?" Kwon echoed.

"Yeah. Volkman was trying out for a movie part."

"I don't understand," Cox said.

"I find myself in the unusual position of mirroring Detective Cox's admirably succinct statement," Kwon said.

"Maybe you guys better talk to her," Webb said. "I'll catch you later."

"Busy day off?" Cox asked.

"Just some things to take care of," Webb said. He unlocked his car and opened the door.

"Don't leave town," Cox said.

Webb raised an eyebrow. "I wasn't planning on it. But out of curiosity, is that advice or an order?"

"Good advice and orders are essentially indistinguishable," Kwon said. "The consequences of disobeying either differ only in the particulars. We may need to contact you for a follow-up statement, Detective Webb, and should that occasion arise, we may need to be able to reach you on short notice. That, I believe, is the thrust of Detective Cox's words. Good day, Detective."

* * *

Webb hadn't known where he was going before running into those two, but their conversation had given him an idea. He'd told Kwon and Cox to get an agent. That was something every actor had. Volkman certainly did, too. He wouldn't have gone to a major audition without one.

Unfortunately, Webb didn't know which agent had been representing Volkman. This was going to take some more legwork. On the plus side, agents were supposed to be easy guys to contact. He looked up the Screen Actors Guild and gave them a call. He drove while the phone was ringing, not wanting to hang around waiting for the other detectives to come up with more ways to waste his time. After an almost reasonable amount of time on hold and two transfers, he had the name and phone number of Volkman's agent. The agent was Freddie Schmitz, who worked in Beverly Hills.

Webb sighed. He hated Beverly Hills. But he called Schmitz's office.

"Freddie Schmitz's office, my name is Annalise," said a very perky female voice. "How may I help you?"

"Hello, Annalise," Webb said. "My name is Detective Webb. I'm with the LAPD. Is Mr. Schmitz available to meet with me? I need to ask him a few questions."

"I'm afraid Mr. Schmitz's schedule is very busy," she said. "I can get you a meeting... let's see... how's two weeks from Monday?"

"I need to meet with him today, ma'am."

"That's quite impossible, sir. I apologize, but Mr. Schmitz is really not available today."

"I'm with LAPD Robbery-Homicide," Webb said. "I'm investigating the shooting death of one of the actors he represents. It's very much in Mr. Schmitz's best interests to meet with me as quickly as possible. He can reach me at this number. Please tell him immediately."

Annalise was silent for a moment. Evidently Webb had gone off the usual script of such telephone calls. "I'll need to talk to Mr. Schmitz," she said at last.

"Do that, ma'am. Thank you." He hung up and lit a cigarette.

Webb wasn't surprised when Annalise called back before he'd finished his smoke to tell him an unexpected opening had appeared in the very busy Mr. Schmitz's schedule.

"Can you come to his office at 10:15?" she asked.

"That'll be perfect," Webb said. "Thank you."

*   *   *

Webb hadn't spent a lot of time around Hollywood types, which was just fine with him, and probably fine with them, too. But he knew what to expect. That was why he wasn't surprised when his 10:15 meeting didn't start until quarter to eleven. These jerks measured power and status in small, petty ways, and they were always playing their silly games. Keeping him sitting on his thumb for half an hour was just Freddie Schmitz's way of telling this annoying detective that he, Schmitz, was a powerful man and Webb was a nasty little interloper.

It irritated Webb, but if it was supposed to impress him, it didn't. Terry Volkman hadn't been an A-list celebrity, Schmitz wasn't the top agent in Hollywood, and Webb was more concerned with the real world, the world where things actually mattered.

At 10:45, Webb stopped pretending to read the four-month-old copy of *People* magazine he'd found in the waiting room. He looked at Annalise, who was young, pretty, and certainly not a natural blonde, and cleared his throat meaningfully.

"I'm sorry, Mr. Webb," she said. "I did let Mr. Schmitz know you were here. I'm sure he'll see you as soon as possible. It's just that this is a very busy morning for him, and this meeting was set up at the last minute. I'm sure you understand."

Webb understood all right. He took out a cigarette and flicked his lighter.

"Mr. Webb, I'm sorry, but there's no smoking in this office."

Webb, temporarily deaf, lit up and took a slow, satisfying drag. He felt better at once.

Annalise, now slightly flustered, said, "Mr. Webb, I really must insist—"

Webb pursed his lips and blew a stream of second-hand smoke her general direction.

Annalise poked a button on her phone and put it to her ear. She said something quietly and listened to the answer. Then she hung up.

"Mr. Schmitz will see you now," she said. "Please put out your cigarette and go through the door on your right."

Webb stood up. "Thank you, ma'am," he said. Seeing no ashtray in a no-smoking office, naturally, he stubbed out his cigarette in the soil at the base of a potted fern.

Freddie Schmitz was wearing an open-necked polyester shirt, accessorized with a gold necklace and a pair of mirror sunglasses. He stood up and walked around his desk to meet Webb with an extended hand and a big smile, showing perfect dentistry.

"Freddie Schmitz. What can I do you for?"

"Harry Webb, LAPD," Webb said, shaking the offered hand. "Thanks for seeing me on such short notice."

"Hey, no problem, Harry, baby. Anything I can do for our civil servants."

"I appreciate that. I just have a few questions about Terry Volkman."

"Oh yeah, Terry." Schmitz's grin only got wider. "Terry and me, we're tight. Like this." He held up the first two fingers on his left hand.

"Good. So you can tell me what movie he was auditioning for."

Schmitz's smile flickered, like a bad fluorescent bulb. "I think there's a misunderstanding, Harry. Terry wasn't up for any parts."

"He wasn't?" Webb frowned.

"No. I mean, let's be honest here. You know Terry. Great guy on set. Seriously. You need a sandwich? He'll get it for you. Wardrobe malfunction? He's your guy. He wants to act? Okay. This town's full of people who want to act, they know they can act, they just need a chance, right? But did you see his screen tests? Here's the juice. I can maybe get him something on the side, a few car commercials, he plays the seedy salesman who works for the competition, whatever. But a movie part? Not gonna happen. Hey, some of us are Brad Pitt, some of us are Lloyd Fenchurch."

"Who's Lloyd Fenchurch?"

"Exactly."

"He told his girlfriend he was auditioning for a part," Webb said.

Schmitz's grin was back to full wattage. "And no guy in La-La Land ever lied to his girl about getting a movie part in order to get laid, am I right? Anything to get 'em in the sack."

"I don't think he was lying," Webb said quietly.

"You saying he went to an audition without telling the Fredster?" Schmitz shook his head. "No, no, no, Harry, baby. That is not how this works. I scratch his back, he scratches mine. That's show business. That's *the* business. A guy deals under the table, he never works in this town again."

"Sounds like Volkman wasn't working in this town anyway," Webb said dryly.

"You kidding me?" Schmitz exclaimed. "Hey, at least he had a job in the industry. You think it's just fetching coffee? Being an errand boy? I know people would *kill* for that job, baby."

"Really? Like who?"

Schmitz blinked. Then he laughed. "I forgot for a second. You're a for-real cop. It's great. I mean, you *look* like a detective. You got a face that's a map of the world, if the world's made of dirty concrete and broken dreams. And you know it is. I could make money off that face. I could represent you, baby, you ever want a change of career. Bit parts to start with, sure, maybe do some TV cop gigs. Get you a walk-on, maybe it turns into a recurring role, who knows? Sky's the limit, baby."

"No thanks."

"Technical advisor, then? We got cop shows all over this town. I can get you a gig. Sweet deal. We're talking high five figures. I can get you eighty, eighty-five large, no problem. And that's just for starters. Benefits, too. Health, dental, the works."

"I've got a career. Who'd kill for Terry's job?"

"It was just a figure of speech. People don't really kill each other in the movie business."

"Mr. Schmitz," Webb said. "You may know the movie business, but I know the killing business. And Terry Volkman is most definitely dead."

"See, Harry, baby, that's just what I'm talking about. You even talk like a real cop. Great dialogue, and I bet you come up with it yourself. Ad-lib the whole thing, don't you?" Schmitz faltered. "Wait, Terry's dead? For real?"

"He was killed last night."

Schmitz leaned back against his desk. "Oh. Oh, man. And I could've gone out on a limb and got him that gig on the Syfy channel doing that alien thing. They're about to wrap. This publicity would've been a huge boost. An actor's last pic. I mean, Brandon Lee in *The Crow*, Bruce Lee in *Enter the Dragon*... other actors, too, not just that family. Man, the Lees were unlucky. It would've been a monster. Well, of course a monster, it was a monster movie, y'know?"

Webb raised an eyebrow and waited for Schmitz to run out of breath. It was amazing how much some people could talk while saying so little.

"So Terry's dead, and for nothing," Schmitz said sadly. "What a waste. I mean, if a guy's gonna die in this business, he should have the decency to do it for the art, you know? So, you figure out who killed him?"

"I killed him."

That succeeded in doing the impossible. It shut Freddie Schmitz up for a full fifteen seconds. Webb counted them by the tick of the clock over the door.

"So... I'm missing something here," Schmitz said at last, swallowing and glancing at Webb's hip where he apparently assumed a gun was hiding under his coat. "If you... shot him, and I'm assuming you shot him. I mean, why would you stab him? Or hit him in the head, or whatever. Why are you asking who'd want him dead? I mean, you know why you shot him, I'm assuming. And you'd have a good reason, I mean a really excellent reason for doing it, I'm sure. Because you'd need an excellent reason to kill a man, right? You wouldn't just kill a guy because he annoyed you, or talked too much, or anything like that?"

"Seemed like a good idea at the time," Webb said. "Just so we're clear, there was no audition on your busy schedule for Terry Volkman, particularly not last night?"

"I told you that already." Schmitz rallied a little. "Look, I'm serious about the technical advisor shtick. It's a gold mine. I know they don't pay you guys what they should, with all the long hours and the hard work you do, not to mention the physical risks. Isn't it time you cashed in on that? It's no sin to want to get paid for your work. I mean, it's not like you're stealing anything, am I right?"

"Right," Webb said thoughtfully. He was thinking about what Ms. Winter had said about Fantasy Feathers. One and a half million dollars missing. He couldn't think what that could possibly have to do with a botched audition and a police shooting, but one coincidence on a case was one too many as far as he was concerned. He and Kwon were in agreement about that.

"So I'll get Annalise to plug you into our database," Schmitz was saying. "Something should be coming up soon. I'll get in touch with my people, we'll do lunch. It'll be great. We're gonna go places, Harry, baby. This could be the start of a beautiful friendship."

"I'll keep that in mind," Webb said. "Thanks for your time, Mr. Schmitz."

He shook hands with the agent, successfully resisted the urge to wipe his hand on his trench coat, and got out of the office. On his way out, he saw Annalise cleaning the ash out of the potted plant. She gave him a bright, slightly forced smile.

"You have a good day, Mr. Webb," she said. "If you don't mind my saying so, you look like you could use one."

"That's the truth," Webb said. "Sorry about the smoke, and the plant."

"That's okay. It's not the worst thing anyone's done in this office. You wouldn't believe what some people will do for a movie part. Did everything go okay?"

"Apparently Mr. Schmitz thinks I have a bright future in show business."

Her smile became more genuine. "Oh, he says that to everybody. I got that spiel and here I am, still doing secretary work for him, three years later. I never did get that star-making role."

"Sorry to hear that."

"Oh, it's not so bad. I meet movie people sometimes, the pay's pretty good, and Freddie's really not such a jerk once you get to know him. I even had a couple of walk-on parts."

"You're one of those glass-half-full people, aren't you," Webb said.

She shrugged a little sheepishly. "Mom always said optimists do better in life, and have more fun along the way. You're more of a glass-half-empty guy, I can tell."

"I'm a glass-on-the-kitchen floor guy," he said. "I look at my life, all I see is jagged pieces."

"That's the saddest thing I've heard in... well, in a week, at least." Annalise stepped up to him and, to Webb's consternation, put her arms around him and gave him a quick hug. "It's not all bad. You'll see. Maybe you just need a change."

"Like a divorce? Already working on that."

"No, I mean a positive change. New scenery. Maybe a new town, new job? If Freddie was serious, I can at least set up a profile for you in our system. Maybe acting would agree with you better than policing."

"Maybe some other time." But he did find himself smiling at her and feeling marginally more cheerful for the first time since he'd shot Volkman. "Thanks, Annalise. You're wasted in this job. I hope you get your big break."

"And I hope you get whatever it is you need. Your day's going to get better, Mr. Webb. I've got a feeling."

Chapter 5

Webb had discovered cigarettes were a pretty good metric for just about anything. Need food in a World War II prison camp? Ten cigarettes would buy you a chocolate bar. Want a bag of chips in a modern US prison? A dozen cigarettes. A measuring stick? A cigarette was seventy millimeters long. An easy way to estimate time? One cigarette, five minutes to smoke.

Webb spent two cigarettes' worth of time thinking as he sat in the parking lot of the movie agency. He was down to his last Camel. That was okay. He could stop at a gas station on the way. But on the way where? All he had were dead ends.

He wasn't even sure he was trying to solve a case. What was there to solve? Volkman had clearly committed a crime. He'd paid for that crime immediately, with his life. If anybody had done a murder it was he, Webb, himself.

Webb wondered whether he was the first cop in history to be deliberately investigating himself for possible homicide.

What was he supposed to do? Turn himself in? But no one thought he'd done anything wrong. Kwon and Cox were just going through the motions. The only reason they were suspicious of him was that he was acting suspiciously. Everyone knew he'd be fine. So why what he worried?

He was worried because someone was getting away with something. And that was a stupid way to feel. People got away with stuff all the time, especially in LA. That was the way the world worked. Remember that famous movie line?

"Forget it, Harry, it's Chinatown," he muttered. Maybe that was the best thing to do. It was his problem because he'd chosen to make it his. Like he didn't have enough trouble.

As if on cue, his phone buzzed. He looked down at it and saw the name Catherine on the screen. Great. He sighed. That was just what his morning needed. Annalise might be a wonderful, sunny person, but she was a lousy fortune teller.

He considered not answering it, but that would only postpone trouble. He put the call through.

"Webb," he said.

"Harry, it's me."

I know. I'm a detective, remember? Plus, we have this thing called caller ID. And if we didn't, I'd probably know my soon-to-be-ex-wife's voice. That was what he wanted to say. What he said was, "Something you need, Cath?"

"I just saw the headline."

"What headline?"

"In the LA Times."

"Cath, I'm living out of a suitcase in a motel. The only staff, as far as I know, is a minimum-wage idiot who watches soaps in the manager's office twenty-four seven. I don't get the Times delivered to my door. I don't think they even have a maid."

"Stop being dramatic, Harry. Of course they have a maid. It's Los Angeles. I don't care where you're staying, they can afford to employ a couple of illegals under the table."

"You're right, Cath. I'm too dramatic. Everyone tells me that at the station. Harry Webb, always bringing the drama."

"Sarcasm doesn't help our communication, Harry. Remember what the marriage counselor told us?"

She said I was too emotionally closed-off, that I lived at work and only slept at home, he thought. "As I recall, she said she charged a hundred fifty an hour," he said.

"She said we needed to keep our channels of communication open. She said you needed to talk to me."

Like you ever listened to a word I said, he wanted to say. He said, "My point is I haven't seen the Times. What headline were you referring to?"

"There was another police shooting. Harry, they said it was you."

"The Times shouldn't be printing the name of the alleged officer before the investigation is complete."

"That's all you have to say, Harry? The alleged officer?"

"You're a lawyer, Cath. I thought you liked it when people talk like that."

"Was it you, Harry?"

"I'd like to consult with my legal counsel before answering any questions."

"You're not funny, Harry. This isn't a joke. Did you shoot someone last night?"

"If I say yes, will you think I'm being dramatic?"

"Harry, I'm sorry I said that. God, I feel like this is my fault. I practically threw you out of the house, you've probably been drinking, and now somebody's dead because of it."

Now who's being dramatic? Webb wanted to say. "Cath, nothing's your fault," he said. "Okay, a guy pulled a gun on me last night. I told him to drop it, he fired, I shot him. That's it. End of story."

"You got shot at?!"

"I'm a police officer, Cath. I carry a gun. That happens to us sometimes."

"Are you okay?"

"Actually, I'm at the hospital with holes right through me."

"Oh my God! Which hospital? How bad are you hurt?"

"I lost eight pints of blood. They ran out of Type O, so they had to rig an emergency transfusion while they looked for a donor. I think they used an orangutan."

There was a pause.

"Harry, that wasn't nice."

"Guess you should've married a nice guy."

"I called because I was worried about you."

"I'm fine, Cath."

"You never believed in us. You never really committed."

"I believe in what's in front of me. I follow the evidence."

"You have to believe in more, Harry. You have to be an optimist for a relationship to succeed, and you're not."

"Oh, right. Believe the sun will come out and it'll keep you warm, something like that?"

"Thank you, Harry. For reminding me why I threw you out of the house."

"Don't mention it. You can have the damn house. I never liked that house."

"I was hoping we could do this amicably."

"That's just because you can't bill yourself for the hours you put in on your own divorce."

"Harry, that's a dirty thing to say."

"What? Reminding you that you make your living off human misery? So do I, remember? If everyone was nice to each other, we'd both be out of a job."

"I've got some paperwork for you to sign."

"Now that's the woman I married. Don't forget to invoice yourself."

"Do you have to make everything difficult?"

"I think so, yeah. It was in the fine print on our marriage license."

"No it wasn't. I read the license, Harry."

"Of course you did."

"Where can I send the papers? Are you going to tell me where you're staying, or did you change your name and move out of LA to get away from me?"

"Say that again."

"What? The part about getting away from me?"

"No, changing my name."

"You don't have a maiden name, Harry."

"Whatever. Look, Cath, I'm at the El Serrano. It's in the phone book. And yeah, they'll deliver mail to my room, because you're right. They do have a maid."

"All right. I'll do that. You take care of yourself, Harry. I hope you're not smoking and drinking too much."

Webb shook the last cigarette out of his pack and pulled out his lighter. "Hardly smoking at all."

"I'll get the papers to you. And I am sorry. About the shooting."

"I'm fine."

"Goodbye, Harry."

"Bye."

He hung up. Then he called his partner.

"Gutierrez."

"Hey, Jimmy, it's Webb."

"Oh, hey, man! How's it going? I gotta tell you, if I was on a day off, I wouldn't keep calling my office."

"That's why you'll never make Chief of Detectives, Jimmy."

"Hey, you're supposed to be my mentor. Aren't you supposed to build me up?"

"Sorry, kid. Can you do something for me?"

"Sure thing. What's up?"

"Kwon and Cox are the guys on my case, right?"

"Yeah. How'd you know?"

"I know things. What I need you to do is run a plate for me."

"Okay. What's the plate number, and what's that got to do with Kwon and Cox?"

"I don't know the plate number."

"Um... kinda hard for me to run it then, man."

"But I think it'll be in Kwon and Cox's file."

There was a silence.

"Jimmy? You still there?"

"Yeah, man. I just... you're asking me to go into their files?"

"That's what I'm saying."

"You want me to ask them to look at their file on you?"

"I didn't say I wanted you to ask their permission."

"I don't think I should do this, man."

"It's not illegal, Jimmy."

"Yeah, but if they see me and ask what I'm doing, what am I supposed to say?"

"You'll think of something. Look, I need that plate, and I need to know who the car belongs to. It's a red Mazda convertible that was at the scene of the shooting. Get the plate, whether it's from the photos, or the witness statements, or whatever. It'll be a woman, she said her name was Maureen Sinclair, but it isn't."

Webb heard Gutierrez swallow.

"Okay, I'll do it," he said. His voice cracked slightly. You would've thought he was a rookie soldier getting an order to charge a German pillbox in some old war movie.

"I knew I could count on you. Thanks."

Webb hung up and waited, wishing for more cigarettes. Two nonexistent smokes later, Gutierrez called him back. The kid was breathless with the reckless daring of what he'd just done.

"Red Mazda, plate 9JZX429," Gutierrez said. "They hadn't run it yet. Looks like it's registered to a Marie Lewis."

"Thanks, kid," Webb said and hung up. A moment later, he thought he maybe would have done better to say something more. Gutierrez could have gotten in significant departmental trouble if he'd gotten caught monkeying with another detective's files. He'd have to do something nice for the youngster once he went back on active duty.

In the meantime, though, he had more police work to do. Webb entered the license plate and name into his onboard computer. A moment later, he had an address.

Maybe it was a fool's errand, but Webb's hunch told him Maureen Sinclair, or Marie Lewis, or whatever her name was, had something important to say about Volkman. Now, finally, he had somewhere to go.

First, though, he needed another pack of smokes. Maybe two.

Chapter 6

Fortified with a case of Camels and a cup of gas-station coffee, Webb pulled up to Marie's address an hour later. It was a run-down bungalow with crumbling stucco walls and a scraggly yard badly in need of a gardener.

He parked and walked up to the front door. He didn't have a plan, which was bad. The advantages a cop had going into an interview were preparation and experience. At least he still had a whole lot of years to fall back on. But what was he going to say?

Oh, hi, Maureen. Or Marie, or whatever your name is. Just got some questions about that shooting. Like, did you rehearse it with Volkman ahead of time? Did he know his gun was loaded with blanks, while mine was stuffed full of .38 Special full metal jacket?

He rapped the knocker against the front door three times, hard. Maybe the sound of brass on wood might clear his head.

He waited. No one answered.

"This address is no good," he muttered. Marie Lewis must have moved. Or maybe she didn't even exist. If Maureen had one fake identity, she could easily have others. That way, if anyone started looking into her, they'd end up chasing their tails all over LA.

Webb couldn't legally enter the house, not without a warrant. If he did, anything he might find would be inadmissible. Assuming the DA even bothered to file charges. And he, Harry Webb, would probably be kicked off the LAPD. If he was lucky, they'd call it retirement and he could still collect at least some of his pension.

So he did the next best thing. He snooped. He worked his way around the side of the house, catching his coat on overgrown bushes, and peered in the windows. He saw cheap, shabby furniture in the living room. No sign of Maureen. He moved on to the bedroom window and leaned around the frame.

"Hey! What're you doing back there?"

The shrill voice made Webb jump. In some part of his brain he went back to being an awkward teenage boy. Blood rushed to his cheeks and he turned, already thinking of fumbling excuses for why he'd be peeking into the pretty woman's bedroom.

He saw an old lady looking over the low hedge between the Lewis house and the one next door. She was holding a pair of clippers in her hand and scowling at him.

Webb reminded himself that he was an adult, a police detective for God's sake, and straightened his back. The best way to get away with things, he'd learned, was to pretend you had every right to be doing whatever you'd been caught doing. It unnerved people and made them back off.

"LAPD, ma'am," he said, flashing his shield. "Harry Webb, Robbery-Homicide. What's your name?"

"Bertha Parker," she said. "Young man, the police have no business prying around peoples' houses."

"I'm looking for Marie Lewis," Webb said. "It's important I speak with her. Do you know her?"

Bertha sniffed. "Well, I don't know that I'd say that. We're not exactly familiar. Though I do tell her to mind that yard of hers. If you let weeds grow in one part of the neighborhood, the next thing you know, there's nettle-leaf and groundsel and knotweed all over the place."

"Letting weeds grow in your yard isn't a crime, ma'am."

She put her hands on her hips. "Well, it should be! What am I paying your salary for?"

"When's the last time you saw Marie?" Webb asked, refusing to be drawn off the subject.

"She left this morning," Bertha said. "In that little red car of hers. I saw her, driving down the street with the top down, letting her hair go every which way. You can tell a lot about a woman's morals by the state of her garden, you know."

"I'll keep that in mind, ma'am," Webb said, thinking that botanical profiling was a subject the FBI had yet to consider.

"She's going somewhere," Bertha added.

"What makes you say that?" Webb asked sharply.

"She had a suitcase," the woman said. "I saw her load it into the back of her car. And she was all dolled up in a red dress. If I'd worn something like that out of the house when I was growing up, my mother would have slapped some morals into me, let me tell you. Now, I don't want you to think I spy on my neighbors, but I couldn't help noticing."

Thank God for nosy neighbors, Webb thought. "Any idea where she was going?"

"Probably staying over at some *man's* place."

Webb sighed. "Thanks for your help, ma'am."

He slid behind the wheel of his car and fumbled for a fresh Camel. He knew the next step. He had to find out whether Marie/Maureen had someplace to go in LA, or if she was leaving town. He brought up his onboard computer and entered her name, looking for next of kin. No matches came up, which was disappointing but not surprising. He'd have to find out about friends, and that probably meant trying to contact Fantasy Feathers again... assuming anyone was still there to answer the phone.

Something hard hit the drivers-side window, right next to Webb's head.

His heart jumped in his chest and he reached for his .38, knowing if this was an ambush, it was already too late. His hand closed on nothing and he belatedly remembered his gun was still locked up in Evidence.

The rapping at his window came again. He turned his head and saw an LAPD detective's shield three inches from his eyes. The shield was held in a slim, light-brown hand. He traced the hand up its sleeve to a familiar face.

Webb sighed again and rolled his window down. "Detective Kwon," he said, not even pretending to be glad to see him.

"Detective Webb," Kwon said. "A second unanticipated meeting in front of another Los Angeles residence certainly strains the bounds of credulity."

"I don't believe it either," Detective Cox said from behind his partner. "And I'm lookin' right at it."

"I eagerly anticipate a justification of this serendipitous confluence of events," Kwon said. "We are well outside the realm of coincidence."

"Are you married, Kwon?" Webb asked.

Kwon's eyebrows quirked ever so slightly. "What possible bearing does that have on our present situation?"

"I'm just wondering how you talk to your girl," Webb said. "When you're alone together. Does all that fancy talk get her going?"

Cox snickered. Kwon glanced at his partner, who immediately dropped the smirk off his face and looked as serious as death.

Kwon returned his attention to Webb, all business. "Marie Lewis. How do you know her?"

"I don't," Webb said. "Like I said in my statement, I met her at the bar for the first and only time. We talked, she gave me a fake name, and she asked for my help dealing with a guy who was hassling her."

"You dealt with the guy, all right," Cox said. "Two in the chest."

"What did she offer you?" Kwon asked.

"I didn't get anything," Webb snapped.

"That's not what I asked, Detective Webb," Kwon said softly. "I asked what she offered."

"Look, it's all in my statement," Webb said. "Read it."

"We have already perused its contents," Kwon said.

"Then read it again. Or peruse it if you'd rather. Scan it, decipher it, absorb its contents. Do whatever the hell you want with it and leave me alone. I'm busy."

"You seem eager to divest yourself of our company," Kwon said.

"Yeah, and you wanna get rid of us, too," Cox said. "I wonder why."

Because he's a prick and you're an asshole, Webb thought. What he said was, "I want to find Miss Lewis as badly as you do, maybe worse."

"Now that's the first thing you've said that I believe," Cox said.

"Though he phrases it differently than I would, I also question your prior veracity," Kwon said. "I would prefer to advance an alternative hypothesis to the account previously provided."

"This ought to be good," Webb said.

"I envision an unhappy marital situation," Kwon said. "An isolated detective, facing an exorbitant pecuniary penalty for the dissolution of his conjugal arrangement. Desperate and alone, he enters into a nefarious compact with a female of dubious character. She will supply his monetary deficiencies and provide intimate favors. In return, he agrees to dispose of an unwelcome suitor."

"You think I hired myself out as a hit man to Marie Lewis in return for money and sex?" Webb said in disbelief.

"Succinctly put," Kwon said.

"Are you out of your goddamn mind?"

"Look how it looks," Cox said. "You meet this dame in a seedy bar."

"It's not that seedy," Webb muttered.

"She's all over you, even though she's smokin' hot, and you're... well, just look at you. You step outside and just happen to run into this other dude. He's got a gun that's loaded with blanks, so you're in no danger, but it looks like you are, so you can smoke him and nobody'll say nothin.' Then you go to make sure there's no loose ends, so you talk to Volkman's girlfriend. We find you there, which is maybe a good thing for her, 'cause maybe you're thinkin' to clip her, too. Then you go to this chick's house to collect on her debt."

"That'd be some trick," Webb said. "She's not here. Kind of hard for me to get blood money when she's making a run for it."

"Hey, nobody said you was a *good* hit man," Cox said with a sneer.

Webb looked back and forth from Cox to Kwon. Neither one gave any sign of this being a joke. "Check my call history," he said. "Check hers."

"Already did," Cox said. "But you know better than to use your own phone for something like that."

"Check my financials!"

"We're workin' on that," Cox said. "But like you said, if you didn't get paid, there won't be nothin' to find there."

"Bring in Marie Lewis!"

"We're workin' on that, too."

"Not very hard," Webb shot back. "Right now you're hassling an LAPD detective as if you were an Internal Affairs jackass. And for what? I didn't take a contract to kill Volkman. I never knew the guy, and I'd never met Marie Lewis until last night! You know I shot him. Hell, everybody knows I shot him! It's not exactly a secret. It was a righteous shooting and you know it. You want to arrest me? You'll be the laughingstock of the Department."

"Clearly, what we require is a further interview with Ms. Lewis," Kwon said. "Finding her is the key to unraveling this situation."

"And that's the only thing you've said that I agree with," Webb said.

"You're a suspect, smartass," Cox said. "We don't care if you agree or not."

"Suspect?" Webb repeated. "Are you deaf, or dumber than you look? I shot him. How many times do I have to say it?"

"We know," Kwon said. "The question is *why* you shot him."

"I shot him because he fired a gun at me!"

"Loaded with blanks," Cox said.

"Tell you what," Webb said. "Let's go out in a parking lot, in the middle of the night, in the rain, after you've had a couple of beers. I'll draw on you and fire, and you can tell me if I'm using blanks or not."

"Your inebriation is a further factor," Kwon said thoughtfully. "I expect Internal Affairs will be desiring an interview."

Webb wanted to tell them about the missing one point five million dollars from Marie's workplace, but at this point, it would only make them suspect him more. That, as far as they'd know, would be one-and-a-half million more reasons for him to have killed the guy. Maybe they'd think he was trying to track Marie down in order to kill her. Once a detective got a particular theory in his head, it could be harder to get rid of than a nicotine habit.

"We're going in circles here," he said. "You going to waste more of our time, or you going to take me in? Either way, I'm sick of the both of you."

Cox looked at Kwon. Kwon looked at Cox.

"We will not be detaining you at this time, Detective Webb," Kwon said. "However, I must insist that you remain within this municipality."

"Don't leave town," Cox added.

"Are you kidding?" Webb retorted, starting his car. "You already told me that. And I live here. I'm just starting to wish I didn't."

*   *   *

Webb didn't have the slightest idea where he was driving, but the motion of the car made it feel like he was getting somewhere. He drove, smoked, and tried to think. Raindrops began to spatter the windshield.

Now he was a murder suspect. That was a new one on Harry Webb. Leave it to those two morons to tumble to that conclusion. Though, now that he thought about it, it wasn't an unreasonable theory. It did fit the available information. Only Webb and Marie knew it wasn't true. The whole thing made a very tidy setup.

"Setup," Webb growled. And just like that, everything fell into place. He understood. It was unbelievable. One moment he was wandering around in a fog, the next it was all totally clear.

The case was solved in his head. Now, if he could only find the mysterious, elusive Maureen Sinclair. And get some proof.

He called his partner again.

"Gutierrez," the youngster said, picking up on the first ring.

"Careful, kid," Webb said. "Answer the phone too fast and the brass will think you don't have enough to do. Next thing you know, you'll have half the Department's paperwork on your desk."

"Webb?" Gutierrez's voice dropped to a whisper. "What's going on, man? IA was just here. Going through your desk. They took your computer!"

"Forget it, Jimmy," Webb said. "It's Chinatown."

"Forget it? This is serious! And what the hell does Chinatown have to do with anything?"

Gutierrez apparently hadn't watched any of the right movies. "Nothing," Webb said. "That's the point. And it's got nothing to do with you."

"What kind of trouble are you in?"

"The best kind. Female. Now focus, Jimmy. I need your help."

"I can't help you go behind the Department's back." Gutierrez sounded scared. "Those other two detectives, Cox and Kwon, were here too. A while ago. Those guys aren't IA, Webb. They're Robbery-Homicide, same as us!"

"I know," Webb said wearily. "I just talked to them."

"I thought it was a clean shooting!" Gutierrez hissed.

"Nothing's clean in this damn town," Webb said. "No matter how much it rains. Relax, kid. I'm not going to ask you to do anything illegal. I need you to put out a BOLO on a car."

"What car? What the hell is going on?"

"Same car I asked you to run earlier. You still have the plates?"

"Yeah, somewhere here."

Webb heard the sound of rustling paper. For a guy who hadn't been a detective long, Gutierrez had managed to make his desk extremely cluttered.

"Okay, got it," Gutierrez said. "Registered to Marie Lewis. Red Miata?"

"That's the one," Webb said. "Put the word out. She's a person of interest in a felony burglary. If she gets spotted, have the uniforms bring her in and give me a call."

"Why don't you call it in yourself?"

"Because our own guys are watching me. I can't do anything through official channels right now. Keep up, kid."

"Okay," Gutierrez said reluctantly. "This isn't some hazing thing you do to the new guys, is it?"

"I told you, Jimmy. This has nothing to do with you. If all you find is the car, and Marie's not in it, let me know where it is."

"Copy that," Gutierrez said. "You coming in?"

"No. I've got somewhere to be."

"Where?"

"I'll be in touch." Webb hung up. No point compromising the kid more than he had to. He was feeling a little better, because he knew what he needed to do now.

"The shooting wasn't the point," he said to the empty car. "This all goes back to Fantasy Feathers and their million five. Follow the money."

* * *

The same security guard was still standing outside Fantasy Feathers, arms crossed. His T-shirt was wet and rain was running down his bald skull.

"You look cold," Webb observed once again. "I hope they're paying you a lot."

The burly guy shrugged. "Can't complain," he said. "I've had worse gigs."

Webb couldn't resist. "Such as?"

"Did concert security for 'NSYNC a few years back. Picture getting swarmed by ten thousand rabid teenage girls."

Webb shrugged. "That doesn't sound so unpleasant."

"You kidding? They're like hyenas. They'll tear you apart before you're dead. I still got the scars."

"Ms. Winter still here?"

The security guy shrugged again. "She hasn't come out this door, and her car's still here."

"Thanks. Do yourself a favor, get a raincoat or something."

Webb found the owner of Fantasy Feathers in her office, which was now almost completely packed up. The old lady glanced at him with annoyance that quickly turned to surprise when she recognized him.

"Detective!" she exclaimed. "I wasn't expecting to see you again so soon."

"I've just got a couple of questions about your missing money," Webb said.

"I can't tell you where it is," she said. "That's what makes it missing, dear."

"What form was it in?"

"I beg your pardon?"

"Was it an electronic transfer? Stacks of bills? Gold bars? I don't know how you movie types keep your money."

"If only I had stacks of gold bars," she said, smiling. "Or sacks of bullion. The closest I ever came was when we did a pirate-themed video. This was back when that first Disney pirate movie came out." Her smile grew wider. "I remember getting a very angry letter from a mother who'd wanted to rent that movie for her son and got ours instead. I hope he found it educational."

Webb raised his eyebrows. "How old was the kid?"

"I don't recall exactly. Fourteen, maybe."

"Then I sure hope he learned something."

"My accountant is currently in communication with one of your colleagues in Financial Crimes," she said, coming back to the topic at hand. "It appears the shortfall was transferred to another movie studio over a period of time."

"What studio?"

"Detective, I don't really see the point of your inquiries," Winter said. "My accountant and attorney are fully cooperating with your colleagues. Why not let them handle this? You seem like more of a street gumshoe, if you'll pardon the observation."

"You're right," he said. "That's why I'm Robbery-Homicide. The financial crimes I care about are bank robberies and armored-car jobs. But humor me. I'm trying to solve a murder here."

"Very well," she said. "I have nothing to hide. Hmm, 'Nothing to Hide' would be a good title for a feature. Maybe starring a female witness in a major crime, one who falls for a mobster. Pity I'm out of the movie business."

"The studio name?" Webb reminded her.

"Pinot Noir Films," she said, her mouth twisting slightly. "A rather obvious pun on the title. But then, it appears to be a fake. They've never made a movie, nor are they likely to. It was just a way of laundering their ill-gotten gains, I imagine."

"Pinot Noir," Webb repeated. "Do you have a phone number?"

"Detective," she said with patient pity. "Don't you understand? There is no one to answer their telephone. There is no telephone. There is no studio. It's all a put-up job."

"But they have a bank account," he said.

"Obviously. Otherwise they would have had nowhere to put the money. *My* money."

"What bank?" Webb asked.

"According to my accountant, First Republic, on Figueroa."

"Thanks." He started for the door and paused in the doorway. "Don't leave town just yet, ma'am."

"Am I suspected of something?" she inquired, seeming more amused than nervous at the idea.

"No. But if you wait around, I just might be able to get your money back."

Chapter 7

Webb was in his car, halfway to downtown, when his phone rang.

"Webb," he said, hoping for good news but expecting more trouble.

"Hey, it's me," Gutierrez said. "Got a hit on your BOLO."

"You've got her?" Webb asked, and for a moment the rainclouds seemed just a little lighter.

"No, sorry."

Webb sagged back again. "Okay, what do you have?"

"The car. Patrol unit reports seeing it in a parking lot."

The excitement was back. "Copy that. Do we have eyes on it now?"

"No. The car pulled out as he was driving in. He hit the sirens, but the driver sped up. By the time he got turned around to begin pursuit, it was gone. We can't do high-speed chases downtown, Chief's orders."

"Right," Webb said heavily. "So now she knows we're onto her."

"She was coming out of a bank," Gutierrez went on. "It was—"

"First Republic, on Figueroa," Webb interrupted.

There was a short pause.

"Hey, boss," Gutierrez said. "If you knew where this girl was, why'd you have me put the word out?"

"I didn't know until a few minutes ago," Webb said. "I'm on my way there now. Anything else?"

"Nope."

Webb hung up. He poked a fresh cigarette into his car's lighter, hoisted it, and closed his lips around it, tasting the smoke. He was closing in, but still running behind. Maybe he'd get lucky. Because he was such a lucky guy.

At the bank, he showed his shield to a teller, who fetched her manager. He was what Webb would have been as a bank executive: still overweight and balding, just dressed in a more expensive suit. The manager was polite without being helpful, which was about what Webb had expected.

"I'm sorry, sir," the guy said. "We obviously take our clients' personal information very seriously, so I can't divulge any of it without a court order."

"Of course," Webb said. "And of course you follow proper federal guidelines regarding large withdrawals and deposits, reporting all of them over ten thousand dollars and investigating any sizable withdrawals."

"Well, naturally," the manager said.

"The purpose of those laws being to prevent money laundering for criminal enterprises," Webb continued.

"Of course," the manager said. He was looking nervous now.

"Pinot Noir Studios is a money laundering front," Webb said bluntly. "This will be obvious when the LAPD's Financial Crimes detectives come knocking on your door in a day or two. Of course, by that time, the money will be long gone. I already know Marie Lewis took money out. I even know approximately how much. All I need to know is whether she made an electronic transfer, or whether she made a cash withdrawal. Can you just tell me that?"

"How much money, sir?" the manager asked.

"One million, five hundred thousand dollars. Give or take."

The manager put a finger under his collar to loosen it. "That's a very large withdrawal," he said. "Many banks don't have sufficient liquidity to accommodate such a request. And we would have been very punctilious in verifying the customer's credentials. But yes, I can confirm a comparable amount was withdrawn, as cash, earlier today."

"Marie Lewis has one and a half million in cash," Webb said.

"I didn't say that," the manager said.

"You didn't have to." Webb was already on his way out the door.

He slid back behind the wheel of his car and started the engine. Marie knew the cops were chasing her now. Her car was distinctive. If she was as clever as he thought she was, she'd ditch the car. That meant she was either headed for a car lot, an airport, or a bus station.

The car lot would buy her a little time, but not much. A cop could quickly find out what car she'd bought or rented, and then they'd be right back on her tail. An airport or bus station was a better bet. The airport would only work if she had a fake ID that would pass TSA scrutiny. But you didn't need ID to get on a bus. Plus, even if they tracked her car to the depot, if she'd bought a ticket with cash, she could have gone anywhere.

The only downside to all that was that she'd be traveling with a bunch of strangers, carrying over a million dollars on her person, which was such an absolutely insane idea that it just might work. After all, no one would expect it.

And there was a Greyhound depot two miles away, in downtown LA. He could be there in ten minutes.

It was thin, and Webb hated thin police reasoning, but thin was better than invisible. It was worth a try. He turned on Figueroa and stepped on the gas. He thought about using the siren, but decided not to. His Crown Vic was unmarked. Just maybe, if he could avoid spooking her, he could sneak up. Assuming he'd guessed right, and her bus hadn't left, and any number of other things.

"And Cath says I'm not an optimist," he muttered.

*   *   *

In Webb's experience, most of the places a detective went were depressing, but some were worse than others. Slums, homeless shelters, emergency rooms after midnight, and bus stations were all near the bottom of his personal list. Los Angeles was, first and foremost, a gigantic, sprawling temple to America's Twentieth-Century worship of the automobile. When people were asked what they thought of when LA got mentioned, Hollywood and traffic were usually the first two words out of their mouths. So what did it say about Angelinos so desperate they had to use public motorized transportation?

Webb wanted to get out of LA, but if he ever did, he wouldn't take the bus.

He parked in the lot next to the depot and looked around, but didn't see a red Miata. That didn't mean a thing. If she knew the cops had made her ride, she would've left it somewhere inconspicuous, probably in a parking garage a couple blocks away. However, if she'd walked partway, that might've bought him a little time.

The Greyhound depot was a squared-off, ugly pile of cinderblocks, the bottom four feet painted the red of dried blood, the rest a dingy cream color. Some well-meaning artist had tried to liven up the roofline with a colorful mural, but it wasn't doing anything for Webb. As he walked to the entrance, he passed a couple of orphaned backpacks, a lone suitcase standing on its little wheels with its handle extended and no owner in sight, and a Hispanic guy bent double, clutching his head.

"You okay, buddy?" Webb asked. Getting no response, he tried again. *"Estás bien?"*

The man muttered something in a broken mix of Spanish and English about cockroaches in his ears, which told Webb two things: he wasn't okay, and there wasn't a thing Webb could do for him. The detective went around him and entered the station.

He saw a mostly-deserted open space divided up by nylon rope-lines. Glancing to either side, he spotted the bus-loading area and a waiting room. He made for the buses first, walking quickly out of the building and under an overhang which kept the rain out, but also trapped the diesel fumes in. Webb lit a cigarette to try to drown out one type of smoke with another. It didn't work.

Two buses were idling. Webb climbed the stairs onto the first one and flashed his shield to the driver.

"Just looking for someone," he said, scanning the seats. He didn't see anybody who looked like Marie, but walked the length of the coach and looked to make sure. He also flipped open the door to the restroom at the back. Nothing.

This was a fool's errand. The woman was gone and there wasn't a damned thing he could do about it. Internal Affairs was going through his hard drive right now, though God knew what they'd find. He didn't even have any porn on it. The worst they'd get was some acrimonious four-way e-mails between him, his soon-to-be-ex-wife, and their respective lawyers. And then there were Detectives Kwon and Cox, trying to nail him for Murder One. They wouldn't find anything, but that wouldn't stop them jumping to conclusions.

"Speaking of fool's errands," he said under his breath as he got off the bus and started for the second one. No DA in southern California would even dream of indicting on the basis of their hypothesis. He wasn't going to jail. But a murder accusation would follow him around, a lead weight dragging what was left of his career down to Santa Monica and right off the end of the pier into the ocean. He could forget about ever getting promoted in the LAPD. It would've been nice to make Lieutenant before he retired. He'd been close; another year of keeping his nose clean might've done the trick.

Webb sucked a frustrated breath through his Camel, inhaling the mix of tobacco and diesel. He was feeling a little light-headed. And he could sure use a drink.

The second bus was the same as the first; mostly empty, not a familiar face in sight. Webb thanked the driver and let his feet thump down on the blacktop at the foot of the stairs. His cigarette was burned down almost to the filter. He reached up to swap it out for a fresh one and tried to think what the hell to do now.

Marie Lewis walked out of the waiting room onto the pavement.

The unlit Camel fell from Webb's fingers, forgotten. He stared at her. She was even more beautiful than he remembered. That flawless complexion; those deep, dark eyes; that lustrous hair, done up in fancy waves and curls better suited to a long-ago decade; and that body, swaying toward him like a cobra under a fakir's spell. She was wearing red, of course, a skirt just short enough to make a man look and think, the fabric pulled tight against her fantastic body. In her left hand was an overnight bag, in her right a suitcase.

"Maureen," he said. It wasn't her name, they both knew that, but here and now, it was the one to use.

She froze. For an instant, he saw surprise flit across her face. Surprise, and something like fear. But then she smiled, and in spite of everything he knew and suspected, the smile warmed Webb's jaded heart right through.

"Harry," she purred. "I wasn't sure if I'd see you again. That would have been a pity. And after everything you did for me."

"Leaving town?" he asked, nodding toward her bags.

"I got a job offer," she said. "I'm going to be shooting on location, very short notice. I've been thinking about you, though. I'm so glad to run into you. Whatever are you doing here?"

"I'm running down a lead on a robbery-murder case," he said, stepping toward her and extending his hands. "Here, let me get those for you."

Her hand tightened on the overnight bag, but she gave him the suitcase. "Thank you," she said. "You're a dear."

"Pinot Noir," Webb said quietly.

She paused. "How sweet of you to remember my drink," she said.

"Quite a coincidence," he said. "You see, the LAPD is looking into Pinot Noir Studios. Apparently it's a false front, a fake studio. It seems that's something that happens in the movie business. Some studios don't actually make movies. There's all kinds of reasons for it, but all of them come down to hiding or laundering money. See, somebody's been siphoning money out of this other studio."

"Oh, Harry," she said. "I wouldn't know anything about that. I've never been good with money."

"Me, either," he said. "That's probably why I'm going to wind up paying alimony to two ex-wives. But someone with access to the Fantasy Feathers accounts was able to move a whole lot of dollars into Pinot Noir's coffers. Then, just a little while ago, someone cleaned out Pinot Noir's account. In cash."

Maureen didn't blink, but Webb saw her hand clench just a little tighter. "Harry," she said. "It's sweet of you to see me off, but my bus is about to leave, and I really don't have time to hear all about your case. I'm sure it's frightfully interesting, and I'd love to hear more about it when I come back to town, but maybe another time?"

"Terry Volkman," Webb said. "He didn't make advances toward you. The guy was a creep, sure, but he was basically a pedophile. His taste ran to younger girls than you. Terry wanted to be an actor, but he couldn't get any decent parts. So you engineered this whole song-and-dance. What did you promise him to help you transfer the money? I'm guessing you said he'd star in Pinot Noir's first big picture, and that one-point-five million would be the seed money to make it happen. He just had to pass an on-site audition.

"Terry was kind of an idiot," he went on. "He'd have to be, to fall for that. But then, I nearly fell for it, too, so what's that say about me? You actually set a guy up to commit suicide by cop. It's kind of brilliant, when you think about it. Because you didn't have to get your hands dirty. All you had to do was say a few lines."

"Harry," Maureen said. "I don't understand. You're not making any sense."

"And we'd have a hell of a time prosecuting you for murder," Webb said. "Because I killed him, not you. If the worst came to the worst, you could even tell the police it'd been my idea, that I'd offered to kill him for you." He shook his head. "And if I hadn't guessed right, you'd be on this bus right now, on your way out of town, rich and clean."

"What are you saying, Harry?"

Webb sighed. "I'm saying it's over, Maureen. Or Marie, if you prefer. Marie Lewis, I'm placing you under arrest for grand larceny and conspiracy to commit murder."

She wasn't smiling any more. "Harry," she said. "Don't do this. I'm innocent, whatever you think."

"I don't know what to think," he said. "But I know what happened."

"There's no proof of any of this. It's all wild suppositions and guesses."

"You've got the proof right there in your hand," he said, nodding to the overnight bag. "One million, five hundred thousand pieces of proof. The bank will connect you to Pinot Noir, and that'll be plenty for our forensic accountants. They've got a boring job, and I don't really understand it, but they're really good at what they do. And then there's Audrey Knowles. She's a strung-out, messed-up kid, but she knows all about the phony audition. She loved Volkman and I guarantee she'll testify. Once you and Volkman are linked to the robbery, it won't take a genius to figure out what happened in that parking lot."

She licked her lips. "Come with me, Harry," she whispered.

"You're coming with me, Marie," he said. "That's how this works."

"No, get on the bus. Right now. Get out of this town." She stepped toward him and lifted her hand to his face. Her eyes were suddenly alive and sparkling with promise. "Come with me, somewhere else. We can go anywhere. You want to start over, don't you? Leave this dead-end job in this lousy town. Leave your good-for-nothing wife. Come with me. I'll make it worth your while."

She leaned in close and whispered, "Every night. You can do whatever you want, and I'll love it, Harry. I'll beg for more. You want me on my knees? I'll get down on my knees for you, Harry." Her voice went still softer. "You want money? I'll give you one hundred thousand dollars. Cash."

"A hundred grand, huh?" Webb said. "That's a solid offer."

"Not enough? Two hundred thousand. Right now."

"That reminds me of a joke," Webb said. "A man sees a beautiful woman in a bar. He walks up to her and asks, 'Would you spend the night with me for a million dollars?'

"The woman thinks about it and says, 'Yeah, I would.'

"The man says, 'Okay, would you spend the night with me for ten bucks?'

"She slaps him in the face and says, 'What kind of woman do you think I am?'

"He says, 'We both know what kind of woman you are. Now we're just discussing price.'" Webb shook his head. A little part of him actually regretted saying it, but he said the words anyway. "I'm not that kind, Marie. I'm not for sale."

She actually smiled at that as she stepped back. It was a sad smile. "But of course you are, Harry. Everyone is. You just don't know your price yet, or what part of you you'll have to sell. That's the way it is."

"So is this," Webb said. "Turn around, ma'am, and place your hands on the side of the bus."

Her hand went into the overnight bag and came out holding a pistol. It was a small, elegant gun, fitting nicely in her hand. A Walther PPK, just like James Bond used.

"I'm getting on that bus, Harry," she said. "And you're not stopping me."

It was Webb's turn to smile sadly. "And then what, Marie? I've got backup already on the way. Even if you get out of this station, where are you going to go? If you shoot a cop, there's nowhere they won't find you. They'll be waiting at the next stop. You know that. It's already over."

He stepped toward her and held out his hand. "You'll do some time, probably ten to twenty if you plead out. You'll still have some life left when you hit the street. But if you shoot me, they'll throw away the key and you'll die in prison."

She stared at him with those dark, luminous eyes, and the moment stretched all the way out into eternity. Webb waited. In that moment, he almost didn't care whether she pulled the trigger or not.

Then his hand closed over the barrel of the Walther and she let go of it. He put the gun in the pocket of his trench coat and pulled out the cuffs.

"Turn around," he said as gently as he could. "Don't worry, I won't make them too tight."

"You could have had everything," she said softly. "Is it worth it?"

"Probably not," Webb said truthfully. "But it's the Job."

"I don't hear sirens," she observed as he clicked the handcuffs shut around her wrists. As he'd promised, he made sure they weren't too tight.

"I was bluffing," he said. "I'm the only cop here. I didn't call anybody. Hell, I'm not even carrying."

Marie laughed bitterly. "Harry," she said. "You should have been in show business."

Chapter 8

Webb got out of the Crown Vic and stood at the curb. He rested a hand on the car door and looked at the house. It wasn't his house, not anymore. If it ever had been. Here at the end of the day, the sun had finally shaken loose from the clouds. Golden light slanted across Los Angeles, the gorgeous, deep gold cinematographers called "magic hour."

He took one final drag on his cigarette and dropped it, grinding it out with the toe of his shoe. Then he walked up the sidewalk and rang the doorbell.

She opened the door and it struck him, as she stood there looking at him, how pretty she was. Not Hollywood beautiful. Not the sort of drop-dead gorgeous that haunted adolescent daydreams. Not beautiful like Maureen Sinclair. But pretty. She had a light spray of freckles on her cheeks. Her hair was brown, but it was a deep, rich brown, with just a hint of auburn. Her eyes had small wrinkles at the corners, but life was a rough road to drive, and who didn't show the mileage?

"Hi, Cath," he said.

"Harry," she said. "I didn't know you were coming. You should've called. I've got plans for this evening. I was just on my way out."

"That's fine. I'm just passing through. I won't keep you. I just..." He had to swallow the sudden lump in his throat. That was funny. It hadn't happened to him before.

"Just what, Harry?" She cocked her head to one side, like she always did when he wasn't making sense. It was one of her most endearing, and sometimes annoying, gestures.

"I just wanted to talk to you for a minute."

"Okay. Here I am. Let's talk." Her body language was guarded, wary. She didn't invite him in.

"I wanted to let you know, I'm not going to fight you for the house. You can have it."

Two little lines appeared between her eyebrows. "Are you sure?"

"Hell, Cath, you always liked it more than I did. We bought it because you wanted it. I would've preferred something closer to downtown, you know that."

"Harry? Have you been drinking?"

"Actually, no. I could use a drink, come to think of it. And I'll probably have one after this, but right now, I'm stone-cold sober."

"Good for you, Harry. I've been worrying about your drinking, especially since you moved out. You're an alcoholic, Harry."

He smiled wryly. "No, Alcoholics go to meetings. I'm just a drunk. I've been smoking like a chimney, if that's any consolation."

She made a face. "I can smell it on you. And that's not funny, Harry. Those things will kill you."

"I should live so long. Anyway, that's one of the things I came to say. The other is goodbye."

"Don't be so dramatic, Harry."

"I mean it. I'm done."

His soon-to-be-ex-wife frowned. "I know. We're getting a divorce, remember?"

"I don't mean with you. I'm done with the whole mess. Los Angeles, the LAPD, all of it. I'm moving. Out east."

"When did you decide this?"

He thought about that. "I guess I've been deciding it for a while. I wasn't sure until earlier today. I had a conversation at a bus station."

That got a slight smile. "With whom? Some panhandler?"

"Nope. A murderer."

The smile vanished. "Are you okay, Harry?"

"Yeah. But she made me an offer."

"A female murderer? What is that, a murderess? Or would it be a *femme fatale*?"

"Yeah, *femme fatale* is about right."

"What was the offer?"

"The best sex I'd ever had, plus two hundred grand."

It startled a laugh out of her. "You're joking!"

"No joke. The thing is, I was tempted."

"Of course you were."

"What's that supposed to mean?"

"Nothing! Just that you're a man hitting middle age, going through a midlife crisis. Of course you'd be tempted by an offer like that."

"I didn't come here to fight, Cath."

Her eyes softened, and for a moment Webb wanted to get down on his knees and beg her to take him back. "I know, Harry," she said. "I'm sorry. That was mean."

"It wasn't anything she offered," he said. "It was the idea of starting over, of getting out of here. I wanted it so badly, I seriously thought about throwing everything away. And then I thought, if that's what this place is doing to me, I've got to get out of here, or next time I really will do something bad. She said I had a price. I'm starting to think she was right."

"Do you have a plan?"

That was just like her. Catherine Simmons—she'd kept her name, naturally. Successful divorce lawyer, planner. He remembered she liked to plan her calendar six weeks in advance, minimum, right down to what she'd eat for lunch. Her grocery lists read like epic poems.

"I talked to Lucano," he said. "He knows a captain in the NYPD, a guy called Holliday. You know, like the Wild West gunslinger?"

"Doc Holliday," Catherine said, nodding. "Val Kilmer in *Tombstone*. I love that movie."

"Anyway, this Holliday's a precinct captain in Manhattan. Lucano said he'd put in a good word for me if I want to transfer. Hell, it's not like I can keep working here after what happened. I'd punch Kwon, and then I'd have to shoot Cox. Plus, everyone will always wonder if I really was in on it with Maureen... Marie, I mean."

"Harry? I don't understand."

"Of course not. But you can read all about it in the papers. The point is, he'll help me get in with Holliday. I'm an experienced detective, and apparently the NYPD has a few openings. I won't have to start on the ground floor. I'll be a

Sergeant from the start and I'll make Lieutenant before long. Maybe this is what I need. A change of scenery, a little reset button."

"But what about the kids?"

He blinked. "We don't have any kids, Catherine."

"I meant from your first marriage."

"Oh, right. They'll be okay. They're in high school now. I hardly see them as it is. I'll come back for the holidays, and for birthdays. Their mom's always done better by them than I could. But I'll say goodbye to them, too. I'm on the way over there next."

"Then I won't keep you." She smiled at him. "You're right, Harry. Maybe this is just what you need. I hope things work out for you there. You know, thousands of people come to Los Angeles to chase their dreams. They never tell you where to go if you already live here."

He chuckled. "That's a good point. I'll send you a postcard."

"You do that, Harry. Who knows? Maybe I'll see you again. I'll look you up if I'm ever in New York." Then, surprising both of them, she stepped in close, raised her face to his, and kissed him lightly on the cheek. It wasn't a passionate kiss, not a lover's kiss. It was a kiss of memory and goodbye.

He tipped his hat. "I'll leave the light on," he said. Then he turned, in the last rays of the afternoon sun, and walked away from her. He got behind the wheel of the Crown Vic, started the engine, and drove away.

About the Author

Steven Henry learned how to read almost before he learned how to walk. Ever since he began reading stories, he wanted to put his own on the page. He lives a very quiet and ordinary life in Minnesota with his wife and dog.

Also by Steven Henry

Fathers
A Modern Christmas Story

When you strip away everything else, what's left is the truth

Life taught Joe Davidson not to believe in miracles. A blue-collar woodworker, Joe is trying to build a future. His father drank himself to death and his mother succumbed to cancer, leaving a broken, struggling family. He and his brother and sisters are faced with failed marriages, growing pains, and lingering trauma.

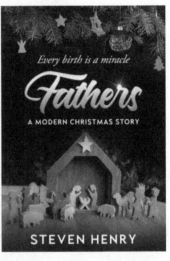

Then a chance meeting at his local diner brings Mary Elizabeth Reynolds into his life. Suddenly, Joe finds himself reaching for something more, a dream of happiness. The woodworker and the poor girl from a trailer park connect and fall in love, and for a little while, everything is right with their world.

But suddenly Joe is confronted with a situation he never imagined. What do you do if your fiancée is expecting a child you know isn't yours? Torn between betrayal and love, trying to do the right thing when nothing seems right anymore, Joe has to strip life down to its truth and learn that, in spite of the pain, love can be the greatest miracle of all.

Ember of Dreams
The Clarion Chronicles, Book One

When magic awakens a long-forgotten folk, a noble lady, a young apprentice, and a solitary blacksmith band together to prevent war and seek understanding between humans and elves.

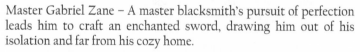

Lady Kristyn Tremayne – An otherwise unremarkable young lady's open heart and inquisitive mind reveal a hidden world of magic.

Robert Blackford – A humble harp maker's apprentice dreams of being a hero.

Master Gabriel Zane – A master blacksmith's pursuit of perfection leads him to craft an enchanted sword, drawing him out of his isolation and far from his cozy home.

Lord Luthor Carnarvon – A lonely nobleman with a dark past has won the heart of Kristyn's mother, but at what cost?

Readers love *Ember of Dreams*

"The more I got to know the characters, the more I liked them. The female lead in particular is a treat to accompany on her journey from ordinary to extraordinary."

"The author's deep understanding of his protagonists' motivations and keen eye for psychological detail make Robert and his companions a likable and memorable cast."

Learn more at tinyurl.com/emberofdreams.

More great titles from Clickworks Press

Death's Dream Kingdom
Gabriel Blanchard

A young woman of Victorian London has been transformed into a vampire. Can she survive the world of the immortal dead— or perhaps, escape it?

"The wit and humor are as Victorian as the setting... a winsomely vulnerable and tremendously crafted work of art."

"A dramatic, engaging novel which explores themes of death, love, damnation, and redemption."

Learn more at clickworkspress.com/ddk.

Share the love!

Join our microlending team at
kiva.org/team/clickworkspress.

Keep in touch!

Join the Clickworks Press email list
and get freebies, production updates, special deals,
behind-the-scenes sneak peeks, and more.

Sign up today at clickworkspress.com/join.

CPSIA information can be obtained
at www.ICGtesting.com
Printed in the USA
LVHW041115080122
708048LV00006B/364

9 781943 383863